DUNE
HOUSE

DUNE HOUSE

A Vintage Mystery

Eunice Mays Boyd
with Elizabeth Reed Aden

First published by Level Best Books/Historia 2021

Copyright © 2021 by EUNICE MAYS BOYD with ELIZABETH REED ADEN

This novel is entirely a work of fiction. The names, characters and incidents portrayed in it are the work of the author's imagination. Any resemblance to actual persons, living or dead, events or localities is entirely coincidental.

EUNICE MAYS BOYD with ELIZABETH REED ADEN asserts the moral right to be identified as the author of this work.

Author Photo Credits: For Elizabeth: James Studios (Madison, WI); For Eunice – old family photo

First edition

ISBN: 978-1-68512-061-0

Cover art by Laura Duffy Design

This book was professionally typeset on Reedsy. Find out more at reedsy.com

For Marilyn Reed Roberts, who helped me build Dune House.

Praise for the Vintage Mystery Series

FOR *MURDER BREAKS TRAIL* (1943)

"No scientific sleuthing this, but a blending of clues, coincidences and concentration...A better than most brain workout."—*Kirkus Reviews*

"As pretty, suspenseful and smoothly written a mystery as I've read in a long time."—Chicago *Sun*

"... well-tangled murder plot... Good entertainment."—New York *Herald Tribune*

"An exceptional who-done-it, which won honorable mention in the latest Mary Roberts Rinehart mystery novel contest, has been skillfully built into a book that is hard to put down until the last page"—Philadelphia *Evening Bulletin*

Chapter One

The cable car lurched along the foot of Russian Hill, the work-bound passengers outside gripping the handles for dear life. It lurched past streets grown over with grass, too steep for automobiles. Across the house-filled hollow there was enough fog on Telegraph Hill to turn Coit Tower into the smokestack of a ship.

The cable car jounced another block, and the smokestack was gone. Down Greenwich Street, the tower became a finger—one finger upraised.

That reproving finger, the scold of the cable in its slot...

On the front platform of the car Lark Williams was, for an instant, a shivering child again, her Aunt Sophie looming over her. Lark had to remind herself that she was twenty-three years old now, and a married woman.

A fat, genial-looking man squeezed between her and a brown-faced Naval commander, and the car jerked on. It had been five years since Uncle Thad died and Lark had run away from Aunt Sophie's chicken ranch and her lashing tongue. Five years of San Francisco: business school for one of them, and then four years at Rollin, Rollin & Hildreth, attorneys at law.

The cable car heaved itself from Mason Street into Washington, and Lark tightened her hold for the next turn at the end of the block that would shake off the napping passengers in the left-hand outside seats. Up the street she saw a young couple belting after the cable car, hand-in-hand.

That was what marriage should be. She wouldn't have minded keeping on with her job if she and Aubrey could go to work together like the two now panting aboard. She smiled when she saw the grip man slow to let them catch up.

1

Marriage wasn't meant to be just six weekends in three months. It was meant to be two cups on the breakfast table and heating the baby's bottle, calling Aubrey at his office to bring home an extra lamb chop. Lark had never had that kind of life, with her father dying before she was born and her mother when she was still young. Uncle Thad and Aunt Sophie had barely spoken to each other, or to her. But she and Aubrey had to wait four years to make their marriage public. In four years, Aubrey's partner would retire. If she'd only known what she was getting into… but she had no right to think such things, Lark told herself sharply. Aubrey had warned her; he'd been more than fair.

It was a vicious circle. Aubrey couldn't marry without reducing the alimony payments to his first wife. If he applied for a reduction, she would bring out scandals that had been suppressed at the trial that would make his scandal-fearing senior partner dissolve their partnership. Even if Aubrey had been younger, Lark wouldn't have asked him to start over. It didn't go with his plumed-hat and lace-at-the-sleeves air that she wouldn't change for anything. The simplest thing was to keep their marriage secret until his partner retired. She still had "Lark Williams" on her mailbox, and the nearest her husband had ever come to her apartment was the curb outside the door.

The cable car flung around the corner to Powell Street; she should have braced for the turn, and only being wedged in kept Lark from pitching off.

They began to climb Nob Hill, Clay Street, Sacramento. Across each fog-dimmed intersection, the Bay Bridge thrust its long steel band, reinforcement for the next block of houses. Like a needle, thought Lark, and the blocks were long beads, the kind a baby plays with.

As she watched a slim man in occidental gray wriggle up the crowded step, a newspaper three pairs of shoulders over caught her attention—the picture of a large house spiked with towers like unlighted fireworks. Between the shoulders she could read the word "Dune."

Dune House, of course, was a landmark on the beach. Fenced off from the public by ocean and wire in a mile-long rectangle of dunes that the roads had to skirt, the house stood alone on a cliff, facing waves of sand instead of water. Dune House's owner, old Miss Julia Paget, was Rollin, Rollin, & Hildreth's wealthiest client. What had Miss Paget done to make the papers print a picture of her house?

The long steel needle out in the Bay threaded another blockful of houses. From one of the many doorways a woman in a flowered wash dress dashed out waving a briefcase. A man stepping off the curb took it with a husbandly peck at her cheek before he swung on board.

Lark wondered wistfully if Aubrey would ever forget his briefcase. But she wouldn't find out for four years unless that gold-digging social debutante who had married him married again and stopped demanding those alimony payments. The girl in flowered cotton was lucky; she didn't have to meet her husband in Carmel or San Jose or Fresno for hole-in-the-corner weekends.

The cable car, fretting in its slot, clacked to the top of the hill and started down. But Lark was too absorbed to notice that all of the passengers were now sliding south instead of north. Not until a chopped-up rainbow blazed at her from the sidewalk did she recognize the flower stand on Geary, and knew she had ridden a block too far.

* * *

In the reception room of Rollin, Rollin, & Hildreth, the bright heads of Red and Dizz—short for Dizzy Blonde—sprang apart as Lark opened the door.

"Oh, it's you," the redhead said, looking relieved. "Have you heard about Oscar?"

"What about him?" Lark asked. "I didn't hear a sound in his apartment last night and he wasn't on the car this morning. Don't tell me Oscar Fry has done something exciting."

"Just tried to commit suicide is all," Dizz drawled.

Lark gasped.

"Right next door?" she said, "and I didn't know it?"

The other two women began talking at once, but the redhead's voice drowned out the blonde's.

"No, here in this very building," Red said. "Yesterday. He jumped out

3

the window of that empty office on the next floor. They found him in the court below with a terrible concussion and a broken arm. They don't know whether he's going to pull through or not. If someone hadn't heard him groaning..."

"He didn't come back before we left last night," Dizz said. "I didn't think anything about it then, but—"

"He's still unconscious," Red said. "The hospital told Mister Hildreth. Mister Rollin won't like this one bit."

Red knew all of the details; she ran the small office switchboard.

"Can he help it if he's unconscious?" Dizz cried. "I guess if you fell six stories..."

"Don't be silly, Dizz," Red said. "What does Mister Rollin care whether Oscar's unconscious or not? But he *is* going to blow a gasket when it gets in the papers that Rollin, Rollin, & Hildreth's law clerk tried to commit suicide."

"Why on earth would Oscar, of all people, want to kill himself?" Lark asked.

"At least not for love," Red laughed. "You've never let him date you, have you Lark? Out of gratitude for getting you his apartment, perhaps? He keeps asking Dizz and me for dates, but no soap."

"Maybe that's why," Dizz said. "He found out he's got no sex appeal and tried to end it all."

"He more likely lost his shirt at the races," Red suggested.

"Poor Oscar," Lark said softly. "Think of him in those two rooms on the other side of the wall from mine, brooding on—whatever he had to brood on, and then..."

Lark looked up suddenly.

"He was lucky not to be killed!" she added. "After all, six stories and a concrete court..."

"Spring cleaning did it," Red said. "When the window washer got down to the second story he was using a ladder instead of that belt, and when he quit at four o'clock, he left the ladder up."

"You mean Oscar hit the ladder?" Lark asked.

"And bounced," Dizz said. "So Oscar only got a concussion and a broken arm. But if he doesn't come out of that concussion—"

"Jiggers," Red interrupted.

The door opened again and a tall man walked in, red-faced, with a gray suit and hair a little grayer.

"Good morning," he said stiffly.

"Good morning, Mister Rollin," the girls chorused.

He walked stiffly across the room and through a mahogany door on the left.

The blonde winked at Lark.

A buzzer sounded behind Red. She did something with her hands and said in a sweet voice into the telephone, "Yes, Mister Hildreth."

She said it again, and then did something else with levers and cords.

"Now Rollin's getting the dirt," she grinned at Lark and Dizz, setting down the headphone she hadn't bothered to put on.

She bent close to Dizz and they began to murmur, their eyes on Mr. Rollin's closed door.

Poor Oscar, Lark thought, what would drive a colorless soul like him to suicide? Ironically, he was as inept at suicide as he was at life. If Mr. Rollin would only think of human emotion instead of the wrong kind of publicity in the papers...

Papers... Miss Paget.

"Has one of you girls got a newspaper?" Lark asked. "I left in too big a hurry. I saw a picture of Dune House in one of them this morning. Did Julia Paget die or something?"

"I've got one," Red said, reaching on top of the nearest file case. "Old Julia's advertising for an heir."

"Advertising for—"

"I'll bet Daddy Rollin's having kittens," Dizz chortled.

Red flapped open the folded paper.

"Here's a picture of the missing heir at three or four months old," she said. "Around forty years ago. Ought to make it easy."

The box behind her buzzed again. She pulled out plugs while Lark looked at the photograph of a fat baby in a long white dress lolling regally back on brocade. The baby had a few tufts of hair and dimpled knuckles and long, lace-trimmed sleeves. An adult hand in one corner served as an anchor. In large letters above the picture Lark read, "ARE YOU THE MISSING HEIR?"

Below, in smaller print, it said: "Julia Paget, wealthy spinster, tries to trace her brother's child, last heard of in France in 1906. Miss Paget does not know whether her niece, now middle-aged, is alive or dead. Dig through your old photographs, San Franciscans; maybe *you* are heir to millions."

"There's more on the back," Red said, "with the picture of the house. Gosh, I wish I was that kid, even if I had to be forty. Think of all that Paget money."

"What are you so quiet about, Lark?" Dizz demanded. "Don't tell me you've got that picture at home?"

"There's something familiar about it," Lark laughed ruefully, "because Mother had one of a long-dressed baby floating in brocade, I guess. If I compared them, one baby's arm would be up, and the other one down, or something. Things like falling heir to millions don't happen to me."

"Me either," Dizz said.

Red offered them comfort.

"Oh well, they say old Julia's pretty queer," she said. "Maybe the millions wouldn't be worth it."

The buzzer behind her rang again, and she uttered her sweet-toned, "Yes, Mister Hildreth?" Then, not quite so sweetly, she repeated, "Yes, Mister Hildreth" and turned around.

"You're the lucky one, Lark—again," Red said. "He wants you to bring in your book."

"Seems to me he always wants you," Dizz said enviously.

"Guess he doesn't like dizzy blondes," Red gibed. "Boy, I wish he liked redheads."

"You'd think he'd go for blondes," Dizz observed enviously, "with his black hair."

"Maybe Lark's a better stenographer," Red said judicially. "Or maybe she's got more of what it takes."

Lark felt herself flushing.

6

"Don't be an idiot, Red," she said.

"I suppose *you* haven't got a case on Hildreth like Dizz and me—not *very* much," Red said, in her judicial voice. "You know, Lark, there's something sweet and sort of downy-looking about you, like a young bird."

"Could be the name," Dizz remarked.

But Lark had reached the mahogany door opposite Mr. Rollin's and opened it.

The man behind the desk stood up tall and crossed the beige rug. He passed her and leaned against the door. His black hair, darker than the wood, was winged with white.

"Good morning, Lark," he said softly.

Then she was in his arms, choking.

"Oh, Aubrey," she said, "when are we going to say good morning *right?*"

He lifted her face in both hands, clipped black mustache and slate gray eyes very near.

"Lovely little girl, you can't want it half as much as I do," he said. "If Ninon would only decide she'd rather have a new husband than alimony... it's not fair to you, this kind of life."

Lark hushed him. She may have had the same thought herself for a brief, unhappy moment on the streetcar, but not while she was with Aubrey.

"We've been over all that," she said, "and decided it was better to have it this way than not at all."

"I ought to have the guts to get that alimony reduced and let Ed Rollin throw me out," Aubrey said. "You and I both know the scandal Ninon's holding over my head isn't based on truth. What does public opinion matter?"

"A lot to a lawyer," Lark said.

"I know, dear," Aubrey said. "That's the hell of trying to start over. I shouldn't have fixed up such nice juicy grounds for Ninon to get a divorce in the first place, and I should have objected to that stiff alimony. If she hadn't run me ragged all the time about being a miser..."

"You had to show her," Lark said. "I never told you, Aubrey, how much Red and Dizz admired you for that."

Or how much they admired him, period, she thought. And it wasn't only Red and Dizz. Sometimes Lark thought of all the debutantes he could have chosen from. Perhaps marrying one of the girls in his office had been a reaction—trying to get as far away as possible from that socially successful Ninon, who had been such a failure as a wife. Aubrey seemed to like Lark's lack of sophistication. He said she was honest and refreshing, "as inartificial as your namesake, Lark."

Lark finished in a rush.

"Red and Dizz know what the firm takes in, and how much you get—and how much of that Ninon gets," she said. "They look at you as a regular Don Quixote or Sir Galahad."

Aubrey Hildreth laughed, his white teeth whiter by contrast with his tanned skin.

"Red and the dizzy blonde, they're a grand couple," Aubrey said. "But I wish I didn't have to wait for Ed Rollin to retire to take you out of this office and give you the things the wife of the junior partner of Rollin, Rollin & Hildreth ought to have."

Lark didn't mean to sigh, and turned her lips up quickly in a smile.

"Now, if only I were the missing Paget heir," she said. "Did you see that piece in the paper?"

"I'll say I did," Aubrey said. "Rollin's fit to be tied."

"The tantalizing part of it is, there's something awfully familiar about the picture of that baby," Lark said. "There's even a hand in one corner..."

She broke off, staring at Aubrey's left hand spread against the door to keep out visitors, his college fraternity ring...

"That's what makes it so familiar!" Lark cried. "There's a ring—the same sort of ring, on both hands, and—"

"Both whose hands?" Aubrey said. "What are you shaking about?"

"I might be the Paget heir, Aubrey!" Lark said. "Oscar and I were looking at family pictures the other night. He brought his over and I showed him mine. Why, I've got a picture like that one in the paper at home, one my mother left. You know I don't know anything about her. What if she was the missing Paget baby?"

"She'd have been lots nearer the right age than you, dear," Aubrey said. "But what's all this chatter about rings?"

"Yours reminded me," Lark said. "The hand in the picture at home has a ring on it, and so has the one in the newspaper. And they look like the same kind of ring! Miss Paget's brother is dead. If his share of old Captain Paget's estate came to me—"

"Now, hold your horses, Lark—" Aubrey said.

"But if it did, we'd be wallowing in money," Lark said. "Ninon's alimony would be only a drop in the bucket."

"Don't get excited, Lark," Aubrey said. "Any baby's mother might wear a ring that looked like someone else's, and all baby pictures look alike. Your mother and I'd be about the same age, and I could show you some of my pictures that you'd say were dead ringers for that until you got them together. That's what going to happen to people all over the country—they'll drag out their family albums and get all excited, too. We tried to keep Julia from sticking out her neck, but she develops a conscience—after forty-odd years—and decides her brother's kid ought to have some of the money her brother didn't get. She put two million dollars in a trust fund to revert to her in five years if Ulysses Paget's child isn't found."

"Aubrey, do you care if I go back home—right now—and see if that picture of mother—" Aubrey said.

"You won't be any good here until you get it off your chest," Aubrey said. "Go ahead, darling. But don't tell Red and Dizz why you're going."

"Oh, Aubrey!" she said, throwing both arms around his neck. "If we could get all that money—"

* * *

The light fog was gone although the sky was still gray as Lark rode back up Powell Street. The long needle of the bridge showed more clearly now its threading of steel, and beyond it she could see the Berkeley Hills, green with spring. The pagodas of Chinatown were redder, more sharply pointed.

The clack in the cable slot matched the clack in herself. That picture of her mother wasn't just any baby picture—whatever Aubrey said. Or the hand in the corner, any hand with a ring. The print was blurry—she shot another look at the tight accordion of newspaper in her hand as the car flung around a turn—but the ring was oval. Wasn't the one at home oval?

Of course, as Aubrey said, when you actually got to comparing...

She jumped off the cable car before the grips had stopped it. She ran up the outside flight of steps with both keys in her hand, and ran up the two inside flights. Then at last the door of her apartment was opened and closed, and she was reaching up on the closet shelf for the little package of photographs and snapshots that was all she had left of her mother.

The faded pink ribbon, almost jerked in two; mussy tissue paper... then her mother's last photograph, plump and young before Dad died; a snapshot of herself; Mom and Dad on their wedding day...

Here it was! The anchoring hand was in the same corner. The ring oval in both... the folds of brocade were the same... the gray background was the same... the babies' dresses were the same. Their left fists... their right fists.

Shaking, Lark set down the photograph and newspaper side by side. She ransacked her desk for a magnifying glass and trained it on the adult hand in the corner of the photograph.

On the flat oval stone of the ring was the faint shadow-shape of a tiny seahorse. She turned the glass toward the ring in the newspaper picture. Through the blur of print like this morning's fog, she could barely make out a smudge on top of the stone. But no amount of peering could give the smudge shape.

Except for those two details—and perhaps a clearer print would make them agree—the pictures were exactly the same.

Chapter Two

L ark rolled down the window in the car door beside her, the wind rushing in tart with seaweed and salt. The park and amusement concessions were far behind now, Fleishhacker Pool and the zoo giving way to blocks of small new houses, the north wall of one the south wall of the next, across the dunes row after row, like turnips and carrots and beets.

On the right, beyond the blowing green of beach grass, past light dry sand and dark shiny-wet sand, miles of gray-green water heaved up and down and broke at thin green edges in white foam.

Aubrey slowed the car to let a girl on horseback cross the boulevard, and Lark's eyes returned to the house on the cliff far ahead. She was near enough now to make out the up-jut of towers.

"It's like a lighthouse, isn't it, Aubrey?" Lark said. "Julia Paget's place up there on the cliff, like a whole nest of lighthouses."

"Now listen, dear—" Aubrey began.

But Lark went on staring up at the cliff.

"Lighthouses are built to warn people away, and here we are..." she said.

"Dune House isn't a lighthouse," Aubrey reminded her as the boulevard reached the Paget fence and turned sharply away from the ocean.

On other days, that fence had been only the boundary of the land of Aubrey's most important client, deflecting the highway away from the beach. Now it was something more personal. Tall iron posts, strong mesh like magnified chicken wire. Each post had two arms, one extended inside the fence and one out. From arm to arm ran strands of wire. Three perching gulls flew up as Aubrey's car passed.

"I don't think I ever noticed how that fence was built before," Lark said. "No one could get around those horizontal wires on top, could they, if they wanted to climb in?"

"Worrying about your millions already?" Aubrey teased.

"Dune House is famous, Aubrey," Lark said. "I'm not trying to be funny."

"Okay, darling, put your mind at rest," Aubrey said. "Those top wires are all barbed—close together."

Lark gave a little shiver. One set of arms with wires like that should be enough. It was odd that another set extended inward.

The road climbed a dune toward a sky gray with high fog, and half a mile away the big house on the cliff was rubber-stamped against it. The mound of sand dipped, and the gray page with the imprint was turned.

But the fence still ran faster than Aubrey's car. Something about it, with the treeless dunes and towered house beyond, made Lark shiver again.

Aubrey put on the brakes. They were in a hollow between dunes. The gardener who planted the rows of houses on the city side had somehow missed this tier of blocks. The world here was only sand, beach grass, and lupin bushes not yet blooming, with a road and a fence leading out.

As they stopped, Aubrey took her by the shoulders and turned her to face him.

"Are you getting cold feet, Lark?" he asked. "Would you rather not claim the trust fund Julia set aside for Ulysses Paget's child?"

"I may not be able to claim it," Lark said. "If Miss Paget's picture doesn't have that sea horse on the ring, like mine—"

"With all the other details the same, I don't think you need to worry," Aubrey said. "Do you want to skip the whole thing?"

"It means so much to us," Lark said. "It's only—oh, I don't know! I guess it's just the gray day, and thinking of all those towers as lighthouses... and the way that awful fence keeps running along and running along. I know it's silly, and I'm sorry. Let's drive on and forget it."

His arms went around her, holding her hard.

"You know I wouldn't tell you your claim looks good if it didn't," Aubrey said. "Ed Rollin said so, too. But if you want to call it off—"

"Of course not," Lark said. She straightened, held herself stiff for a moment, then relaxed against him. "I guess it's just reaction. After all, when you've been poor all your life and then the Paget millions jump at you… you know how it is. You said your mother had quite the struggle, and when your father's people took you—"

"Except the Hildreths aren't in the Paget class, my dear," Aubrey said. "They're practically shabby-genteel. But I know what you mean. Ever since you brought that picture back to the office, we've about talked you to death."

"I felt so mean holding out on Red and Dizz," Lark sighed. "They knew something was up."

She thought of the girls' excitement, shrill as Chinese music in and out of the rumble of Aubrey's and Mr. Rollin's questions every time Aubrey's door was opened.

"If you hadn't insisted…" she finished.

"They'd spread it all over town," Aubrey said. "We don't want it in the papers until it's proved."

He paused.

"Do you want to go on?" he added.

"Of course I do," Lark sighed again. "We can't pass up a chance for all that money. I only hope we won't have to fight to get it. I hate a fight."

"You have a husband to fight for you now," Aubrey said.

For a moment, the only sound that came in through the window was the swish of passing cars. A derisive honk brought Lark's head up from Aubrey's shoulder.

"Don't miss them," he smiled. "Can't you do a little necking with your husband?"

"How I wish, when we go in there," Lark said, nodding toward the fence, "you could introduce me as your wife."

Aubrey shook his head, his mouth firm beneath the line of black mustache.

"Miss Paget would blow her top," he said. "No matter what your evidence is, she'd swear it was a put-up job. You working in our office is bad enough, or will be in her eyes, but if she ever found out you and I were married…"

13

"I don't see how she could think anything was wrong," Lark said. "Finding out I'm probably related to her is as much a surprise to us as anyone. I should think it'd seem a wonderful coincidence that the wife of her own lawyer should turn out to be her missing grandniece."

"It would to you, darling, if you were in her place, but you don't know Julia," Aubrey said. "Even though you never heard your mother's maiden name or had any idea what the sea horse in the picture stood for—even though I never saw any of your mother's pictures, let alone that one, or so much as set foot in your apartment—if we admitted we were married, Julia would decide there was a rat to smell."

"But, Aubrey," Lark protested, her hands coming together, her fingers locking. "You mean that we have to go on keeping our secret until Mister Rollin finally turns seventy and retires, like we planned in the first place? Won't this make any difference?"

"Don't get upset—of course it will make a difference," Aubrey said. "But we've got to keep still, if you really want that money, until it's turned over to you. Then we'll produce our marriage license and set up housekeeping as Mister and Missus Aubrey Hildreth. We'll shout it from the housetops—"

"Mister and Missus Aubrey Hildreth," Lark repeated softly. "Doesn't that sound... just right?"

"Perfect, my lovely little girl," Aubrey said. He picked up her clasped hands and held them for a moment against his cheek. He stepped on the starter. "Miss Paget's expecting us at three."

The fence began to run again, always ahead of the car. The clustered towers were stamped on another gray page of sky, and now a second building with two or three modified towers appeared inside the fence across from the truck-garden rows of small houses.

"Here we are," Aubrey said. "Garage doors don't make that old stable look any less like a place to keep horses, do they?"

"Doesn't Miss Paget keep horses?" Lark asked. "I read in the paper that she has a car for errands downtown, but people drive between the house and gate in carriages."

"In a victoria, my sweet," Aubrey confirmed. "I've taken plenty of buggy rides behind her spankin' grays with Leo or old Adam at the controls. Julia doesn't go for modern inventions. Wait until you see the Maison Paget—or Museum Paget, I should say. Hello, Adam. Callers keeping you busy today?"

A small door had opened in the stable behind the garage doors. A man had come out who must have been tall when he was young, but who was now stooped in his dark green uniform. He peered at Lark from under shaggy eyebrows, smoothing a few long gray locks of hair across his bald head before answering Aubrey.

"Them reporters have about drove me wild," the man said, "but they petered out around noon."

"Have many people been around with photographs?" Aubrey asked.

"The things some folks think looks like other things make you sick," the old man snorted. "Miss Julia says not to let them in unless the pictures they got looks like the one in the paper. By cripes, Mister Hildreth—beggin' your pardon, miss—some show up with pictures of kids in short pants, and some with no picture at all."

"I knew she'd get a lot of cranks," Aubrey said. "Lucky she has you to keep them out. This is Miss Williams, Adam. Miss Paget's expecting us."

"She told me," Adam said.

The gatekeeper sent another hooded glance at Lark, then turned to the open door behind him and yelled, "Leo!"

"All ready, Mister Hildreth," came a voice from inside the dark stable. Another green-uniformed man showed his profile for a moment at the doorway.

Lark involuntarily glanced at the fence. That strong netting—the tall posts with barbed wire overhangs—the great house inside—and the uniformed guards at the gate. Guards? Why had she called them guards?

The road for the moment was free of cars. The ranks of new houses on the city side were as silent as ranks of stones. The Paget dunes seemed creepily still.

"What's wrong with the fence, miss?" Adam said gruffly. He was fitting a key into the padlock on the gate.

Lark found herself staring up at the fence, fingers interlaced.

"Wrong?" she said. "Why—nothing. It just seems so—strong."

The old man gave a barking laugh.

"You bet it's strong," he said.

"The barbed wire," Lark faltered. "Like roofs on each side…"

"It only had one when the fence was built," Adam said. "The one inside."

"But then… people couldn't climb in?" Lark asked.

Aubrey put his hand on her elbow.

"Come on, Lark," he said, taking a step toward the gate.

The old man went on talking.

"That wasn't why it was built, miss," he said. "That outside arm wasn't added until after the reporters began to get brash. That fence wasn't built to keep folks out. It was built to keep them in."

Chapter Three

In the muffling sand there was no friendly thud of hooves, no brisk clip-clop. Only the jingle of bridle silver, the leather creak of harness, and the fainter creak of well-greased wheels told the ear that the carriage was moving.

"Make yourself comfortable, Lark," Aubrey urged. "Lean back and relax."

Relax? Lark thought. In a place like an institution? She should have known from the first time she saw the fence—without Adam having to say it—that it was built to keep people in. Mesh like chicken wire, far too heavy for chickens; and the house on the cliff, far too large for one family, aloof past its rolling dunes.

In spite of the way the sand slowed the horses, the house kept coming nearer, looking, with its many small towers and one tall one, more than ever like a lighthouse nest full of young. Lighthouses, built to warn people away...

Aubrey's calm voice broke in.

"Is your hat well-anchored, Lark?" he asked. "A victoria's not a closed car."

His casualness was more effective than his admonition to relax. Lark reminded herself that any number of families had skeletons in their closets. She was letting her imagination run away with her when she ought to be singing hallelujahs. If she could satisfy Miss Paget that she was Ulysses Paget's granddaughter, and the money was made legally hers, there would be nothing she and Aubrey couldn't do or have. She settled back against the bottle-green upholstery, stroking the smooth broadcloth with an almost proprietary air. Dark green, like the suit of the driver on the high seat in

17

front. She must remember to think of it as livery, not a uniform.

"There's always wind here," Aubrey said. "Look over there at the sand."

Ahead, between them and the ocean, sand blew like fog off a long bare dune. From every open patch of sand that dappled the beach grass and lupin, the fine mist rose. As the team pulled west, an arc of sun coming out of the clouds gave all the lower air a silvery cast, and the great towered house rising out of the luminous dust had the look of a mirage.

"Now I see why they call it Dune House," Lark murmured. "It seems to belong to the sand instead of the cliff or ocean."

"The important thing to Julia is that it belongs to the Pagets," Aubrey said. "They say old Captain Paget built out here because of his seafaring youth, but he and Julia have always been so snooty, I'll bet it was to get away from the hoi polloi."

"Do you think my being a stenographer—?" Lark began.

Aubrey's voice dropped, too low for the coachman to hear, almost too low for her.

"You'd still be a Paget, my dear," he said. "Providing you can prove it."

The wheels turned softly through the sand, dropping little showers back from each spoke. A lone gull, less gray than the sky, dipped down and veered off to sea.

"This road ought to be paved," Aubrey remarked. "But you'd never catch Julia Paget doing anything so modern. Her father had it corduroyed and graveled twice—when they built the house before Ulysses ran away."

"What did Ulysses Paget do," Lark asked, "that make his father cut him out of his will?"

"He married a burlesque queen; didn't you know?" Aubrey asked.

"Yes, but surely that wouldn't be enough to—" Lark said.

"It was, for Julia and her father," Aubrey laughed. "Ulysses was a pretty wild young blade anyway, I gather, but the marriage is what really got them. No Paget was going to smirch the family name and get away with it—at least not on Paget money. I'd be willing to bet, from what my grandmother said, that Ulysses wouldn't have married the gal if the Captain and Julia hadn't raised such a fuss."

"And now Miss Paget's sorry?" Lark asked.

Aubrey snorted.

"Julia was never sorry for anything she did in her life, as far as I know," he said. "But she hates to think of Paget money going to anyone but a Paget, and she got some anonymous note a while ago that made her think Ulysses' child might still be alive."

"Too bad mother isn't," Lark said with a sigh. "Oh, Aubrey."

She slipped her hand into his behind the coachman's back.

Suddenly the hand over hers was withdrawn and her husband was at least three inches farther off in his corner of the carriage. Lark felt the way she had the first time she saw the ocean when she was six, and a wave knocked down her sand castle.

"See that tallest tower?" Aubrey said loudly. "The one that looks all windows? That was Captain Paget's pilothouse. Julia spends half her time up there surveying her acres with a spyglass."

"A spyglass!" Lark said.

"Either there or in one of the second-story front windows," Aubrey said. "She likes to keep track of what's going on."

Lark felt suddenly naked in the open carriage crossing the dunes. No wonder Aubrey had drawn away. If Miss Paget had a hearing device to go with her spyglass—a sort of periscope ear, like the driver's... Lark sat up quickly and made her own voice loud.

"Look, Mister Hildreth," Lark said. "The sun's gone again."

The silver light was gone, too; Dune House was no longer a mirage but a tremendously substantial building they had almost reached. She could see now that a line of green in front of it, irregularly hidden from the carriage by dunes, was a hedge. The road went up in a last steep pitch, and the gray team was all at once higher than the victoria.

Then the carriage was on the slope too, and the horses were going through the hedge.

The first thing that startled Lark was the flat green reach of the lawn. The second were the sounds: hooves thumping, wheels crunching. They were off the sand at last, on hard dirt and a graveled drive.

Directly ahead, hardly fifty yards now, the gun-metal-colored house looked incredibly large.

"It's gigantic," Lark said. "And so dark. You'd think Miss Paget would want something more up to date. It's not as if she couldn't afford it. This house is so—ugly."

"I doubt if it's ugly to her," Aubrey said. "She wants things exactly the way her father had them when he built the place in the Eighties. She even wants to do the things he did, like taking mulled wine to go to sleep instead of hot milk. Not in a thermos, either. Her maid stays up to heat it whatever time of night Miss Paget decides to go to bed."

Lark shivered suddenly.

"I'm cold," she said. "And don't say it's my imagination. I can't help feeling as if that house cuts off the sun. Only there isn't any sun."

"You'll warm up inside," Aubrey soothed. "There's a fireplace in every room."

But I want sun, Lark thought stubbornly. The green expanse of lawn was bare. No trees broke through the plush. No flowers patterned it. The formal shrubs against the house were green and blossomless.

As the horse trotted smartly into the curve before the house, Aubrey leaned forward.

"How's Miss Paget today, Leo?" he asked. "Feeling—uh—well?"

Lark hadn't even heard that Miss Paget was ill. And how oddly Aubrey spoke! Something in his tone, his little pause...

The man on the high seat in front answered without looking back.

"Seems to be fine today, sir," he said. "Not at all—uh—depressed."

Depressed! Then it wasn't a physical illness? A woman who wanted everything done as her father did it, that fence built to keep people in.

She caught Aubrey's arm, crying out before she could stop, "Miss Paget's not crazy, is she?"

"Good Lord, no," Aubrey said. "What gave you that idea?"

"He—he said she wasn't depressed today," Lark said.

"Leo and I were being tactful," Aubrey laughed. "After all, she hires and fires us both. I meant, was she in a bad temper? And all Leo said was no."

"But you—the papers—everybody says she's strange," Lark said.

"If all strange people were crazy," Aubrey said. "You don't need to worry on that score, Lark. Julia's as sane as you are. Here we are; give me your hand."

On the ground, Lark looked up again. The house seemed even larger. How could she walk in and ask for two million dollars? A girl from a run-down chicken ranch who'd always had to earn her living.

"You look fine," Aubrey murmured as if he knew what was on her mind. "The wind didn't do a thing except rouge your cheeks."

He spoke too soon. The March wind, proverbially changeable, gave him an uppercut that knocked his hat flying. The team jumped, and the carriage flashed down the drive, but not before Lark had seen Leo's face as he grabbed Aubrey's hat. She knew now why he hadn't looked back when he answered Aubrey, why he kept his right cheek turned away.

A long scar ran across it, pulling up his upper lip.

Still in the road, but on the other side of the lawn by now, the team began to slow.

"Aren't horses wonderful?" Aubrey said, a trace of envy in his voice. "When a thing like a hat blowing off starts a runaway, don't motors seem boringly safe?"

"Boringly safe!" Lark exclaimed. "Wonderfully, happily, comfortably safe! Everything about this place gives me the creeps, Aubrey. There's your hat by that bush. Let's snatch it and run."

"Lark, you're not going to let a horse's skittishness get you. When we're right at the door…"

She sighed and straightened simultaneously.

"Of course not," Lark said. "I'd be an idiot to miss a chance like this."

The rear wheels of the victoria vanished through the hedge, and Lark turned toward the house. A dozen wide marble steps with bronze railings, great bronze double doors in the face of a pseudo-stone tower. Lark grasped one cold railing far more tightly than balance required and started up.

Beside her at the top, Aubrey had no more than raised the knocker when the great doors began to open.

21

Lark braced herself for more bottle-green livery, perhaps another crabbed old man like Adam; not, she hoped, another scarred face like Leo's.

But the hand on the knob was feminine, the uniform black, with white apron and cap, the woman in it young and rosy faced. She smiled, as all women smiled at Aubrey.

"Come in, Mister Hildreth," she said. "Miss Paget's expecting you and Miss Williams in the boudoir."

The vestibule they passed through was all marble mosaic. Lark tried not to stare at the bright geometric patterns and brighter stained-glass windows on each rounded side.

Inside, through another set of double doors, these of carved wood, she cried involuntarily, "Oh, the sun did come out! But where's it coming *from?*"

They were in an enormous round hall with a massive stairway rising from the middle like a tipped-back Y. The figure of a life-size, nearly nude woman standing on the newel post gave Lark her second start before she saw that it was only a statue holding up a lamp. From far above it, gold light slanted into the center of the room, gliding the stairs and statue and a great disk of red carpet, touching the sides of floor-to-ceiling pillars spaced in a circle about it. Beyond the pillars, out of the golden light, the room was a shadowy cavern.

"It's a skylight," Aubrey said, his hand on her elbow, urging her after the maid.

Lark followed through the dimness out into the gilt circle. As her eyes traveled up to a huge, inverted Chinese hat of yellow glass, she was conscious of two rows of balconies below it. Scalloped with deep arches, one curve above the other, they ran about the light well. It was like a small-scale Colosseum, with herself and Aubrey, the maid, and the life-size statue on the stairs down in the arena.

In the gilding from above the rosy maid looked yellow and Aubrey's skin a dark tan. The lamp-bearing statue—Lark was near enough now to see red and greenish studding like jewels in the girdle and headband—looked like gold.

"I hope you're impressed," Aubrey murmured as they started up the heavily

22

carpeted stairs with Lark still staring at the statue. "There are gas jets in that yellow glass globe she's holding up—good old nineteenth century gaslight. And the gal herself is bronze washed in eighteen-carat gold. Incidentally, those red stones are garnets and the blue-green ones are aquamarines."

"It makes you feel funny, doesn't it?" Lark said.

She put out her hand to the bannister, then jerked it back. Instead of smooth wood or metal, her fingers had met fabric napped like fur. The handrail was covered with red plush.

Plush-topped railings... gaslight... gold-washed statues... boudoirs... and something else that wasn't quaint or queer. There was something about this house she didn't like—beyond this crawly plush and the cavern shadow beyond the light—something she couldn't name.

Where the stairway branched at the fork of the Y they followed the trim young maid across the flowered carpet of the landing and up the climbing roses to the left.

Lark wasn't entirely sure what a boudoir was. Uncle Thad's romantic novels that she used to sneak up into the chinaberry tree when Aunt Sophie wasn't looking had led her to expect something vaguely naughty. But the boudoir caps that sloppy housewives wore over curlers somehow didn't fit in with that picture.

They were up the stairs now, turning right along the second-floor balcony. The yellow light was filtered by the balcony above. Lark could dimly make out closed doors and tapestries and pictures in heavy gold frames.

At one of the doors toward the front of the house, the maid stopped and knocked.

"Come," called a voice, more in command than invitation.

The maid opened the door, said "Mister Hildreth and Miss Williams, madam," and stepped back for them to enter.

Aubrey stepped back too and gave Lark's arm a little push. There was no one to hide behind now.

Lark's first fleeting impression, before her eyes found the occupant of the room, was that it was a small living room cluttered with tables, chairs, and cabinets, with bric-a-brac and framed photographs.

Then she saw the woman sitting in the bay window. There was no boudoir cap on Julia Paget. Her hair was a graying yellow, like gold plating wearing off a silver spoon. She wore it parted loosely in the center and pulled into a pointed knot on top of her head. Her face was heavy, sagging over the jaw line. A big bust strained at fetters of candy-box gold lace over blue brocade, hung with three or four strands of pearl beads and a platinum chain. She fumbled at the chain and brought up a platinum and diamond lorgnette case, flicked out the glasses and, with a practiced gesture, examined the girl in the doorway.

Lark tried not to squirm. Perhaps she should have worn her spring hat with the flowers instead of the four-ninety-eight black felt she thought was so smart. Perhaps no hat at all.

"This is Lark Williams, Miss Paget," came Aubrey's voice.

The lorgnette was lowered for an instant.

"Take off your hat, child," Julia Paget directed.

The felt had been a mistake. Lark laid it on the nearest of the many small tables—a checker-board marble mosaic—and loosened her soft hair.

The lorgnette was raised again. "Here, child." One small hand, spectrumed with diamonds, tapped the table beside her.

Lark thought of Uncle Thad's booming voice and noisy slaps of the thigh: *Here, Spot. Here, Blackie. Here, Shep.* Of the yapping and fawning… but perhaps Miss Paget merely wanted Lark's hat on that other table. Picking it up from the marble-top, Lark brought it into the Bay.

The lorgnette tipped up and Miss Paget frowned.

"Ulysses' hair was as light as mine, and this girl's is brown," she said. "But she does have blue eyes. Of course that Georgette creature… and whomever their daughter married… let's have that photograph, child."

The zipper of Lark's handbag kept catching, but finally the photograph of the long-dressed baby on brocade was in the imperious hand. With the other, equally weighted with diamonds, Julia Paget opened a carved jade box and took out a magnifying glass and another photograph. Her lorgnette tipped down.

Lark bent over her shoulder. Sharply clear now without any newspaper

24

blurring, Miss Paget's photograph gave back detail for detail. The glass rested on the corner with the hand. There it was in the other picture, as it was in her own, the last detail—the tiny seahorse on top of the ring.

Lark straightened and her eyes shone at Aubrey.

Julia turned Lark's picture over. It was blank. She reversed her own, and Lark saw, written in faded ink by a careless hand: "Juliette. Age six months. Looks like Ulysses, n'est-ce pas?"

"How like that woman to air her smattering of French," Julia said contemptuously. "She'd never been near Paris until Ulysses took her. And naming the baby for me—with that nasty burlesque twist like her mother's."

"But my mother spelled hers J-u-l-i-e-t," Lark said. "At least that was on her headstone."

"Sounds Paget," her hostess declared. "Find a chair, Aubrey. You sit here, child. Aubrey tells me you have no information about your mother except what's on your headstone, not even her marriage certificate."

Lark nodded, groping for the indicated rocker.

"I was only six when mother died," she said. "I can't remember anything she ever said about her people or where she came from. I know I was born on a ranch in Texas a month after my father died. I don't think the ranch was paid for, from what Aunt Sophie said. As soon as Mother was strong enough, before she was, I guess, she got what she could from the ranch and we moved to Dallas. I'm afraid she started working too soon, because one of my earliest memories is of her lying on the bed trying to comb my hair and explaining how to go to the corner grocery for milk. Poor mother, she was always so gentle and tired, and finally, when she got to the end of her rope, she wrote my dad's brother in California, and he sent her money to come out, but she died after we'd been there a month."

Julia frowned. She had been listening with the expression of one who doesn't like beer having to drink it.

"Who is this Aunt Sophie you mentioned?" she asked.

"Dad's sister-in-law, his brother's wife," Lark said.

"Neither your uncle nor aunt knows anything of your mother?" Julia asked.

25

"Uncle Thad's dead now, too. All they knew was that Mother and Dad were married when Dad made a trip back East, but they didn't know where, or what her name was before it was Williams. They didn't even know how old she was to put on the headstone. Poor Mother was so sick that month she was with them."

"But you can tell from the other pictures Lark has that her mother was about the right age," Aubrey said. "I brought them along."

Aubrey took her little store of photographs out of his briefcase and handed them to Miss Paget.

"See that longish plaid skirt and plain jacket and the hair bulged out over the ears?" he said. "That would be in the early Twenties. The face was extremely young... see? Now take this—"

Lark waited while Aubrey talked on and the platinum lorgnette was aimed at each picture.

Julia kept nodding and finally looked up at Lark.

"What does your birth certificate say about your mother?" she asked.

"Why, I..." Lark turned to Aubrey.

"We ran into a sticker there, too," he said. "When Ed Rollin made that trip to Mexico for you in 'forty-three and had to take a secretary with him, we found Lark didn't have a birth certificate. The courthouse in her county had been burned, and the mail bag taking the other copy of her certificate to the Bureau of Vital Statistics was lost in a train wreck. Those things do happen, you know. But Ed wasn't going to have just any stenographer he could get in Mexico, and didn't want either of the other girls in the office. They're a little—uh—conspicuous. So he had the doctor who attended Lark's mother looked up—too old for the service, fortunately—and a new certificate made out. But the doctor didn't have her mother's maiden name in his records, and of course he couldn't remember it. So that's all the good Lark's certificate does us."

Julia Paget sat still with her small hands out like claws on the arms of her chair. Lark wondered if another woman would have indulged in finger-tapping. Something about those ring-splattered fingers, curved down so hard that they dented the damask upholstery, wouldn't let her gaze leave.

26

Finally, with a physical effort, she pulled it away to the milky jade box from which the photograph had been taken.

The magnet of the claw-like fingers drew Lark's eyes again, and she brought them back once more to the table—to the jade box and the black felt she'd never want to wear again, to a leather-covered cylinder with concentric rings of metal in the end toward her, something smooth and shiny at their center like an oversize dewdrop... the spyglass, of course, the one Aubrey said Miss Paget kept track of things with.

Lark's gaze jumped to the window. Where had the carriage been when she'd reached for Aubrey's hand? Down almost at the stable, she saw the horses and victoria coming out from behind a dune. But they hadn't been behind a dune on the way up when she'd made that blunder, for Aubrey had pointed out Captain Paget's pilothouse, pointed it out loudly for her benefit, but not in time.

Suddenly, as if Miss Paget had reached a decision, her tense hands relaxed.

"What sort of things did your mother leave, child?" she asked. "Any letters or family things? Any keepsakes?"

"Only a few books and her clothes—not new, of course, but not old enough for family things," Lark said. "The books were all from Dad, with just her first name and—the sort of little messages a husband writes to his wife."

Lark tried not to look at Aubrey when she spoke.

"And then there was that package of photographs and snapshots that Mister Hildreth showed you," she added.

"No jewelry? No silver?" Julia asked.

"Just her wedding ring with nothing engraved on it," Lark said. "If Mother ever had anything else, she must have sold it while we were having such a struggle in Dallas."

"Lark was only a child when her mother died, Miss Paget," Aubrey said. "She and her aunt weren't on the best terms, and if there was anything else left, Lark might easily not have known it."

"But surely Aunt Sophie wouldn't keep anything that was Mother's!" Lark exclaimed.

Aubrey looked thoughtful.

"Your Aunt Sophie Williams doesn't strike me as being particularly scrupulous," he said. "It might not be a bad idea to have a quiet look around that chicken ranch and check up on your aunt's expenditures since your mother died."

"That was sixteen years ago," Lark said.

"I know, but your aunt and uncle weren't too well off, and the tradesmen or neighbors would have noticed a sudden splurge," Aubrey said. "Of course, if the price of eggs was good that year—"

Aubrey shrugged.

"Maybe a piece of jewelry the neighbors never saw before… women are fond of jewelry," he added. "Was your brother wearing any when he left, Miss Paget, something you'd recognize again?"

Julia Paget's face looked as hard as the bronze bust of Julius Caesar on the mantel.

"He had a stick pin set with one of the best Paget diamonds," she said. "We used to tease him about looking like Diamond Jim Brady when he wore it, but of course that woman was always after him to put it on. When I think of her getting that diamond…"

She stopped, then went on with great expression.

"He took the platinum and diamond watch fob I gave him for his twenty-first birthday the month before, and his pearl studs and all his cuff links, even the square emeralds and rubies that an Indian Maharajah gave Papa."

Lark noticed that she pronounced "Papa" with the accent on the last syllable.

Miss Paget went on cataloguing.

"He took a fine diamond and ruby ring Papa gave him when he came of age," she said, "and all his stick pins, some of them very good. That was all, I think, except for the Paget crest ring he always wore. It wasn't valuable, just an amethyst with the sea horse inlaid in gold."

"Oh, that's the one in the picture!" Lark exclaimed, picking up the photographs on the table. "Look, on the hand in the corner… with the magnifying glass."

Julia Paget's lorgnette came up again.

28

"But Ulysses was dead—killed in a runaway on the Riviera two weeks before the baby was born," she said. "I know what day that was, the exact hour and minute. His wife was so near her time they let her stay on at the consulate. The Paget name did that, the way it got him his position in the first place. Of course, as soon as the child was born, with Ulysses gone and all, she had to leave."

Julia took a closer look at the picture.

"My brother was dead," she said. "How could—? That's not Ulysses' hand. No Paget ever had knuckles like that."

All at once she began to laugh, unpleasant laughter that shook her thick shoulders, its only sound like the panting of a dog.

"It's Georgette—that creature he married," she said. "I saw her once. She came out to the house; we didn't have a fence then. And Venetia and I peeked through the portières. Papa was trying to buy her off, and Venetia and I heard it all. I remember those ugly hands, as large as a man's, and so badly shaped... she wouldn't know that it isn't proper for a woman to wear a crest."

Julia began to shake again in another paroxysm.

Lark hadn't known it either and could see nothing to laugh about now. And after all, if "that Georgette creature" was her grandmother...

She looked uncomfortably at the tables and chairs with fringed covers and upholstery that cluttered the room. More tassels and fringe on the sofa and curtains and the draping over the mantel. The silk damask on the walls, behind a stippling of framed photographs, made her think of *The Arabian Nights*.

"That photograph you're looking at," Julia said, "is Alexandria, King Edward's wife, you know. She autographed it for me."

"It's amazing, Miss Paget," Aubrey said smoothly, "the number of celebrities you've known. If Lark can qualify as your grandniece she'll be a lucky girl, quite apart from the trust fund involved."

Julia gave him an approving glance, flicked out her lorgnette, and returned to contemplation of Lark.

"You know, in many ways she's very Paget," she said. "The widow's peak—even if her hair isn't blond, the way it grows to a point on her forehead... like mine, see?"

Julia pushed back the fading fluff and let it droop again.

"Ulysses' peak was even deeper," she said. "And she has the Paget small bones. Look at those wrists and ankles."

Aubrey looked, leaned nearer Lark and murmured, "Mmmmm."

Lark flushed.

"What's that?" Julia asked sharply.

"A touch of cold," Aubrey said, giving her his most charming smile. "You know how a throat behaves. Or maybe you don't. You're never ill, are you, Miss Paget?"

"The Paget constitution," Julia said; her tone held no patience for others. "None of us was ever ill. Poor Mother, of course, but she was a Drew. Papa'd be living yet, I do believe, if he hadn't gone sailing and been caught in that squall. Ulysses was in that runaway, and Venetia had that fall."

Lark's lips were already rounding to ask who Venetia was when Aubrey shook his head.

Julia turned suddenly toward her.

"You're never ill, are you, child?" she asked.

"Why, I—no, I never have been," Lark stammered.

The older woman nodded graciously.

"The Paget in her," she said.

The Paget in her! But nothing was proven. It surely couldn't be as easy as this—when she didn't know her mother's family's name, when the only name she did know—Juliet—was spelled wrong, when she had nothing but these pictures, and ever her own birth certificate was a substitute?

"You—you really do believe—?" Lark swallowed.

Aubrey spoke up with no more emotion than as if he had nothing at stake.

"Don't you think, Miss Paget, that we'd better try to dig out a little more about Lark's background before you decide she's a Paget," he said.

That was smart, although Lark barely kept herself from saying so. For all the public knew, she was one of the many stenographers in Aubrey's office. He was right not to seem eager.

"As far as the trust fund goes, of course," Miss Paget said impatiently, "one hardly turns over two million dollars without proper legal formalities. But as far as the girl herself is concerned—she has the picture, and the Paget bones and hairline and health—I'm ready to believe she's Ulysses' granddaughter."

Lark sighed, not so much in relief at Julia Paget's acceptance as at the thought that in only a few minutes she and Aubrey could leave, get away from this turreted, creepy house and its mistress; get away from the endless dunes, and the wind, and the fence built to keep people in…

"Unfortunately, our clerk's in the hospital," Aubrey said, "or I'd have him start right away. But I'll get hold of the private detectives we employ and give them all the information we have on Lark's mother. Her maiden name may be on job applications in Dallas. And there's that ring you said wasn't valuable—the one with the crest. It must have meant a lot to Missus Williams, and if she couldn't sell it for much… I keep thinking Lark's Aunt Sophie should be checked on. I'll get hold of the men right away—"

Lark jumped up.

"Why don't I call Red now and have her phone them?" she said. "They could have someone at the office by the time we get back, Mister Hildreth—"

"Phone?" Miss Paget interrupted distastefully. "Did you by any chance think you could telephone the city from here?"

"Why, I—I—" Lark floundered. "Would it inconvenience you, Miss Paget? Perhaps I should have asked you first."

Were they out of the city limits here? Surely no one who owned that gold-plated statue downstairs would object to a ten-cent toll charge?

"I don't know why I never mentioned—" Aubrey began.

Julia stopped him with a gesture and stood up. The inch or two she rose above Lark seemed like twelve. The thickness of shoulder and breast no longer gave the impression of fat, but of hardness, of a power that was physical, too. Oddly, the small hands and feet, instead of contradicting that look of power, increased it, pointed it up.

"You don't understand, my dear," she told Lark; even her voice seemed more powerful when she stood. "Our telephone line merely runs to the stable. We live here as my father did—without electric lights and radios and canned soup."

31

The word *soup* must have meant more than soup in her mind. The way she said it...

Suddenly Lark thought of a crocodile—the heavy body, the small, out-of-proportion hands and feet—a crocodile lying in wait. This woman who handled vast sums of money must be used to handling people. Her apparent acceptance of a girl who had so little to recommend her—could there be another reason behind it? Suppose the whole story of an heir was a hoax to get hold of someone for a special purpose. Those moments of quiet while Julia Paget's hands had gripped the arms of her chair—if she'd reached some decision..."

"Well?" the woman demanded. "What's the matter?"

"I—I—" Lark stammered again. What had they been talking about? Oh yes—a detective. "I was trying to help get things started. If they had a man there when we got back—"

Julia Paget interrupted.

"When Mister Hildreth gets back, you mean, my dear," she said. "Not you. You're going to stay here with me."

Chapter Four

L eaning on the glass, Lark counted three different shades of green outside the window: the flat green lawn, the hedge on the brink of the cliff, and the gray-green sea teetering darker and darker in the twilight.

It was better to keep her mind on things she could actually see than let it spear one wild notion after another and be carried off on a rocket chase as if she'd harpooned a whale.

The way Miss Paget had accepted her—without any real proof—and then keeping her here, a stranger in a household that didn't believe in banks. Aubrey had told her long ago of the big safe in the dining room for the Paget silver and the smaller one in the pilothouse for money and jewels and papers. The old captain hadn't trusted banks. For all his daughter knew, Lark might have dynamite in her handbag.

The woman's actions weren't normal unless, of course, she was working out some scheme that needed an outsider's help. If the role in it she'd assigned to Lark was something Lark couldn't accept, what then? Would Miss Paget merely try argument and persuasion, or bribery perhaps—or would she try threat?

Lark's mouth felt oddly dry. Better bring her mind back to concreteness—to the lawn and the hedge and the sea, even darker now than when she had looked at it last.

Aubrey must have reached the office an hour ago, while she was still in the boudoir with Miss Paget having tea—little cakes, exquisitely frosted; jasmine tea out of Meissen cups, with souvenir spoons from Italy to stir it;

the massive silver service—and all the time the feeling of having her table manners watched.

It had been a relief to be sent to this quiet bedroom and left alone. But her thoughts had not been relieving.

A knock at the door jerked Lark away from the window. Her soft "Come in" was too soft for the size of the room. She crossed the flowered carpet and turned the knob.

A woman stood in the corridor, her head and upper body silhouetted against the light well through one of the scalloping arches supporting the gallery above. Light was coming up the center well now instead of down it, and was much brighter.

It took Lark a moment to recognize the maid Kezzie, the older woman Miss Paget had run for this afternoon to call the carriage for Aubrey.

"Are you ready to have the gas lighted, miss?" Kezzie asked.

Raising a long metal holder with a tiny flame at one end, the maid came forward and Lark stepped back.

Kezzie laid something on the bed in the shadow of the high footboard and lifted the long holder to the gas fixture. Lark heard an uprush of gas, and light flared in the room.

The harsh brightness made the woman's angular features witchlike and her black parted hair look like paint.

"Miss Paget sent you a dress, miss," Kezzie said.

"Doesn't she like my suit?" Lark asked. Adding "either" in her mind, Lark glanced down at her carefully chosen gray wool.

"It's hardly the thing for dinner, miss," Kezzie said.

Lark's head came up. There was nothing disrespectful in Kezzie's words or in her expressionless face. Only something in her tone, perhaps a gleam in her small black eyes.

"I wasn't expecting to stay," Lark said, "so I have no other clothes with me."

"Of course not, miss," Kezzie said. "But I think Miss Venetia's things will do nicely. You look just her size."

Venetia again—the one who'd had "that fall." If Kezzie had been the pretty girl who'd opened the door this afternoon, Lark would have asked about

34

Venetia. She didn't like to ask Kezzie.

The tall woman laid the gas lighter, with the flame out now, on a table and bent over the bed, arranging the dress she'd laid there. Beneath her hands the skirt fanned out, full and diaphanous, a silvery gray that even in the glare of the gas made Lark think of moonlight.

The maid straightened, and Lark felt bony fingers at the back of her neck. Her first impulse, sharply controlled, was to pull away.

"Your jacket, miss," Kezzie said. "And now the skirt."

Lark started to unbutton her blouse and felt the bony fingers at her throat.

"Now the blouse," Kezzie murmured. "I've drawn your bath. May I help...?"

"Oh, no," Lark said. Hurrying toward the door indicated, Lark remembered to say "thank you" before she closed it between them.

Her own reflection met her inside, a big-eyed girl in a slip who walked with her through a mirror-lined dressing room to an open door at the other end.

The room she entered was so large that, for an instant, she thought Kezzie must have given her the wrong directions. Then she saw the sunken tile tub like a miniature swimming pool. The gas was bright here, too, repeating on the wainscot the blue opalescent gleam of the tub, glittering on the metal wash bowl and faucets that shone like polished silver. Wall paintings on plastered panels, closed wooden shutters, plush curtains at both windows...

A door across the room sent her hurrying over marble mosaic. Here was another dressing room with its wardrobe doors all mirrors; beyond, another bedroom, dim in the twilight, as large as the one she had left. Kezzie must have come that way to light the gas and fill the tub. What solid doors these were to shut out the sound of running water.

Lark bolted both doors to the bathroom and came back to the blue edge of the pool.

But she couldn't bathe forever. The time came when she had to return to the lighted room and Kezzie and the moon-colored dress.

"Now, if you'll please take off your slip again, miss," Kezzie murmured, "Miss Venetia's has its own."

35

It looked like a silver snare about to catch her. Before Lark could even tell herself not to be silly, she was enclosed in a rustling lavender-scented straightjacket. Her head emerged from silver-gray taffeta, and she drew a long breath, instantly cut off around the waist.

"Sorry, miss," Kezzie said. "I have to get it hooked. Miss Venetia wore a corset."

"I guess I can breathe," Lark said. "But when I think of eating…"

Kezzie's disapproving silence suggested that Venetia didn't eat.

The long garment made a polished cast of Lark's body to the knees and then frothed into sudden fullness.

The cobweb of the over-dress was descending on her now, and the silver paled to moonlight. Venetia as well as Miss Paget must like old-fashioned things. *Must like* or *must have liked?* There was something about the way Kezzie spoke and about the dress itself… the cobweb was shirred at the neck and tiny waist, and at the sleeves there were quaint little puffs like dandelions gone to seed. The smell of lavender came stronger, spicy in Lark's nostrils.

Kezzie picked up something hidden by the footboard.

"I wonder if you can wear her slippers, miss," Kezzie said.

She held them out, and Lark gasped.

"No one's worn such pointed toes since I can remember!"

"Naturally not, miss," Kezzie said. "It's been over forty years since Miss Venetia—was taken."

"She's—dead?" Lark asked.

Kezzie nodded. "The ocean got her."

The water that Lark had watched darken, whose muted boom she heard now…

The scent of Venetia's clothes was all at once suffocating. Lark hurried through the rest of her dressing.

Kezzie opened the hall door.

"I'll go down with you, miss, and show you the way," she said.

At the head of the stairs Lark hesitated. The roses of the carpet spilled down the left-hand fork before them and climbed the right. Below, at the base of the Y, the golden lady held up an orange-yellow ball of dazzling light. It stamped the shadow of each arch across the balcony where she stood and, on the third-story balcony above, she could see the pattern repeated. The great Chinese hat of the skylight that had been so softly golden in the daytime was now no more than a dun-colored ceiling.

"I'll see you don't get lost," Kezzie said.

But Lark already felt lost, descending the padded stairs that gave back no creak or footstep sound, as muffling as the sand of the dunes. Aubrey was miles away, back there in the world she left.

There was no longer a gilded circle in the middle of the downstairs hall. Now all the pillars supporting the balconies stood out in their marble smoothness only slightly less red than the carpet. The huge circular room, not so packed with furniture as the two bedrooms and Miss Paget's boudoir, looked almost as vast to Lark as a department store. The walls were rods away—not walls, she corrected herself, the wall: one sweeping circle, hung with deeply framed paintings, tapestries and bas-reliefs, and broken only by doorways whose massive frames were splashed with gold. Except for the wide opening into the vestibule where two wooden doors were pushed back, all the door frames—five on each side and one behind the stairs—were hung with dark portières the shade of the Paget livery.

"They're in the Maple Parlor," Kezzie said. "Third door on your right from the front."

They?

The portières in the third doorway were as motionless, as stagnant green, as all the others. Lark started doubtfully toward it as Kezzie returned toward the stairs.

Over her shoulder Lark looked from the maid's black back to the green portières, fighting an urge to run away, to walk slowly enough for Kezzie to reach the upper hall—and then not go through the portières. Run instead to the closed double doors. Run, in the drowned Venetia's moonbeam dress, down the graveled drive, down the long road across the dunes.

She glanced back at Kezzie. Instead of being halfway upstairs, the maid stood by the newel post looking more pinched than ever beneath the voluptuous statue. She stood there, waiting.

Lark walked on toward the portières, one slow foot before the other. Now, in another step, she would reach them. She looked back again.

Kezzie was still there.

Lark's hands touched cat-fur plush and slowly drew the curtains apart.

She saw a big rectangular room, crowded like the others with furniture and bric-a-brac. Above cream-yellow woodwork the walls were pale blue silk hung with heavily gold-framed pictures. The birds-eye maple wainscot seemed to have a thousand eyes, all fixed on her.

Then she saw the human eyes.

Toward the far end of the room flames climbed from a grate beneath a marble mantel and a mirror as large as a window. Leaning against the blue lambrequin—wasn't that what mantel drapes were called?—was a man in a dinner jacket, with his face turned her way.

Lark dropped the curtains and stepped in.

Julia Paget looked up from a chair by the fire.

"Oh, there you are, child," she said. "Come let me look at you."

Beneath Miss Paget's stare, the young man at the fireplace, and all the maple eyes, Lark made her way forward.

"Venetia's dress fits you perfectly—I knew it would," Julia said.

She gave herself a congratulatory nod. Flicking out her lorgnette, she examined Lark but made no move to introduce the watching man or the small woman about Miss Paget's age whom Lark now saw almost hidden in a big chair with its back to the door.

The man, not as tall as Aubrey or as handsome, looked on with his mouth turned down, while the little woman in the big chair seemed mystified.

"Miss—ah—Williams, I believe?" Julia murmured. "My cousin, Benson Drew."

Lark looked down at the little woman in the girlish pink dinner dress. But it was the man who said, "How do you do?"

"And—ah—his mother, Rowena Drew," Julia added.

This time the little woman nodded, offering a tentative smile.

"I shall call you Lark, of course," Miss Paget announced. "And you must call me Aunt Julia."

The flames climbed on up the chimney, but they—and Julia's eyes—were the only things that moved.

At last the man said to Lark, "So, you're the successful candidate, Miss Williams?"

"Cousin Lark, Benson," Julia corrected. "You're not properly welcoming your Cousin Ulysses' granddaughter."

"What—Julia—Ben—I don't understand..."

The wail came from Mrs. Drew.

Lark was shocked to see how the little woman had shrunk, quivering and white in her chair.

Benson Drew bent over her quickly.

"Don't get upset, Mother," he said. "You know Cousin Julia said a month ago that she thought her brother's child might be alive."

"But this girl—now—in Venetia's dress—" Miss Drew stammered.

Benson laid one hand on his mother's shoulder and faced Julia.

"The costume *is* a little odd," he said. "Are you giving a masquerade for her debut?"

Miss Paget laughed—that silent, panting laugh.

"I must say, Benson, you're taking this well," she said. "You would have been the heir if there'd been no Paget left. Actually, you've behaved almost as if you were a Paget yourself."

Benson bowed. "The accolade."

"Too bad I can't say the same for your mother," Julia said, looking scornfully at the shaken woman in pink. "But then, she's not even a Drew. You saw the paper this morning, Benson?"

He nodded. "Perhaps I should have told Mother," he said, "but I didn't expect your ad would be answered—successfully—so soon."

Lark's eyes met Julia's. The older woman shook her head.

"What do you mean by an ad, Ben?" his mother asked. "Julia's ad?"

"Cousin Julia had the papers print a picture of Ulysses' baby to see if anyone could match it," Benson said. "I suppose, Cousin Julia, you've checked to make sure Miss Williams' picture is genuine. Its age and all that?"

Julia Paget didn't even pause.

"Of course—or at least Aubrey Hildreth has," she said.

Or would as soon as Miss Paget got hold of him, Lark thought. Benson Drew's skepticism was a lot more normal than his cousin's too-quick acceptance. But of course he stood to lose millions. Or did he? Perhaps this was Miss Paget's scheme, and the whole reason why Lark was being kept at Dune House. Would Lark be used as a catalyst to speed the Drews' reaction, and then, when the fun was over, be laughed at, perhaps doled out a few dollars, and sent back to her typewriter at the office? There was something evil about this house. She had felt it from the first.

Miss Paget was speaking again.

"Really, Benson, you must learn to call Ulysses' granddaughter Cousin Lark, or Lark, if you like; you young people are so informal. And Lark, my dear, you must call your cousin by his given name, too, and his mother Cousin Rowena."

Rowena Drew made a sound like a squeak, and Lark saw her son's hand tighten on her thin shoulder.

He couldn't be much older than she was, Lark decided, but his mouth was more bitter than Mr. Rollin's. He was strongly built. The hand on his mother's shoulder was large and looked muscular, though not in the same way Uncle Thad's hands did or even Oscar Fry's—as if it were used to work. Poor Oscar, she must find out what hospital he was in and call up to ask about him... but she couldn't call from Dune House.

"That dress needs something, child." Julia had her lorgnette out again. "How did Venetia—? Oh, yes, I remember. Benson, will you pull the bell cord?"

The young man leaned over his mother again.

"Don't worry, Mother," he said. "Everything's going to be fine."

Benson walked to the door Lark had entered and pulled a cord she assumed was just another tassel in this plentifully tasseled room.

Before he was back at the fireplace, the pretty maid Lark had seen first came in through another set of portières.

"Dinner is served, madam," she told Miss Paget.

"Tell Yep to take the soup back and keep it warm," Miss Paget said. "Then run and find Kezzie and tell her to bring me Miss Venetia's pearls."

"Venetia's pearls!" Rowena gasped.

"Be quick, Eileen," Miss Paget commanded. "Miss Lark is to wear them for dinner."

Eileen went out by the way she had come, and silence crowded the Maple Parlor.

"I remember you wanted to wear them years ago, Rowena." Julia leaned back in her chair. Her long green dress, almost the shade of the portières and the Paget livery, overflowed it. "But of course, when Ulysses' own granddaughter..."

The silence came back, although not quite perfect silence, for Lark could hear Rowena breathing.

It seemed weeks before the hall curtains were pushed aside and Kezzie came in, walking stiffly, with a blue velvet box in her hand.

Julia opened it and drew out four long strands of pearl beads secured with a platinum clasp.

"Come here, child, and bend over," Julia said, fastening them around Lark's neck. "Papa sent a man all through the Orient to match our pearls. His daughters had to have the best."

She touched the strands looping into space from her own outcrop of bosom.

Real pearls, Lark thought, looking down, not imitation. How lovely they were on the moon-colored dress—ethereal—out of this world. She shivered suddenly. That silly phrase was too descriptive of the girl who had once worn this dress and these pearls, as Lark was wearing them now.

She looked up and met Benson Drew's eyes—greenish, she saw in the gaslight, not gentle, not at all soft.

"Very well, Kezzie," Julia said. "You may tell Eileen to serve the soup."

In a leisurely moment they followed her through portières on the ocean side into a dining room that made Lark gasp. A tremendously long table stood on a partnered Persian rug as large as Aunt Sophie's chicken yard.

"We're usually served in the alcove." Julia waved toward the end of the

41

room and a set of bottle-green portières wider than any of the others. "This table seats sixty—a little large for four. But the first night Ulysses' granddaughter is with us, we have to receive her in state."

Eileen was taking soup plates out of a dumbwaiter near a carved wood mantelpiece where another fire flickered and four places at the end of the table looked lonely and a little ridiculous.

Miss Paget led the way past a long row of oil paintings and a sideboard top-heavy with silver toward the four distant plates. She came to the end of the table at last, though not to the end of the rug, and, taking the head chair, motioned Lark to sit on her right and the Drews on her left.

"Tell Yep," she commanded before Eileen had set down the last wide-lipped bowl, "that he can't use the excuse of sending things up from the kitchen to get careless. The soup's not hot enough."

Perhaps Yep would have a better chance, Lark thought, if the soup hadn't had to go up and down in the dumbwaiter two or three times.

"He thinks he owns the place after he's been with us fifty years," Julia complained. "Oh, well, Yep's a good cook... I saw you looking at the paintings, child. How do you like that portrait over the mantel?"

Lark looked across Julia's thick shoulder, past the mantel-shelf's great slab of carved wood, for once undraped, into a massive gold frame about the face and bare shoulders of a blond young woman.

"Why—that's you, isn't it, Miss Paget?" Lark asked.

"Aunt Julia." The correction was amiable with approval. "I knew you'd recognize it. Everyone says I look just like it yet."

The hair, gold then instead of silver, dressed much as it was now... eyes with the same expression, though without the whitish age circles that clouded the brown... mouth the same, as straight then as now... the shoulders, even at that time, beginning to show the thickening of power... the face, then without any sag of the cheeks, already heavy chinned—the whole expression showing earlier stages of what it had crystallized into now.

"Yes," Lark said slowly, "you do still look like that."

Across the table she caught the flash of Benson Drew's green eyes and the down curve of a mocking smile.

"She does," Lark repeated. "Her expression is the same."

Benson Drew turned to his mother.

"Maybe Miss Williams *is* a Paget," he said. "She knows what to say."

Lark flushed, but Julia disregarded the Drews as if they were so many grains of salt on the damask.

"That portrait was done while Papa and Ulysses and Venetia were still with us," Miss Paget said. "The young painter wanted to marry me—poor thing."

Lark contradicted her silently. Not "poor thing"—brave young man if, after putting all he'd put into that face, he still wanted to marry Julia Paget. He must have needed money badly.

All through the fish course, the meat course, and the salad, Lark kept looking from the portrait over the mantel to the woman at the head of the table. The way that painted promise had been fulfilled was uncanny. Lark couldn't help wondering how Papa and Ulysses and Venetia had liked the early stages.

By dessert Rowena had recovered her outward composure—whether from the claret served with the food she had seemed only to push about on her plate or the attentions of her son, Lark couldn't tell. It was odd to be sitting here in a borrowed dress in this great paneled room gleaming with silver and crystal and delicate china, among people she had never seen before three o'clock today. If she was in truth Ulysses Paget's granddaughter, the thick-shouldered woman at the head of the table was her great-aunt, the bitter-mouthed young man across it some kind of cousin, his frightened-looking little mother a sort of cousin-in-law. Were they the answer to her childhood longing for a family?

Julia tinkled the silver bell she had rung so many times during dinner, and pushed back her chair. They all rose, and she linked her arm with Lark's.

"Come, child, let's go back to the Maple Parlor," she said. "From now on, Rowena, we'll have a fourth at whist. Papa was so fond of whist, my dear. He played it every night."

"But, Miss Pa—"

"Aunt Julia."

"Aunt Julia," Lark's tongue repeated, while her mind kept repeating *from now on*. Years of after-dinner whist at Dune house... of being out of contact with the world, with Aubrey... years of—.

She was crazy, she told herself sharply. Proving that she was Ulysses Paget's granddaughter wasn't going to take years, and as soon as that was settled, the money put aside for her child would be turned over to her. She and Aubrey would announce their marriage and set up housekeeping for themselves. It wasn't going to take years, just a few more days, or maybe weeks of trying not to antagonize Miss Paget, and all this Dune House nonsense would only be a nightmare from which she had finally awakened.

Lark dropped her voice though she and Julia were several steps ahead of the Drews. "We don't know yet—"

The heavy arm squeezed hers.

"Hush, child; it does Rowena and Benson good to sweat a bit," Miss Paget said. "Don't say anything to them about things not being certain. Understand?"

Her feet had stopped, and her arm stopped Lark. The thick neck stiffened, her chin tucking down into three. Her eyes shone from narrow slits.

"Understand?" she repeated.

Lark wet her lips. "If—if you say so—Aunt Julia."

Julia's neck returned to normal, her chin, her eyes. Her straight lips smiled.

"Come here, Benson, and get acquainted with your cousin before we start playing," Julia said. "Step out on the balcony a moment. Rowena and I can always find plenty to say."

She pushed them ahead and took Rowena's shriveled arm.

Lark's blue eyes met Benson's green.

"You can't exactly expect me to warm up, you know," Benson observed. "Though I'd be only too glad to—under other circumstances."

"I'm not looking for—warming up," Lark returned.

"No, I guess not," Benson said. "What you're looking for clinks when it drops on the bar."

Her chin came up. Then her lips, which had started to open, closed. After all, would she have checked that picture in the paper with the one she had at home, or even thought about it, if it hadn't been for the Paget money?

He touched her elbow.

"This way to the balcony we've been ordered to go out on," he said.

They crossed the great hall behind the staircase and went through the last portières on that side.

"This is the smoking room," he told her. "Otherwise known as the Moorish Room, imported in chunks from Granada."

Along walls trimmed with grain leather and carved wooden grilles, they passed deep leather chairs and carved stands on islands of oriental rugs.

"For gentlemen only, of course," Benson added. "And they only smoked pipes or cigars. Cigarettes weren't considered the thing when this place was built. By the way, if you'd like one on the balcony, Miss Williams, I don't think Cousin Julia'd detect it."

"No, thank you," Lark said. "I can take them or leave them."

"And run no risk of annoying Cousin Julia," Benson said. "Very smart, Miss Williams, very smart."

He opened a pair of French doors, and cold air blew at them from the ocean. Lark went through and leaned on the metal railing.

A foot away, Benson leaned beside her.

"Let me know before you get pneumonia," he said. "Then we'll have a good excuse to go in."

Out there, beyond railing, lawn, and hedge, the Pacific was no more than a black line against a less black sky, a line and a rhythmic crashing.

Lark wished Venetia's dress were warmer. In the night it was like a moonbeam, with the pearls drops of dew.

"I take it Venetia was Miss Paget's sister," Lark said. "Was she—like Miss Paget?"

Benson shook his head.

"Very different, according to Mother, and much younger," he said. "Mother says she was lovely—blond and slim and kind, with a voice like a bell."

Lark thought of the silver tea bell in Julia Paget's claw hands.

"I wonder—" she began.

"How she got along with Cousin Julia?" Benson said. "I guess Venetia couldn't take it any more than Ulysses. He ran away, and she died."

"But dying wouldn't be—not being able to take it," Lark objected.

"It would—under some circumstances," Benson said.

What did he mean? Or did she really want to know? She quickly said instead, "Then Kezzie and the cook can certainly take it. If Venetia died forty years ago and Kezzie used to dress her... and the cook's been here fifty..."

"Oh, the servants are paid," Benson said. "They know which side their bread is buttered on."

His face was only a blue shadow in the overcast night. Lark wondered what his position and his mother's were. It sounded as if the family wasn't paid. She glanced up at the mass of house extending half a story below the floor she was on and at least two above it with towers rising still higher.

"It must take loads of servants to run this place," Lark said.

"It does when the whole thing's open," Benson agreed. "But Cousin Julia's closed off a lot of rooms. She only has Adam and Leo outside now, and Yep and Kezzie and Eileen in the house. Leo helps with the heavier inside work, and the laundry's sent out. She says she'd rather pay double wages and have only a few servants that she knows are close-mouthed."

"What's there to keep so still about here?" Lark asked. "I don't see—"

She broke off, realizing that she'd spoken aloud.

"Cousin Julia's always been fussy about publicity," Benson said. "That's why she added those outside arms to the fence. There were too many reporters climbing in."

Lark kept herself from asking for whom the inside arms had been put on as Benson added, "She does live rather oddly, you know, with everything the way her father had it—even her own gas plant in the basement. She'd get a lot of unpleasant publicity if reporters had the run of the place and the servants did too much talking, besides attracting any number of crooks."

Was he looking at her? It was hard to tell, with the only light coming from the open French doors a good yard to the left and the window curtains drawn. Except for the heavy thump of waves on the cliff below, the balcony was still.

Then out of the night came a loud, deep reverberation that sounded alive.

"What's that?" Lark cried.

"A lion roaring in Fleishhacker Zoo," Benson said. "We've got a choice collection here, both inside and outside the fence."

"I hope he doesn't do it often," Lark said. "It's funny, when you think about it—the zoo a step away—and Playland and the park and all those rows of houses the other side of the fence. And yet, ever since we came in the gate, I've felt so strongly we were in another world that I'd actually forgotten we were so near the real one."

"Don't let the ocean fool you," Benson said. "We're looking out on space here. Come on around to the north side and I'll show you."

She followed, one hand on the cold railing, to the corner of the house. The balcony turned with it, and Lark drew in a quick breath. Beyond the dark half-mile stretch of Paget dunes, lights starred the night: lines and lines in the rows of houses; brighter, higher street lights; down the beach the crazy quilt of Playland. A long finger of black meant Golden Gate Park. Then more lights that meant more houses.

"It makes you feel queer, doesn't it?" Lark said. "All those other people living so close, and we seem so far away."

"Let's go in," Benson said. "We must have been here long enough to satisfy Cousin Julia."

* * *

"No use yawning, Rowena," Julia said. "We have to play off the rubber."

It was twelve o'clock. By now one card looked to Lark like any of the other fifty-one. All she saw were hands; dealing, laying down cards—Julia's little hands with pudgy backs and claw fingers; Rowena's arthritic joints on hands, not so small as Miss Paget's, that trembled as she played; Benson's muscular man's hands. How like Julia to play whist instead of contract. Papa had played whist every night—Papa, who had built this house that his daughter preserved as he'd left it.

Whenever Lark wasn't seeing hands, she was seeing walls of grained leather and patterned silk; wainscots of eyes; oil paintings in massive gold frames; crowded, heavy pieces of furniture. Aubrey seemed far away, almost too far away to be real.

"We talk if we want to when we're playing," Miss Paget had told Lark early in the evening. "Papa always did."

Then she snapped at Rowena, "Don't take all night deciding what to lead. We have a full day ahead of us tomorrow, getting Lark the right sort of clothes."

Rowena's faded eyes lighted.

"Oh, I love to shop—where shall we go?" she said.

"'We' means Lark and me," Julia said coldly. "You won't be with us, Rowena."

The other woman's face changed like a child's. Tears filled her eyes.

"Go on and play," Julia prodded.

The card Rowena laid down had a drop of moisture on it, fumblingly wiped off, and in spite of her son's gentle, "Having no spades, partner?" she reneged three times. Miss Paget and Lark won the rubber.

They all climbed the stairs together. At the fork of the Y, Julia Paget and the Drews turned right. Lark turned left. As she opened her door she saw, across the light well, the Drews going up the next flight to the floor above.

The light was burning in her room. Had she left it on?

Then she saw that her room wasn't empty. Kezzie was standing by the bureau, the heavy black line of her brows and the thin pale line of her mouth alarmingly straight.

"What's the matter?" Lark cried. Had something happened to Aubrey? But how would Kezzie know—here, with no phone?

"The pearls, miss," Kezzie said. "I have to put them in the safe."

"Oh, of course," Lark said. Relief made Lark clumsy, working at the clasp. "I'm not used to real pearls."

Kezzie unfastened the necklace and laid it on the bureau. "Let me unhook your dress, miss."

"Thank you," Lark said. "Then it'll take me a minute to pop into bed."

"I always put Miss Paget to bed," Kezzie said. "She told me to help you, too."

"I don't need help," Lark said. "I'll sleep in my slip since I don't have a nightgown... oh... you've brought one?"

On the bed lay a long-sleeved, high-necked white gown.

"Miss Venetia's," Kezzie said.

Then it was going over Lark's head with the same spicy smell as the dress.

"Was lavender Venetia's favorite scent?" Lark asked.

Kezzie nodded. "She used to grow it—out there at the back of the house toward the ocean. The conservatory and the servants' wing cut off the wind. Miss Venetia had lots of flowers."

And Julia had none. Lark thought of the wide plush lawn without blossom or tree. How different the sisters must have been. Venetia slim and kind, with a voice like a bell. And Julia... well, what made Rowena Drew look so cowed and Benson Drew so bitter?

"They were both out there that night," Kezzie said. "Miss Venetia and Miss Julia—out in Miss Venetia's garden. I didn't hear them myself, but the downstairs maid told me the next day she could hear them arguing and quarreling clear up in her room. She heard a scream, and Miss Julia came in. I saw her myself. She was pale as death—and alone."

Kezzie paused. Lark found her heart beating faster.

"Miss Julia said Miss Venetia'd gone over the cliff," Kezzie said.

"You—you mean—out *there*?" Lark pointed to the window overlooking the ocean. The ocean, and the great cliff plunging down... Venetia, who'd had "that fall."

Kezzie nodded. "That was before the hedge was planted. That was *why* it was planted. Miss Julia said Miss Venetia jumped."

Surely Kezzie hadn't accented *said*. That was Lark's own imagination. But what if, forty years ago, Julia had not stopped at breaking spirits?

Kezzie opened the window, and the swish of the sea was louder. "Goodnight, miss," she said. "There's a candle and matches on the table by your bed if you want them in the night."

She reached up toward the light, and the room went dark. In a moment the hall door opened barely enough to let her through; then the latch clicked, and the light from the gallery was gone.

Lark lay tense between linen sheets. What if all this *had* been forty years ago? If Julia pushed her sister off the cliff... Kezzie hadn't said much. But her tone, and the things she'd left out...

In Venetia's long white gown Lark felt her way across the carpet. Julia was still there, in the same house with Lark...

She caught the door knob and fumbled for the key. She must be wrong; there *must* be one...

Shaking, she found her way back to the bedside table, struck a match, and brought a lighted candle to the door.

But she wasn't wrong. The lock had no key.

Chapter Five

Tonight, her second at Dune House, Lark didn't have to wear Venetia's nightgown. She had one of her own without any sleeves, the loveliest she had ever seen. Behind the mirror doors in her dressing room were the prettiest dresses she had ever tried on, and folded in the drawers that were lined with rose velvet was exquisite underwear. Yet every garment fitted to Lark's measure seemed more Miss Paget's than her own.

Lark shivered under handmade lace between smooth linen sheets. Linen was cold anyway, but not even outing flannel would have kept her warm here. When she and Aubrey first drove through the hedge she had felt the chill of Dune House.

She shivered again and turned over. Today had been the sort of day girls dream about, the sort she had dreamed of herself before Aubrey filled her dreams. Lark, too, had worn furs in the Post Street parade and the kind of suit other women stare at. Post Street, Geary, Grant Avenue—in and out of the most expensive shops. No chance to call Aubrey, with Julia never out of sight—walking across sidewalks, down store aisles, sitting in the dressing rooms—while Leo, with his right cheek always averted, picked them up from store to store in the long black car with Paget-green upholstery.

Shops and dresses and fittings all day, broken into only by lunch, with Julia's cake crumbs falling on the same cloth as her own. Then the long drive back to Dune House side by side through streets of jammed-together, bay-windowed wooden houses, with Adam reporting at the stable a dozen more missing heirs who had brought the wrong pictures. Another many-course

51

dinner with the disappointed Rowena and bitter-mouthed Benson, this time in the dining alcove, the food considerably warmer than the night before. Another long evening of whist.

Lark turned over again. How long would it be before Aubrey's detectives would be able to prove something, one way or the other? What if they never could? Would Julia expect her to stay all the time they were working? Would—?

What was that? It sounded like singing.

Lark sat up.

It *was* singing. A woman's voice coming in through the open window—soft—melodious—bell-like. As if someone was out on the back lawn singing bits of opera to herself. Above the muffled crash of waves Lark could barely hear the voice—soft, but true and bell-like.

Funny how she kept thinking of bells. Where...? Oh, yes, Benson said Venetia had a voice like a bell. But he wasn't talking of singing.

Lark was cold, sitting up in the sheer, lace-topped gown. She shivered down into the covers.

But the singing went on. She cocked her head away from the pillow. Tones almost like a part of the ocean sound.

At last, curiosity got the better of the cold. Lark reached for the marabou dressing gown at the foot of her bed and ran across the deep carpet to the window. Leaning out, she searched the starlight. The voice sang on, but nothing showed except the dark patch she knew was grass, and the glinting sea. The servants' wing, jutting out toward the ocean, was dark.

For an hour—she struck matches beside the candle on the bedside table to look at her watch—the singing went on. Finally, still shivering, Lark slept.

* * *

"But I heard it, Aunt Julia," Lark said. It was easier to call Miss Paget Aunt Julia now. They were sitting at breakfast in the alcove off the dining room.

"Songs from *Aida* and *Rigoletto*," she continued, "and that lovely *Lucia* thing. A woman's voice, soft and clear as a bell. I could have sworn it came from the lawn out there above the ocean."

"Nonsense," Julia said sharply. "I'm a light sleeper, and I didn't hear a thing. In fact, I slept particularly well last night. It was your imagination. Between the ocean pounding on that side of the house and the wind howling, you can think you hear anything."

Lark appealed to the Drews. "Didn't either of you hear it?"

Rowena shook her head. She seemed oddly excited, almost as if she didn't trust herself to speak.

Benson only looked amused.

"Our rooms are on the third floor, the other side of the servants' wing from yours," he said. "I'll bet one of them smuggled in a battery set."

"But I didn't hear an orchestra," Lark objected, "though of course the ocean could have drowned it out."

At the same time, Julia repeated "Battery set," her colorless eyes drawn together.

"Radio, to you, Cousin Julia," Benson said. "One that runs on a battery like your telephone, without an electrical plug-in."

Julia stood up.

"I shall go through their rooms at once," she said. "If Kezzie or Eileen or Yep..." Her voice was still coming back as she left the room.

"I didn't mean to get them in trouble," Benson said, jumping up from the table. "I'll go put Eileen wise. She's the likeliest suspect."

His mother and Lark were left alone.

Clutching the edge of the table, Rowena leaned across it.

"My dear, don't say anything more to Julia," Rowena said, her voice trembling and her arthritic joints standing up from the cloth. "I—I wish you'd told me first. You see—her sister used to sing like that—out in that very garden. It was a garden then. Venetia always had flowers, and after she died, Julia had them all dug up."

"I heard about—how Venetia died," Lark said.

"It's dreadful to think of her suicide," Rowena said.

Lark opened her mouth, but before "Suicide!" came out, Rowena said, "A lovely girl like that. You can see why Julia wouldn't want to be reminded.

53

She had such high hopes for Venetia."

"You mean her voice?" Lark asked. "Did she think Venetia could sing opera?"

Rowena looked shocked. "Oh, but that's what the quarrel was about!" she said. "Venetia wanted to sing on the stage, and Julia swore no sister of hers ever would. That's why she built the fence!"

"What do you mean?" Lark asked. "Who built the fence—and why?"

"Julia did, to keep Venetia in," Rowena explained. "You see, Julia had opposed Ulysses' marriage—Julia and Captain Paget—and Ulysses ran away; then, when the old captain died two or three months later and Ulysses a few months after that, Julia said that she was head of the house and Venetia had to do what she said. Venetia was only seventeen, and Julia had control of the money. I was here a lot in those days, though it was a good ten years before I was married. My husband was the girls' Uncle Benson, you know. I was a lot younger than he was and younger than Julia, too; so she couldn't call me 'aunt.' Anyway, she wouldn't... I was thirty when I married and thirty-eight when Ben was born and his father died—"

"But the fence, Missus Drew," Lark said. "You said Miss Paget—"

"Yes, I was telling you about the fence," Rowena said. "When Venetia said she was going to New York to sing—honestly, my dear, I'm still amazed when I think of Venetia taking such a stand; she was always scared to death of Julia. But they say a worm will turn, you know, and there was one thing Venetia was willing to fight for—maybe two."

"But, Missus Drew—" Lark began. Perhaps Miss Paget's treatment of her wasn't all due to malice. Rowena could certainly be trying.

"Yes, the fence," Rowena continued. "As I said, when Venetia announced she was going to New York, Julia locked her in her room and had the fence built. When it was done and the lock taken off her door—poor thing, it was pathetic to see how Venetia would get herself all scratched up trying to climb out."

So that was why the fence was built—to keep Venetia in. Not because anyone was crazy—unless it was Julia, who went in and out at will.

"So you see," Rowena said, "why it's best not to say anything to Julia about hearing a woman sing in the back garden, especially singing opera. *Aida* and *Rigoletto* and *Lucia* were Venetia's favorites. I remember how she used to sound out there, with the roar of the ocean."

Lark thought of the silver voice last night and was colder than she'd been in bed.

"You see, don't you dear," the little woman repeated. "You won't say anything to Julia?"

"I—see," Lark said slowly. She saw perhaps more than Rowena did. Rowena had said suicide. "Then what did Miss Paget have such high hopes of Venetia for if not opera?"

"Oh, to marry and increase the Pagets," Rowena said. "Julia didn't want to marry, but she said Venetia had to, and she was going to make Venetia's husband change his name to Paget."

"I wonder if she could," Lark said. "People are funny about their names."

"*Julia* would," Rowena said. "As a matter of fact, she had already picked out a man who would... why, you know him, my dear. It was Edward Rollin."

Mister Rollin, of the thick stiff back and red face, whose morbid fear of publicity surpassed Julia's. Mister Rollin, so careful of everyone's dignity—but his own when he lost his temper. Perhaps having to be content with a lawyer's share of the Paget millions instead of a son-in-law's had soured him.

"Venetia and I were great friends," Rowena said. "She was three years younger than I, but Julia was so... anyway, Venetia was like me about not wanting to quarrel and argue; one of those retiring, gentle girls, but she did have flare-ups of stubbornness—the way she was about her singing—and that coachman..."

"Coachman?" Lark asked.

Rowena looked embarrassed.

"Well, if you haven't heard..." she began. "Still, I suppose it's better to tell you than to leave you guessing. When Venetia had turned seventeen she fell in love with her father's coachman. Not that she ever *did* anything, my dear, just acted silly. But the old captain was so mad that he cut her out of his will, at least temporarily. Then, after Ulysses ran away with Georgette, Captain

Paget cut him off without a dollar; so everything went to Julia. Venetia was always to be allowed a home at Dune House but wasn't to have her share of the property until Julia died. The old captain said Venetia would be protected from fortune hunters that way and Julia could always be trusted to do the right thing."

The right thing... would that be pushing her sister off a cliff?

Rowena stood up.

"I'd better run along," she said. "When Julia comes back, you won't say anything to her, will you, if you hear singing again?"

Lark shook her head. "Not unless it's necessary."

"It's never necessary, my dear, to harrow people's feelings," Rowena said. "I know Julia doesn't always follow that rule herself, but... she'd hate to think of Venetia—like that... well, I'd better be running along."

She hurried out, and Lark sat on at the empty table. She too hated to think of Venetia—like that... forty years dead, and a voice in the night...

The portières parted. Lark hoped it wasn't Julia coming back. But it was only Eileen.

"Excuse me, miss," she said. "I thought everyone was through. May I bring you some fresh coffee? Or toast?"

"No, thank you," Lark said. "I've finished breakfast. Go ahead and clear the table. Oh—uh—Eileen, do you sing?"

The maid's hand, reaching for a wasp-waisted silver egg cup, paused. Her Irish-blue eyes blinked at Lark. "Sing, miss?"

Lark nodded.

"I heard someone singing last night, and I wondered—" she said.

"I don't have a radio, miss," Eileen said. "Mister Drew said Miss Paget's searching our rooms for one now. None of us have one."

"I mean, do you sing yourself?" Lark clarified. "It sounded like a woman out there on the back lawn singing."

"Oh, no, miss," Eileen said. "I can't even carry a tune. And Aunt Kezzie and I both went to bed early last night."

"Is Kezzie your aunt?" Lark asked. "For goodness sake, when you're so pretty..."

Eileen dimpled.

"Maybe we don't look much alike, miss," she said. "But if Kezzie hadn't been my aunt, I never would have got on here. Miss Paget wouldn't take just anyone. Leo's Adam's son, and I'm Kezzie's niece."

"Maybe it was Kezzie I heard," Lark said.

"But she sounds like me, miss—like a crow," Eileen said. "It runs in the family. And we both went to bed early last night. I'd done a lot of cleaning, and Kezzie was tired from her trip downtown."

"Did Kezzie go downtown yesterday too?" Lark asked. "Clear downtown?" Eileen nodded.

"She took the streetcar, miss, down at Fleishhacker Zoo," Eileen said. "We only have to walk to the gate, and we can always pick up a ride to the zoo if Leo can't take us."

How in keeping with the Paget tradition for the mistress to drive downtown in style and let the help walk a mile through sand, and hitchhike a ride to the streetcar!

"But you're too young and pretty," Lark exclaimed. "You can't tell who might pick you up—and not put you down at the streetcar."

"Leo used to have a fit." Eileen's dimples showed briefly again and then vanished. "But I guess he doesn't care anymore."

"He's the one with—?" Lark broke off. "The man who drives the car?"

"Leo's the man with the scar, if that's what you meant, miss," Eileen said. "He got it in the war. It scarred a lot more than his face, if you ask me, miss. He's different now."

How lucky *she* was, Lark thought, that Aubrey had come out of the war intact, hadn't even been sent overseas before they discharged him in 1944 for being over age. An ache to see him, to get out of this house, throbbed suddenly at her temples.

She stood up. "If anyone asks for me, Eileen, tell them I've gone downtown. I'll be back this afternoon."

Lark tossed the last words over her shoulder, and didn't even see Eileen start to open her mouth, and then close it.

At the door to the hall, Lark hesitated. But she wasn't a weekend visitor to have to consult her hostess on every move. She had told Eileen she was going out.

She parted the bottle-green portières, glancing down at her dress—a navy shantung bought with Julia's money. It had cost more than the suit she came out in, was just as smart for street wear. But she found herself hurrying across the round hall, running up the padded stairs, jerking open her wardrobe doors in a dizzying toboggan of mirrors, rose velvet walls, and a girl in blue shantung. She found her gray suit, the shoes she had come in, her old handbag, the despised black felt hat.

Then she was back downstairs, blindly prompted to run across the gilt circle once more spotlighting the hall. Going through the marble vestibule.

Outside, at the foot of the steps, she hesitated again. There was no secret about her departure, no reason why she couldn't crunch down the graveled drive. But she put her foot on it only three times, crossing to the grass.

She might have called Leo and the victoria. Perhaps she was supposed to. Though was there any reason why she shouldn't walk? As conscious as if she were going toward it of the many-windowed house behind her and the spyglass behind one of the windows, Lark made herself walk and not run across the big lawn; walk and not run down the graveled pitch beyond the hedge; walk and not run through the sand.

Not running became a symbol. Even when dunes hid the house, she kept herself from running. She wasn't running away, she told herself, merely leaving Dune House for the morning and part of the afternoon. Merely going to see her husband and the world beyond the fence. There was no cause to run; she wasn't running away.

But by the time she reached the stable she was breathing as hard as a sprinter. The gate through the fence had a padlock on it, and she turned back to the stable door, lifting the latch.

Inside, smelling of hay and horses, was a long tunnel-like aisle with box stalls on either side and coco mats on the floor—surprisingly, a waxed floor. A horse whinnied, and one of the grays that pulled the victoria stretched his polished neck over a door.

At the far end of the aisle another door opened, and a man in green livery came out.

"What you want, miss?" he asked. It was Adam's gruff voice.

She stepped inside. The mats were as thick as Julia's carpet and made a sound like whispering as she walked. Somewhere on the other side of one of the doors a hoof hit boards.

She waited as Adam started toward her. She could see the slicked look of the fingers of hair he combed up over his bald spot.

"I—" Lark began, then tried again. "I see the gate's locked."

"It's always locked, miss," Adam said.

"I—guess I'll have to go through here, then," Lark said.

"What for, miss?" Adam asked.

"To get out," Lark said. "I'm going to town."

She crossed another mat and the whispering followed her feet.

"It's me you give your pass to, miss," Adam said.

"Pass?" What did he think this was—an army camp?

"Ain't you got a pass from Miss Julia?" Adam asked.

"What on earth would I need a pass for?" Lark asked. "I'm going to town. Excuse me, please."

She started by him, and Adam stepped aside. One hand went up to his bald spot, reslicking the strands of hair.

"Door's right at the end of the aisle, miss… but it's locked," Adam said.

Lark whirled. She stared at the old man in green livery stroking his head. Then she slowly turned back toward the door. She was near enough now to see the padlock.

"You'll unlock it for me, won't you, Adam?" Lark's voice was almost as stiff as her throat.

"Not without Miss Julia's orders," Adam said. "Sorry, miss. That's the rules."

Lark stood still. An hour ago, it hadn't particularly mattered, but now reaching Aubrey and the world outside seemed desperately important.

"Then I'll telephone," she decided. "Miss Paget said there's a regular phone in the stable."

"There is, miss, in the harness room, but the phone booth's locked, too,"

Adam said. He paused, and his old lips stretched into a tobacco-stained grin. "And right now I can't find the key."

Lark's fingers meshed like cogs. But there were other ways, she reminded herself. She could follow the fence, call to someone in one of the little houses across the boulevard, send a message to Aubrey by a passing car... and how would that look? A girl prisoner at Dune House. How would it read in the papers? Helplessly, she shook her head.

A step behind her made her whirl again. Leo came out of the room Adam had come from. He walked, with his right cheek turned away, through another door across the aisle.

Adam cleared his throat.

"Want Leo to drive you back to the house, miss?" he said.

"No, thank you." Lark raised her chin. "I'll walk."

She passed him stiffly down the aisle she had come up. The horse with his head out blew softly. Reaching with a robot's gesture for the latch, she closed the door behind her.

Outside, the towers of Dune House made a jagged cloud on the sky. She started toward it with her chin still up. Walking... walking... walking.

A dune hid the stable and all but the two tallest towers. And suddenly Lark was running. Not toward the house or back to the stable. She ran off to one side—tripping on beach grass, sinking to the ankles in bare sand, dodging among dunes—out of sight for the most part of both house and stable, running toward the beach. There were still other ways for those who couldn't afford publicity. From the highway she hadn't been able to see the spot where the fence joined the cliff. Neither could passing motorists see her—suited, hatted, gloved—trying, like a monkey in a cage, to climb out.

She stopped for breath, toes fighting the sand in her shoes. Hard on stockings... never mind them, she had to get out! Necessity now, not impulse. Locked in, she had to escape.

She stood panting between two high dunes. The beach grass curved and dipped in the wind like another sea. Lark touched a bush of lupin too big to blow out. If she could only reach out and touch Aubrey like that, or a blue-sleeved policeman. Policeman? What did she have to complain of—that the gatekeeper had lost the key to the telephone booth… even if she didn't believe it. That he wouldn't unlock the gate without an order from the owner? He was only hired. Miss Paget would say Lark should have asked her; she would gladly have given permission. Miss Paget would say—

Lark's head jerked around. But of course, Julia wasn't running behind her, silent-footed in the sand. Neither were old Adam or scar-faced Leo. Her own tracks were the only ones she could see—tadpoles, where the sand had caved at each step, in a long, wriggly line between the dunes.

Back there against the sun, the air was silver again, bright with the sand that filled her shoes, that muffled the sound of following steps and swallowed her into a maw of grass and bushes and gray, unpopulated sand.

She began to run again. Run until she had to stop for breath. Pant. And run on.

There was the fence at last, rising on the edge of the cliff. Rising… breaking off.

Lark ran to the break. Saw that the fence ended only because the cliff, too sheer to scale, had taken over.

She ran down the fence toward the beach. Here was the place to try, on flat sand out of sight of the road.

Hooking her handbag over her arm, she set a foot in the mesh, reached up with both hands, set the other foot…

Her head bumped, and she bent her neck, feeling with one hand along the barbed wire of the overhang. A barb pierced her glove—another—another—

Her hat fell off, and she felt a trickle of blood down her forehead—down one arm. Saw the long gash in her sleeve.

She went down a step or two and tried again.

Tried again.

And again.

At last—panting, torn, bleeding—she gave up. The fence built to keep Venetia in kept Lark in, too.

Chapter Six

At lunch, no one commented on Lark's scratches. Was the Paget household too well bred to show curiosity, or did everyone know what had happened? Benson and even his mother might once have come back with the same kind of scratches themselves.

Lark wondered briefly what Kezzie would think of the tattered gray suit now hanging on the back of her other clothes behind the mirror doors. Think—and report to Miss Paget. As she lifted a forkful of creamed sweetbread, Lark saw Julia's eyes fixed on a red gash in her hand.

After lunch she hurried upstairs and shut herself in her room. She paced the afternoon away up and down the flowered carpet, each step on the heavy padding as hushed as it had been in the sand. Once or twice in the great, silent room with an unlocked door, Lark caught herself turning quickly, as she had this morning on the dunes, to see if she were being followed. When Eileen called her to tea at four o'clock, the sharp rap of knuckles on wood made Lark shake until she could hardly grasp the knob.

Tea this afternoon was in the library, the fifth door south of the vestibule, Eileen told her. It might have been a street direction.

Lark's steps were soundless on the carpet along the curved gallery to the stairs, soundless going down them. Pausing by the lamp statue, she counted doorways to the right of the vestibule. She didn't know what lay behind the first two sets of deep green portières. Then came the Maple Parlor and the dining room. The library must be next, directly at the back of the entrance to the servants' quarters.

She might as well be out on the dunes, alone in a muffled world where she couldn't hear anyone follow. Like the sand, the thick red carpet of the hall gave back no sound.

As she raised her hand to the fifth pair of portières, she heard a man's voice. Forcing her fingers to relax, she let the plush drop. She couldn't tear in and throw her arms around Aubrey's neck, not with Miss Paget pouring tea.

At last she was able to walk in with composure, smile politely at her husband, and sedately cross the room to a chair.

As Aubrey stood up he leaned toward her.

"Good Lord, Lark," he said. "What have they been doing to you at Dune House? Do you keep cats, Miss Paget?"

Lark's scratched hands flew behind her back, but she couldn't hide her face. Slowly it turned toward her hostess.

Julia answered, her eyes holding Lark's.

"I'm afraid Lark—had a fall," she said. "You were walking on the dunes, my dear?"

She wouldn't want Aubrey to know that Lark had tried to climb the fence. Julia said a fall. She had called Venetia's plunge from the cliff a fall, too. And now the fence built to jail Venetia was jailing Lark.

"Better stay off the dunes, then, Lark," Aubrey said briskly, "or watch where you're going. Rollin, Rollin & Hildreth never had you looking like this."

It was nice to have someone care, to have someone speak out and bring things into the open.

Eileen came in with the tea tray. She murmured over Miss Paget. Lark caught Yep's name, and Julia broke into a tirade.

Under cover of it, Aubrey asked, "Have you seen the conservatory, Lark? The Dune House begonias are famous." He stood up.

Lark, too, got up quickly, and they moved toward the other end of the room where, for the first time, she saw glass doors opening into greenness.

"For God's sake," Aubrey muttered before they had covered half the distance, "what happened to you? How did you get all those scratches?"

"The barbed wire," Lark said. "I was trying to get out."

Her recitations of horrors began, all the way from maple-eyed wainscots to lions roaring in the night.

"Look, dear," he broke in. They were in the conservatory now, a round glass room tinged with the florally filtered green light that always made Lark think of undersea caves. "Do you want to give it all up? It seems a shame when Julia's taken such a fancy to you, but nothing's been proven yet about your being her brother's granddaughter. You can tell her it was all a mistake—that you picked the picture up on the street, or something—and walk out."

"Walk out!" Lark said. "Don't you know that no one leaves this place without her permission? And she'll never give it to me. I don't know why she wants me here, but she'll never let me go."

"You're getting hysterical, Lark," Aubrey said, reaching for her hand. "If you aren't Ulysses' granddaughter, there's no reason on earth why she'd want to keep you. She's not like me... and we'll live through it even if we can't announce our marriage for *ten* more years."

"Ten!" Lark gasped. "But Aubrey, it isn't going to be ten years before Mister Rollin—"

"Of course not, darling," Aubrey said. "Rollin's going to retire in four years. At least he said he was. I was thinking how it would be if he didn't."

"Well, don't think things like that," Lark said. "It's bad enough as it is. Oh, Aubrey, this is such an awful place! Think of a woman, dead forty years—singing in the night!"

"Now, dear, you know there's some logical explanation of that," Aubrey said. "What Ben Drew said about a radio must be right. I know the set-up's screwy here, but there's nothing wrong. I've been coming out here long enough to know."

Lark swallowed. "Did—did you ever hear how Venetia got 'that fall?'"

He nodded toward the ocean on the other side of the glass.

"Out there on the cliff," Aubrey said. "Gran Hildreth told me. All the old San Franciscans knew."

"But how it *happened*?" Lark said. "Do you know how it happened, Aubrey?"

"Gran said there was a difference of opinion about whether it was an accident or suicide," Aubrey said. "Julia can be pretty hard to take at times."

"What if—" Lark swallowed again. "What if Julia pushed her?"

"Dear girl, people like Julia Paget don't commit murder," Aubrey said. "And certainly she wouldn't kill her own sister—another Paget. Look how long poor dotty old Rowena Drew's been with her—the world's worst whist player, too—and lived."

"Don't joke, Aubrey. I'm frightened," Lark said.

"There's nothing to be frightened of; I'm sure of that," Aubrey said. "But if you are—if you're that unhappy and scared, I'm not going to leave you here, no matter what's at stake." He stood up straighter, looking handsome and firm.

Lark, who had started to release a long breath, leaned suddenly closer.

"Aubrey, you sighed!" she said.

"Nonsense, of course I didn't," Aubrey said. "Julia's right; you have got an imagination. What would I have to sigh for?"

"Because you know that if I leave here I'll never get that trust fund," Lark said. "Miss Paget would be so mad she'd cancel it or something. And you're right. I know you're right."

"Darling, what does money matter—really matter, compared to your happiness?" Aubrey said.

"We know what it matters," Lark said. "We could make our marriage public, do all the things you've always talked about... no wonder you were disappointed. But you're not going to be now. Because I'm going to stay."

"Lark—"

"Yes, I am," Lark said. Her head came up. She was going to live up to his expectations. Besides, he'd been coming here for years, as he said; he'd know if anything was wrong. Just the sight of him, alone, was reassuring.

"Lovely little girl," Aubrey said tenderly. "I'm proud of you. And I know there's nothing to worry about. If there's any worrying to be done, I'm the one to do it, with you seeing so much of Ben Drew all the time. He's a well-set-up lad—and so many years younger than I am."

"You know you don't have to be worried, Aubrey," Lark said. Both her hands went up to his shoulders.

He covered them with his and gently took them down.

"Don't forget the carpets," he murmured. "Julia could be right at the door, and we'd never hear her... why, Lark, look at your hands! Some of those jabs are a lot worse than scratches. Promise me you'll never try to climb that fence again."

"Well, Aubrey," came a voice behind him, "what does Lark think of the Dune House begonias?"

Lark jumped, but Aubrey turned calmly with her hands still in his.

"I was telling her she ought to have her hands dressed," he said. "Some of these scratches are deep."

Julia waved them back to the tea table, Lark belatedly seeing yellow, salmon pink, and orange splashes of begonia as she passed. But not until they'd had tea, and Aubrey and Miss Paget were deep in a discussion over papers, did Lark notice the room she sat in. The library, Eileen had called it. All four walls were covered with red velvet. Lark felt as if her temperature had risen, but probably Captain Paget had considered it cozy for reading. The books were so hidden in massive, carved cabinets behind glass doors that her eyes had to push aside an even greater-than-usual clutter of tables and rocking chairs with tidies to find them.

In the nearest case a yard of blue books met a two-yard stretch of red. Beneath them a long line of tan filled one shelf and half another. Rows and rows of grouped counterparts—like the blocks of new houses on the dunes, Lark thought, bending closer to read titles. The tooled blue leather was Thackeray; the red, Washington Irving; the ten half-calf that took up more than one shelf was Bulwer-Lytton.

She was picking out books she'd read in school from the green Sir Walter Scott's, when Julia dismissed her.

"There's no need for you to sit here, Lark," she said. "Mister Hildreth and I will be going over papers all afternoon and evening, by the look of what he brought. Why didn't you come earlier, Aubrey?"

"Couldn't get away from the office," Aubrey apologized, rising with Lark. "I'm terribly sorry. I'll wait around until you're ready, if you'd like a rest—"

"Whoever heard of a Paget resting?" Julia said. "Run along, Lark. We'll both see you at dinner."

"At dinner, Lark," Aubrey murmured.

She paused in the doorway, watching Aubrey's black head close to Miss Paget's tarnished gold, with its pointed knot on top of her head like an extra nose to turn up at the world. The buttons of Aubrey's dark blue tweed sleeve clicked on the table. He looked up and winked at Lark, and she dropped the portières.

"Well, *Cousin* Lark, you're looking more pleased with life than I've ever seen you," a voice said. "Things going better this afternoon?"

Benson was coming down the hall, a few steps away.

"For heaven's sake," Lark burst out—what story had her face told as she stood watching Aubrey? "Don't call me Cousin Lark! Do you have to call me anything when we're alone?"

"Well, of course, I *could* whistle," Benson said, looking down at her.

Aubrey was right about Benson being well set up, and right, of course, about his age. But his lightish hair, neither brown nor blond, wasn't nearly as distinguished as Aubrey's silver-winged black, and he wasn't as tall—not quite six feet—and certainly no broader shouldered.

"I could whistle," Benson repeated. "It wouldn't be hard to, the way you looked coming out of the library. Wonder if there's something in those old books I've been missing."

He raised his hand toward the portières she had dropped.

"Oh, but they've sent me out," Lark said. "I don't think they want to be disturbed."

"They?"

"Miss Paget and—Mister Hildreth," Lark said.

"So, he's in there!" Benson said. "Is that why you're so pepped up? Though what girls see in men the age of their fathers is a mystery to me. Maybe that's it: mystery. The man with a past... well, if you land Cousin Julia's trust fund, you might land your ex-boss too; or any other man. A couple of million—"

"If you're always like this, Benson, no wonder Miss Paget's hunting another heir," Lark said.

He grinned. "'Tain't the disposition, lady; it's the blood," he said. "Paget to Paget, soda speak. By the way, if it wouldn't be too much during your stay at Dune House—or perhaps I should say, the rest of my stay—could you bring yourself to call me Ben? Benson makes me feel like a butler."

"Instead of a worm?" Lark said sweetly. She turned toward the stairs.

"Got any disinfectant in your bathroom, Miss Williams?" he called after her. "Those scratches ought to be taken care of. Rusty wire can be bad..."

But she was halfway upstairs. He'd known all along what had made those gouges—as she'd thought. There must have been plenty of times when he'd come back bleeding, too.

By the time Kezzie had helped her into one of her new long dresses—a pale chartreuse—and the scratches, disinfected at least three times, were covered as much as possible with makeup, Lark couldn't help being pleased with her many reflections in the dressing room. These were the things—name-dresses, maids, long mirrors—that Aubrey wanted her to have.

Tonight when they were all assembled in the Maple Parlor, he was there—in his office tweed, of course—approving Lark's dress with his eyes. At her side he joined the parade down the long dining room to the alcove.

"How's Oscar?" Lark asked as he pushed in her chair.

"Still unconscious, far as I know... or did one of the girls say he came to?" Aubrey said. "Darned if I even heard what she said, I've been so busy."

Across the table, Rowena looked up. "Who's Oscar?"

Julia said impatiently, "Oh, you know that ratty little man Edward and Aubrey always send out here when they don't want to come themselves."

"Now, that's unfair, Miss Paget," Aubrey declared. "There's never been such a time. Of course, Oscar has to pinch-hit for us sometimes, when we're in court, and so forth. He's our law clerk, Missus Drew—not the type one remembers, I'll admit. He fell out a window the other day and he's still unconscious."

Rowena Drew's eyes turned to Julia, then slowly to Lark.

"So many falls," she murmured.

The dining alcove seemed all at once no bigger than a telephone booth.

Julia reached abruptly for the tea bell, and its silver tinkle pushed the walls back.

"Tell Kezzie, Eileen," she directed when the maid came in, "to bring me down the opal ring set with diamonds—the large Hungarian opal."

Again, Rowena looked up from across the table.

"Venetia's opal?" she asked.

Julia frowned. "The one Papa bought for Venetia."

"Some of the Paget jewels are quite old, my dear," Rowena told Lark. "Very old family jewels. All bought by Julia's father. The Pagets didn't—"

"Sorry, Mother," Benson apologized, sitting up again in his chair. "I dropped my napkin and knocked yours off picking it up... Oscar's been unconscious ever since he fell, has he, Aubrey? I knew a chap once..."

The two men batted unconsciousness back and forth across the table until Kezzie came in with a small box, blue-velvet covered, like the one with the pearls.

Miss Paget opened it. Blue, red, green, and gold fire blazed up from a stone as large as one of her lorgnette lenses. She held the ring out to Lark.

"I knew it would be lovely with that dress. Put it on, child," she said.

The gold band slid over Lark's knuckles, the great opal with its border of diamonds hiding all the lower joint of her finger. The fire and glitter of the stones made her blink.

"It's so shiny!" she cried.

Julia smiled indulgently. "Venetia used to say opals were more gorgeous than diamonds. I'd rather have diamonds. You may have that ring, if you want it, child."

Across the table, Rowena spoke again.

"Opals are unlucky—unless your birthday's in October," she said. "I hope yours is, my dear. Is it?"

"No," Lark said uncomfortably. "It's in May."

Aubrey began to talk about superstition with matter-of-fact, detached interest. His foot touched hers beneath the table.

When they finally rose to leave, Kezzie met them at the door.

"Mister Rollin's here, madam," she said, "waiting at the stable."

"Tell Leo to drive him up," Julia said, turning to Aubrey. "You might as well have Dune House on your letterheads."

He laughed. "Of course, if you won't have a phone… the Scott matter must have come to a boil," Aubrey said. "It was simmering when I left. You'll excuse us if he and I talk a few minutes before we get on with that business of yours?"

"I'll have to," Miss Paget said ungraciously. "My affairs are too important to get less than your full attention, especially with that Santa Barbara sale hanging fire…We may as well have a hand of whist while we're waiting."

Back in the Maple Parlor, Lark drew the low card and didn't play. She sat beside Aubrey, watching his hand. Once or twice she met Benson Drew's sly eyes, and remembered to say something to Aubrey about his cards to make plain that it was merely his playing she was interested in.

Julia took the last trick and stood up. She looked at Aubrey.

"Leo ought to be driving up any minute," she said. "Shall we go back to the library now?"

At the hall door, as Aubrey raised his hand to the portières, Kezzie came through them.

"Excuse me, Miss Paget, but Adam's on the phone again," she said. "He says, since Leo's got the grays, should he drive…"

The rest was lost as Julia stepped into the hall, and the maid and Aubrey followed.

"Now we can play three-handed, Ben, dear," Rowena said happily. "You and Lark and I."

Her son rose. "Sorry, mother; there's something I forgot to do," Benson said. "Can't you and Cousin Lark play double solitaire?" His mouth turned down in that way it did.

The portières dropped behind him too.

His mother sighed. "Double solitaire makes me so nervous," she said. "Oh, well, it's better than sitting here. I can't bear double dummy whist. You take the red deck, Lark."

Lark glanced toward the mantel and the gold clock denting the blue lambrequin. Aubrey and Miss Paget wouldn't be through for an hour or more. Ben Drew—his mother and Aubrey both called him Ben—might not be gone so long, but it was Aubrey she wanted to see.

By the end of the first game only twenty minutes had passed and neither Aubrey, Miss Paget, nor Ben had returned. The second game took longer, and still the portières hung unstirred. Lark and Rowena were laying out their fourth game when Ben came back, and they had hardly started a round of three-handed whist when the hall portières were pulled aside again and Mr. Rollin appeared.

His face was as red as Lark had ever seen it, even in office crises. He marched, thinly erect, down the room.

"Good evening, Rowena," he said stiffly. "... Miss Williams... Ben... I couldn't go without paying my respects."

His voice didn't sound like that of a person paying respects. He went on in the same forced way.

"Ah, dummy whist!" he said. "Wish I had time to stop and make a fourth."

He looked so much as he did when he asked to have papers typed over which he hadn't dictated right that the four front-office desks and Red and Dizz and Oscar came crowding into Dune House with Lark.

"Oh, Mister Rollin," she exclaimed, "how's Oscar? Aud—Mister Hildreth didn't hear the last report."

Edward Rollin's face turned almost purple.

"That—that puppy!" he said. "Do you know that he had the effrontery—came to this morning—" He broke off to swallow.

Surely it wasn't Oscar's coming to that was upsetting Mr. Rollin! Had the poor man died after all, labeled "suicide"—a major crime for Rollin, Rollin & Hildreth's law clerk?

"Only conscious long enough to say a few words—and you know what they were?" Mr. Rollin's thin body shook. "He said he didn't *jump* out the window—or *fall* out. He said he was *pushed*!"

Rowena gave a little squeak.

Ben said, "What do you know!"

Lark stared. She wet her lips. "You mean he died? And it was murder?"

"No-no-no-no!" Mr. Rollins seemed beside himself, but now that she

71

knew about Oscar she thought she understood her employer's excitement.

"He's not dead yet; he relapsed again," Mr. Rollin added. "But the idea of saying someone tried to kill him! Think of the publicity—probably got kicked—be a lot more like it—and the poor fool lost his balance. And he—insolent puppy!"

"Did he say who pushed him?" Ben asked.

Edward Rollin, beyond speech, shook his head.

Poor Oscar. He couldn't do anything to suit Mr. Rollin, not even fall out of a window. Well, perhaps if he didn't die, there wouldn't be anything in the papers. But he said he'd been pushed.

Like Venetia, Lark thought suddenly, and found she was shivering.

"Well," Mr. Rollin said abruptly. "I have to see Aubrey again. Miss Paget wants you in the library, Ben. Too bad to interrupt your game, ladies. Good night."

Ben rose. "Sorry to break up the game, gals, but duty—and Cousin Julia—call."

So it was double solitaire again in the room with the blue silk walls and maple eyes. Double solitaire, and Rowena's "Oh dear's" and "Why wasn't I quicker?" and Lark watching the clock.

Another hour and she was ready to throw all the cards into the air and run under them screaming. She stood up.

"Excuse me, Cousin Rowena"—Cousining and Aunting came easily now—"I have to get a handkerchief," *and get out of this room.*

She almost ran, under a patter of directions about pulling the bell cord for Kezzie, through the portières into the hall. As the green plush dropped, Lark's eyes turned to the library curtains. Closed, of course; she hadn't dared hope otherwise. Anyway, she could go upstairs and have a change of scenery, stick her head out the window and get some fresh air. Or would Venetia be singing?

Lark was shivering again—like an idiot. She started toward the stairs. At the circle of red marble pillars, she stopped.

Across the hall, next to the Moorish Room, light came between parted portières from a room she hadn't seen—closed off, she understood from

Ben on account of the servant shortage.

She hurried past the stairs toward the bright stripe between the curtains.

Inside, white dust sheets made ghostly humps of the furniture. Above them a gigantic, bird-headed statue reared a disk-and-snake headdress. Egyptian designs and hieroglyphics patterned the walls and ceiling.

As Lark looked, one of the sheets gave a flap, and a man's voice said, "No dice."

"Wh—who's there? she gasped.

A pair of dark trousers appeared from beneath the largest hump, rear first, then the back of a dark coat and disheveled lightish hair. The face that turned toward her was Benson Drew's. On the other side of the hump rose a bottle-green suit. Leo's scarred cheek showed for an instant before it was averted.

"What's the matter?" Lark cried. "Are you looking for something?"

"Yeah," Ben said. "I dropped my collar button. Now you'd better go tend to your card game."

"Why don't you say, 'Mind your own business,' and be done with it?" Lark snapped. She turned away indignantly.

But not until she was halfway upstairs and her hand accidentally touched the crawly plush railing did she think of what Ben had said. Dropped his collar button. Did men wear collar buttons now? Anyway, how did he drop it there, in a room unused and closed off?

In her own room she turned the gas low and leaned her head out the window. The wind was more of a gale than the ocean breeze. At least it ought to blow the fog from her brain, if not the hair from her head. Out there in the dark a seal barked, and another one answered.

At last Lark sighed and stood up. She couldn't leave poor old Rowena alone with two decks of cards all night. And Aubrey and Miss Paget might be through with their papers by now. Lark closed the window and combed her hair.

Going downstairs, she could see over the railing that the curtains Ben and Leo had left open were closed. In the great round hall all the portières hung straight and dark and still.

Back in the Maple Parlor, Rowena looked up eagerly as Lark came in.

"Oh, dear, I was hoping Ben and Julia would be with you," she said. "We didn't finish last night's rubber, you know."

And they didn't finish it that night. Kezzie looked in once, bright-eyed, to make sure the windows were locked. But it was twelve o'clock before Julia came back.

"Time you two were in bed," she said sharply.

"Where's Ben?" Rowena fretted.

"I sent him on an errand," Julia said. "Don't fuss, Rowena. Benson's grown up."

"Did—Mister Hildreth go back?" Lark said, trying to act casual.

Julia didn't answer immediately. She took out her lorgnette and stared at Lark.

"Of course he's gone," she said finally. "Did you expect him to tell you goodnight?"

Lark hoped she wasn't as red as she felt.

"Put something on those scratches, child," Julia added. Behind the glass, her eyes moved to Lark's hands. "And don't let Rowena scare you about opals. That's a nice ring, even if it's not an old family heirloom." The lorgnette turned coldly on the faded little woman across the card table.

"It's lovely," Lark said.

The portières parted and Kezzie came in again.

"Go and warm my mulled wine," Julia commanded. "I'll be upstairs in a minute. Come on, Rowena. You too, Lark. It's bedtime."

"Is anything the matter?" Lark burst out.

"What do you mean—*the matter*?" Julia said.

"Oh, I don't know," Lark said. "Maybe because Aubrey and Mister Rollin were both there. And Ben's been gone all evening. And Kezzie popping in. I guess it's something in the air."

"And last night you heard singing!" Julia said. The lorgnette came up again. "It's time you went to bed. Since when, by the way, have you been calling my attorney by his Christian name?"

Lark's face was hot even after she reached her own room. Perhaps for once she'd get into bed without Kezzie's help, since the maid was preparing Miss Paget's nightly drink; but Lark was half white slip and nyloned legs and half a wriggling tube of chartreuse jersey when Kezzie knocked and came in.

Emerging, Lark demanded, "What was the matter tonight? Miss Paget was so cross. And you've never come in to see if the windows were locked before while I've been here. And I saw Mister Drew and Leo in one of the closed-up rooms looking under dust sheets!"

The tight skin over Kezzie's skull looked suddenly tighter, like a bag stuffed to bursting. "Miss Paget says nothing's wrong, miss."

That was an odd way of putting it—*Miss Paget says*. Lark wanted to know what Kezzie said.

But Kezzie was keeping still. A quarter hour of yes's and no's, and she made her longest speech, her only volunteered one. Lark was in bed, the light out, and the maid at the door.

"Goodnight, miss," Kezzie said with the mocking respect Lark had come to know. "I hope you—sleep well, miss."

Lark didn't like the tone of that *sleep well*.

She lay staring into the dark. Whatever had happened here tonight must be fairly important to keep Aubrey from seeing her again. He'd have wanted to see her to reassure her about staying. He knew that no Paget money would ever give them the chance to make their marriage public if she antagonized Julia by walking out of Dune House, and he knew that ridding their marriage of secrecy was even more important to Lark's peace of mind than his own. That was why he'd persuaded her to stay. It was lucky that he'd kept his head instead of getting emotional, too. But telling her goodnight couldn't be classified as losing her head. Something must have happened to prevent it.

What could be going on here, anyway? Surely nothing to get her into this state. Here she was actually wishing she was back in her two small rooms on Lombard Street, back where Dune House was only the home of one of Aubrey's clients—a picture in the papers, still with four years to go before Mr. Rollin retired and she and Aubrey could be openly married, still with all Ninon's alimony to pay...

She kept wishing her door had a key. And if Venetia sang again tonight...

Lark found herself doubled up—tense. Forcing each muscle to relax, in a breath she was tight again.

Perhaps some of the wind that had blown off her powder after dinner was what she needed now. She jumped out of bed and skimmed, barefooted in her nightgown, to a window overlooking the sea.

Wind whipped her hair about and made a great bubble of her gown. This was real. There was nothing mean or frightening or crawly about wind. Nothing supernatural. The ocean boomed its muffled booms, driven by the gale. She leaned farther out, freshened and cold.

One hand caught the sill. Down here in the shrubbery near the house, it came again—a gleam in the bushes. Someone was out there with a flashlight!

She'd known there was something going on ever since she'd seen Ben in that empty room. And then when Aubrey left without saying goodnight... but maybe he hadn't left yet. Maybe that was Aubrey out there on the lawn. It hardly seemed likely, even to a wishful thinker, but if she could ask whoever was there what had happened...

The flashlight moved south around the bulge of the conservatory. Out of sight. She might intercept it at one of the front windows downstairs. For some reason that she was unwilling to examine too closely, she didn't want to step out the front door. If she could be sure it was Aubrey... but it almost certainly wasn't at this time of night after the household had gone to bed.

She thrust her feet into slippers, arms into the sleeves of her marabou robe, and opened her door.

The light from the lower hall was still brilliant. At the landing, the sight of the gold-washed, girdled lady with the lamp was almost like the greeting of a friend. It seemed as if they were the only two in the great silent house. Them, and the person with the flashlight on the lawn.

The candle and matches she'd snatched off the table shouldn't be necessary. Leaving the portières apart ought to give her enough light to find a window and miss the furniture inevitably lying in wait.

That first doorway right of the vestibule, the first doorway south, Eileen would call it...

Lark slid through the portières. Blinking for a moment in the desk, she pushed them wider. In the dimness this room seemed small and without the usual jumble of tables and chairs. There were several oddly light spots on the wall to her right.

She struck a match. This must be the Eighteen Eighties' idea of a powder room. The candle flame showed hooks lining the walls, a closet with a discreetly closed door, and a silver fitted marble washbowl. That bowl and the long row of white towels hanging beside it made the light spots on the wall to her right. One of the towels lay crumpled on the floor.

In the outside wall was a window, heavily curtained. She took a step toward it, and the sole of her slipper gritted on something that sounded like sugar on a kitchen floor. The housewife in her bent toward it. Not light enough for white sugar, not dark enough for brown; it was sand. She ought to know that dune sand by now. Oh, well, this was the maids' province. Eileen would clean it up tomorrow when she put the used towel in the laundry.

Lark moved over to the window and blew out the candle. She pulled aside the curtains, and her fingers met slatted wood. Feeling for the catch of the shutters, she opened them, too. Outside, she could see only starlight and blackness. She waited at the window, but no beam flashed in the dark.

Perhaps from one of the rooms across the hall. She fumbled with the shutters and curtains, felt the sand beneath her feet again, and slid through the parted portières.

The marble mosaic beyond the open double doors of the vestibule was brighter by gaslight than by day. She glanced in as she paused—and stopped so quickly she almost fell forward.

A man's crossed legs had come in sight around the door nearest her. Crossed legs in gray trousers—the leg of a chair—

Clutching the candlestick, Lark took another step.

Sitting on a chair in the vestibule in the gray suit he had worn from the office—still erect and dignified, though dozing with his mouth a little open—was Mr. Rollin. And on his lap—a gun!

Lark almost dropped the candle.

She began to back away—bumped a chair—turned and ran for the stairs. For once she was glad of the deep-napped carpet.

She reached the top, gasping, and stood for a moment holding on to the newel post.

Somewhere she heard a door close.

In one of the arches of the gallery where she stood, something moved. Then she saw it was Eileen, and moisture came back to her mouth.

Lark ran along the curved gallery toward the other girl.

"Eileen," she whispered frantically, "Mister Rollin's sitting in the vestibule with a gun! What's happened? What's the matter?"

Eileen began to wring her hands.

"Oh, miss! Oh, miss!" She whispered too, in the same hushed voice, "I'm scared to death. Adam let a man in right after Mister Rollin—and no one's seen him since!"

Chapter Seven

In the morning, pushing and tugging the great chest away from her door was harder than dragging it there with the strength of fear had been last night. A chair propped under the knob would have been lighter and more effective. But Lark had been too excited to think.

She was thinking now but still excited, tense with a dread she couldn't reason away. What if someone *had* come in and couldn't be found? He surely wasn't in the house—with all its tightly shuttered windows and guarded doors. She automatically multiplied Mr. Rollin by the number of entrances. She'd stay inside where she'd be safe, though it was hardly a question of her safety. Whoever had come in must be someone Adam knew or he'd never have unlocked the gate. There was no more reason to think that a caller at Dune House would want to harm her than there was for the apprehension that had settled on her as soon as Aubrey's car turned into the boulevard and she'd thought of the Paget towers and cupolas as lighthouses—warnings of danger. There had been no sound reason for the daily increase of the pressure of that apprehension, welling up within her until, now that she had something definite to pin it on, it kept bursting out in jets of pure terror. She was being silly—the doors had been guarded, at least the front door had. Maybe Aubrey had guarded one of the others, and that was why he hadn't told her goodnight.

She started to run downstairs. At the bottom, with one hand gripping the lamp statue's foot, she leaned to peer into the vestibule. She couldn't see any legs this morning and hurried to the edge of the downcoming daylight at the circle of marble pillars. The chair that had been in the vestibule last night was gone too.

She crossed the hall and went through the long dining room to the alcove. Julia sat as majestically, as unruffled as ever, at the head of the breakfast table. No one else was there but Ben.

Lark gripped the back of a chair.

"Who was it, Miss Paget?" she asked. "Have they found him yet?"

"Aunt Julia," her hostess corrected.

Ben rose to draw back Lark's chair.

"Where's Mister Rollin?" Lark asked. At the office she'd never felt at home with him, but here, compared with Julia Paget...

"Edward's on his way to work, I suppose," Julia said coldly. "Sit down and eat your breakfast."

Lark had almost forgotten how much the woman looked like a crocodile. Her white-rimmed dark eyes were reptile-cold.

Her neck straightened, seemed to swell, and she trebled her chin. "I said sit down."

Lark sat.

Benson returned to his chair across the table. Lark met his eyes, more sardonic than ever, the down curve of his mouth more pronounced.

"Last night—" Lark began.

"The breakfast table is no place for discussion, Lark," Julia said. "If you wish to see me privately later, come to my boudoir. We'll say no more; here's your Cousin Rowena."

Ben's mother came in, settling her glasses with one hand and patting down gray curls with the other.

"Goodness, I didn't know I was late," she said. "Aren't the rest of you a mite early?"

They were, Lark agreed silently. Yet Miss Paget and Ben had already finished breakfast. If a place had been set for Mr. Rollin, it wasn't there now.

Julia rose. Lark swallowed a cup of coffee that burned all the way down, and rose too.

She'd try to be politic, try not to show how trapped she felt inside the

Paget fence, how terrified she was of this house with its evil something that eddied through the great rooms. She must remember what Aubrey said and not offend the woman who had in her hands the giving or withholding of Lark's chance to make her marriage public without waiting for Mr. Rollin to retire. If she could simply get out even for a few hours... she'd trump up some excuse.

Rowena caught Lark's skirt.

"Uh—my dear..." She waited until Julia was out of sight, then hissed, "Did Venetia sing again?"

Lark shook her head and pulled her skirt free, glancing at Ben. Evidently his mother didn't know about last night. She wasn't the type to let it go unremarked. As for poor Venetia and the singing, Lark hadn't even thought of it after she saw Eileen last night. It was just as well; Venetia's singing would have been the last straw.

Miss Paget had reached the great staircase by the time Lark reached the hall. She hurried after the small feet propelling the weight of a body upstairs.

At her boudoir door, one hand on the knob, Julia turned enough to say, "Close the door behind you when you come," and was sitting in her chair by the window when Lark clicked the latch.

"Miss Paget—"

"Not 'Aunt Julia' at all this morning?"

"Au-Aunt Julia, of course," Lark said. "I have to—go to the office for awhile. Will you give me a pass, please, so I can leave?"

"Leave?" Julia asked.

"Yes, I—really have to go," Lark said.

"Have we made life so intolerable for you at Dune House, child?" Julia asked. "With all your new clothes, and the opal ring, and...?"

"Oh, I didn't mean go forever," Lark said. "I meant—there are some things I must do at the office. I hope I don't seem ungrateful. You've been more than good to me. But Adam said yesterday I had to have a pass to leave the grounds. Will you please give me one now so he'll let me out?"

Julia sat looking at her. The tiny hands, pudgy near the thick arms, were downcurved on the arms of her chair.

81

"And what—" she said, the measured slowness of her voice terrifying, "if I don't?"

"But you can't keep me here!" Lark cried. "You've got no right—" She stopped, corking back a spurt of terror.

"Who's keeping you, child?" Julia asked. "How could I force you to stay? All you have to do is go down to the stable—"

"And have Adam refuse to unlock the gate?" Lark said. The cork came out of the bottle now. "You know as well as I that he won't let me out without a pass. You're not forcing me to stay! But I still can't get out."

Julia began to laugh—that silent, panting laughter.

Lark clenched her hands, then shut her eyes and counted ten. When she opened them, she didn't look at Miss Paget, but out the window at the dunes. Leaning closer, she saw two men come out of the stable half a mile away. They separated, one walking south, the other north along the fence.

"Who's that?" Lark pointed. "Those men by the fence?"

Julia's panting stopped. She stood up and reached for the spyglass on the table.

"Come up to the pilothouse, child," she said. "We can see more from there." She rose and glided in her steamer-like way toward the door on her right.

"But—"

She turned the knob, gave Lark a glance with an imperative lift of the head too smooth to be called a jerk, and Lark followed.

Julia was crossing a bedroom even larger than Lark's, crowded with heavy furniture. She was skirting a table as massive as the library table when Lark saw the spiral staircase. Rising from beside an enormous bed, it bored its way beyond the heavy walnut headboard through a hole in the cupid-freckled ceiling.

She heard the clang of metal as Julia started up the steps. Her voice floated back.

"This used to be Papa's room, but I took it after he died," Julia explained, "on account of the stairs to the pilothouse. I don't like every Tom, Dick, and Harry going up there."

Lark's hand touched the cold metal railing, and her own shoes rang on iron.

"I lock the door when I'm out of my room," Miss Paget announced, "though never when I'm in it. Papa told us so many stories of shipwrecks and jammed stateroom locks that none of his children would any more lock themselves in their rooms than walk downtown naked."

They climbed another yard before Julia boasted, "I'm as much on the job at night as in the daytime. Papa trained me to be such a light sleeper that if my doorknob's barely turned, it wakes me."

If anyone started up these stairs it would wake the dead, thought Lark, wake Papa himself. They were above the bedroom now, clattering through a tube-like space as if they were climbing up a well.

Julia's voice came ricocheting down. "It's not because there's a safe in the pilothouse that I don't want people up there. The safe's locked, of course, like the one in the dining room that everyone passes three times a day. I don't want anyone else using Papa's pilothouse. Of course Kezzie has to go up now and then. I gave her the combination and a key to the inner door so she can get out my jewels, but I'm the only one with a key to the money compartment."

So the ring on Lark's finger had made this journey before, and Venetia's pearls...

"And at night," Julia continued in that hollow rain barrel voice, "I keep Papa's revolver under my pillow."

Was it because the walls were so near that the trip seemed long, or because they were climbing in a spiral? Or was it Papa's revolver? The mere mention of a weapon in this enclosed space... surely they'd come more than one flight. The spot of light on Miss Paget's bedroom floor looked so far down that Lark felt dizzy.

When she looked up again, Julia was gone, and Lark herself was almost at the top. Her eyes found first the black safe opposite the stairs as she came into a smallish round room set so thickly with windows that it looked as if the walls were made of glass. Then she saw Julia, spyglass raised, settling herself at a window in a damask-upholstered armchair.

Everything was spread out below them—dunes and fence and the boulevard and all the little houses. There were the men Lark had seen leave the stable, walking—one south, one north—along the fence.

"Who are they?" Lark cried, pointing. That was one answer Miss Paget could no longer evade.

She laid down the spyglass with a grunt. "That's Adam and Leo—out hunting."

"Hunting what?" Lark asked.

Julia paid no attention. Nodding toward the window in front of her, she said, "There goes Benson… you like your cousin, child?"

He was angling across the lawn, reaching, as they watched, one of the gaps in the hedge where the drive went through. His legs, then his tan sweater, then his lightish hair disappeared for an instant down the drop where enriched earth gave way to sand.

"What's *he* looking for?" Lark asked.

"Tracks, I suppose," Julia said.

"Whose tracks?" Lark asked.

"Last night after Edward Rollin—" Miss Paget stopped. Her fingers spread claw-like on the chair arms.

"I saw Mister Rollin last night—" Lark paused. She was proud of the way her voice stayed down. Now, while she could keep it down, she'd let Miss Paget know in a perfectly pleasant but firm way that she couldn't put anything over. "He was sitting in the vestibule—with a gun."

"Oh, you saw him," Julia said. It was a statement, not a question. Julia leaned back in her chair. Her diamond-studded fingers tapped without sound on the damask upholstery. "Is that why you want a pass?"

Trust Julia Paget! She knew that Lark wanted to get away, and snatched the first excuse. She should have thought up something better. "I left some things unfinished when I came away so suddenly on Tuesday," Lark said with dignity. "But if you'd seen Mister Rollin with that gun—and Eileen said—"

"Yes?" Julia said. "Go on, child. What did Eileen say?"

"That a man came in right after Mister Rollin," Lark said, "and hasn't been seen since."

"Eileen's a fool... with an Irish imagination... I wonder if you haven't some Irish in you too?" Julia said. "As for Edward, he's been back at his office for hours. I wanted him here last night, so he stayed. There's nothing to get worked up over, but I'll give you a pass if you want it."

"Oh, thank you," Lark cried fervently.

"More gratitude in that than you showed for clothes or Hungarian opals," Julia said. "Of course, Adam's not at the stable now. You'll have to wait until he's back."

"You won't—" Lark's fingers came together. "You won't see that he stays away, will you?"

"Child, child, how suspicious you are!" Julia said. "If I give you a pass, will you stay until after lunch? Adam's busy now, and can't let you out."

Surely she could wait a few hours longer.

"All right," she said. Lark sighed, turning wistful eyes toward Golden Gate Park and on toward the ocean. It was queer to see all the people on the beach and riding roller coasters down there in Playland, to know that others even closer, down in Fleishhacker Zoo, were feeding monkeys and giggling at giraffes. Here she was...

Her eyes went to the ocean and stopped, perplexed at a dun-colored swell—moveless, oddly solid, right beside the back windows. Then she saw that it was glass, a shallow curve that came to a peak. No wonder she'd thought the spiral stairs long; they had brought her up above the central skylight. She was overlooking the top of the Chinese hat.

She turned back to the window that Miss Paget was looking through. Down at the fence she could see Adam and Leo still walking and Benson poking through the dunes.

"Haven't they found any tracks or anything yet?" Lark asked. "No trace at all of the man who came in?"

"What man, child—the one Eileen dreamed up?" Julia asked. "Edward and Aubrey are gone. The only men here are Benson and Adam and Leo and Yep."

"The man who came in after Mister Rollin," Lark said.

"I told you Eileen was a fool," Julia said. "If you believed everything she said… it wasn't a man. Adam didn't quite shut the gate after he opened it for Edward, and a dog got in."

"A dog!" Lark said. "Why all the excitement, then? Peeking under dust covers—flashlights on the lawn—Mister Rollin sitting up with a gun!"

Julia Paget began to laugh again, that horrible, silent laughter.

"No wonder you're upset," she panted. "You see, I'm allergic to dogs. If one comes anywhere near me, I get the most violent hay fever. So naturally I take precautions. My hired men hunt them. My friends stand guard to shoot."

Lark was torn between fierce disbelief and feeling like an overwrought adolescent.

"Oh," she said weakly.

"So now, of course, you won't want the pass," Julia said. "Now you know it was only a dog that came in." She had stopped laughing; she sat watching Lark.

"Oh, yes… yes, I do," Lark said. But if it was just a dog. "Even if I don't—go to the office today, I'd like to feel I had a pass if—"

She couldn't say *if I can't stand it any longer.*

"—if I had to leave suddenly and you weren't around to ask," she finished.

Don't offend her… don't offend her. Not because it wasn't politic, but because she was afraid. Yet why would Julia want to harm her, Julia or anyone else? Feeling she must be on guard, not knowing for sure whom to be on guard against… sometimes Lark thought that not knowing was half of her terror.

Julia's lips had made a straighter line. She was standing up. The large body… the small hands and feet… that look of time-biding power.

Lark shrank back. The high glass pilothouse seemed all at once as far away from help as the moon.

Julia was going toward a table. The palms of Lark's hands turned wet. Where was Papa's revolver now—in the drawer that Miss Paget was opening? But all she took out was a writing pad and a box of tagged keys. She wrote on the pad and tore off the top sheet. Then, selecting a key, she removed the tag and held out paper and key to Lark.

"Here's your pass, you silly child, and a key to your bedroom door," she said.

"Of course I'd never lock myself in, after all Papa's tales. But if it makes you feel any better... even though you've nothing to be frightened of. Perhaps you're allergic to dogs."

Lark was going to laugh again.

Her hand closed tightly on her treasures. If she didn't get out before that laugh came...

"Oh, thank you," she said. "I have to—will you please excuse me? Missus Drew wants me to..."

At least her feet weren't incoherent. They started for the stairs, and her hand grasped the cold, curved railing. Once more steps clanged in the long wooden tube—down... down... down the well... faster... faster...

She ran through Julia's bedroom, through the boudoir, down the gallery to her room. There she stopped. How did Julia know Lark had no key? The spy system was too smooth here—as everything was too smooth. It wouldn't be long before she'd have to use this pass.

She went inside and had the doubtful pleasure of turning a key. Now, with the door to the bathroom bolted, she knew that no one could slip up behind her, and right here in her hand was a pass that would open the gate when she had to leave.

But the next minute found her tramping the flowers of the carpet again, asking the same question. Could it have been a dog that had caused so much excitement? Anything could happen here. Even a fantastic story like this one of Julia's allergy could actually be true. It could be true, but...

Lark sighed. If only she had something to do besides think, something to fill her time while she waited for things to be settled. Her feet slowed. What about the Paget picture gallery? Seeing that would be something to remember, one of the few things she'd want to remember after she left Dune House.

She glanced down at the pass in her hand. She'd need a bag to put it in; this dress had no pockets. Her old handbag, scratched like herself by the barbs of the fence... she found it in its rose-velvet-padded cell behind one of the long mirror doors. If the time ever came when she had to use this precious piece of paper, she wouldn't want to take away any Paget-bought hundred-dollar handbags.

As she unlocked the hall door and opened it, wind swooped through the room. In her hurry this morning she'd forgotten to shut the windows, and now the imported lace curtains had all been sucked out into the salt spray and wind.

Dropping her bag on a chair, she gathered in the first pair of flapping white flags and pulled down the sash.

It was funny how some of these Eighties' styles were coming back, she thought, straightening the heavy plush draperies. Aubrey said—she pulled down the second window—that if Julia hadn't built the fence and kept herself so isolated that hardly anyone knew what she had, the Paget picture collection would be famous. There were a good many pictures here, he said, by artists well-known in the Eighties that Lark would want to see. It was tactful of him to say *want* instead of *ought*. He'd seen and done so much in his life, and she so little. Would the quality in her that he called refreshing always suit him?

As she opened her door and reached for the key, she heard another door close. Across the light well she saw Kezzie coming toward her. Lark clicked the key home. She was nearer the stairs. Eyes firmly straight ahead, she started for them, started down. After her session with Miss Paget, she didn't feel equal to coping with Kezzie.

Past the landing, going down the broad stem of the Y, her eyes flew to the vestibule where last night she had seen Mr. Rollin. Another pair of legs was there now—a standing pair, in trousers far too short. Two heelless black slippers and a pair of white socks...

She went down a few more steps. The front door was open, a man in it, looking out. Or was it a woman? A short white jacket above the dark trousers—down the jacket a thin, black braid of hair...

As she paused, one hand clutching the plush-topped rail, he turned—and she saw what he held.

Sun glinted on the long, bright blade of a butcher knife!

For a second she stood there, feet welded to the carpet, hand to the furry rail.

In that second the man—it must be a man—broke into a cheek-cracking smile.

"You're not afraid of ol' Yep, are you?"

Now Lark felt completely the overwrought adolescent. Old Yep, the Chinese cook, had come up from the kitchen.

He came toward her, beaming.

"You're a pretty girl," he said.

She could see now that the tuft of hair from which the queue hung was gray, the face deep ripples from the splash of his smile. She came the rest of the way downstairs and made herself smile in return.

"I've never tasted such good meals as yours, Yep," she said. "…what—do you have that knife for?"

His smile and ripples vanished.

"To catch the dog," he said. "Miss Julia is allergic to dogs."

His eyes were as bright—and as hard—as black glass. "What do *you* want, missy?"

Tit for tat. And it wasn't the picture gallery she wanted to see now, but Eileen. Eileen, who said last night that a man had come in.

"You know where Eileen is?" Lark asked. "I'm looking for her."

He pointed with his knife toward the Maple Parlor. Lark sidled by, and he winked.

The knife made a whistling swing, and Lark shot through the portières.

Eileen, a cloth around her head and a broom in her hand, jumped too. "Oh, it's you, miss."

The furniture in the Maple Parlor was covered with sheets, like the room Lark had seen last night. The air made her sneeze.

"No vacuum cleaners in the Eighties, I guess," Lark said, and sneezed again. "Were you scared I might be the man who came in last night—the one they couldn't find?"

Eileen reddened. "I—I've been thinking I ought to tell you, though I suppose someone else has by now," she said. "I must have misunderstood last night. I thought it was a man I heard them talking about, but they say it wasn't. They say it was a dog that came in, and dogs give Miss Paget hay fever."

So Eileen had that story now too.

"Are you sure?" Lark asked. She tried helplessly to see behind the rosy face and Irish eyes. "Do you think they're—kidding?"

With the edge of her broom, the maid brushed uncomfortably at a blue carpet rose.

"I don't see why they would, miss—all of them," Eileen said. "Kezzie said it, and Mister Ben, and—Leo."

"Leo wouldn't tell you that if there was any danger, would he?" Lark asked. "Didn't you say he—liked you?"

"He used to, miss; but the war changed him so," Eileen said. "He did say to lock my door tonight so the dog couldn't get in my room."

Lark's heart beat faster again.

"But shutting the door would be enough—for a dog," Lark said. "You wouldn't have to lock it."

Eileen looked up, white.

"I never thought of that, miss!" she said. Then her color came back. "But maybe it's a big dog. Leo knows the catch on my door's bad; he tried to fix it for me. A big dog could bump against it, and the door'd fall right open."

But Lark wasn't so easily satisfied. "I thought you could help me figure things out; I want to go to the picture gallery."

"You want to see the pictures, miss?" Eileen asked. "Missus Drew's in there now. Go in the second curtains from the vestibule on the other side of the hall and through the French Salon to the portières at the end. The gallery's there."

She began to sweep again, anxious to be rid of Lark. But perhaps Eileen didn't want her faith in the dog shaken.

Lark crossed the hall, sped by Yep's hiss from the vestibule, "I haven't caught the dog yet," and the sight of his wrinkled face bending over the knife while he ran his thumb along the blade.

In her flurry, she went through the first portières instead of the second and found another cloakroom with a closet and wash bowl and towels like the one she had been in last night. Perhaps one was for men and one for

90

women when they used to give balls at Dune House, she thought.

She slipped out again, trying not to attract Yep's attention, and hurried through the next door. Eileen said the gallery was at the end of the French Salon. This room was very French, with curlicues on gilded, thin-legged furniture, with tapestries and ornately framed mirrors on the walls and cupids on the high ceiling, sporting a chandelier that was larger and dripped even more crystal ice than the glittering stalactite in the Maple Parlor. Away down at the end of the pastel-flowered carpet was another set of portières. She started for them, passing a third set in the middle of the inside wall. These rooms must be built like those on the other side of the house, with that parting of doorways down the center.

Through the one at the end, she looked into a room that seemed narrow because of its great length. The whole ceiling was a skylight of clear glass. Along the walls hung the massive gold frames she had come to expect.

Far down the room something stirred. She saw Rowena move from one picture to another.

Lark stepped in and was startled by the sound of clicking heels. This floor wasn't carpeted. A long rug ran like a strip of parking down the center. Both sides and ends showed polished boards.

Rowena must have heard the clicking too. She looked up and hurried forward. They were still yards apart when she started talking; her words came in twittering jerks. "Have you heard—about the dog?"

That made four—Julia, Yep, Eileen, and now Rowena.

"That's what made them all stay away last night, Lark," Rowena said. "They were looking for the dog, even Edward and Aubrey. You see, Julia gets the most terrible hay fever—"

"Who told you?" Lark broke in.

"Ben did, this morning at breakfast," Rowena said. "I've been so excited. I love dogs, myself, but the way Julia feels... had you heard about it, my dear?"

"Yes," Lark said briefly. "Did Ben tell you to lock your door nights?"

"Why, I always lock my door nights," Rowena said.

Ben knew that his mother would be safely locked in; Leo had warned Eileen. Lark felt a little lonely to think that Aubrey had known about the dog and hadn't told her to lock her door. Hadn't even hunted her up to say goodnight. But if Aubrey knew it was a dog, of course he wouldn't tell her to lock herself in. Perhaps that was the first good sign.

"Were you looking for me, dear?" Rowena asked. "Was that why you came to the gallery?"

"No, I came to see the pictures," Lark said. "I haven't been in here before."

"But, my dear, how thoughtless of me," Rowena said. "Let me show you the Rosa Bonheur and the Bouguereau and the Turner! That's a Romney you're looking at."

Rowena fluttered from picture to picture. Suddenly she stopped and looked behind her; then, with an air of deep mystery, she leaned closer to Lark. "Does anyone know you're here?"

"Why, I don't—" Lark's voice died away. This gallery, set apart from the rest of the house, all the length of the long French Salon from the hall... "Poor old dotty Rowena Drew" Aubrey called the little woman whose eyes were now strangely bright... and Lark had come between her son and the Paget fortune. What if the evil Lark felt in the house arose from Rowena instead of Julia?

"Eileen knows," Lark burst out. "She said you were here."

"Oh, well—Eileen," Rowena shrugged. Her eyes seemed even brighter. She turned toward the portrait beside her of a high-spirited looking young man with fair hair. "Know who that is, dear?"

Lark shook her head.

"Your grandfather," Rowena beamed.

Relief almost made Lark laugh. This poor, harmless soul—imagine thinking her dangerous, when the high points of her life were cozy gossips and putting something over on Julia—even if it was only introducing a girl to her grandfather's portrait.

Lark looked up at the picture, too. So that was Ulysses Paget, with his widow's peak and his diamond stick pin. No wonder Julia and her father hadn't been able to manage his life; those full red lips looked as stubborn as his sister's.

"The same young artist painted him who did the portrait of Julia in the dining room," Rowena said. "Old Captain Paget wouldn't sit, himself, but he wanted all his chil—" Rowena stopped.

"Then where's Venetia?" Lark asked. "I'd love to see what she was like."

"It was beautiful," Rowena sighed, "that portrait of Venetia. Her expression made her face, and that's the sort of thing that's hard to put on canvas. But the artist caught it—the way a fawn looks: timid and gentle and ready to run. The kind of gentleness that means no harm to anybody..."

"Do show it to me," Lark urged.

"I can't, dear," Rowena said. "I'm terribly sorry. You see, after Venetia went over the cliff, Julia had that portrait destroyed. That portrait and all of Venetia's photographs."

Lark looked up again at the painted face of Ulysses. He'd disobeyed Julia, but she'd kept his portrait—and destroyed every likeness of her sister.

Another voice spoke, and both women jumped.

"Miss Paget wants you, Missus Drew."

Kezzie was standing behind them. She must have tiptoed across the bare floor at the end of the room and walked down the rug. Had she wanted to hear what they were saying in front of Ulysses Paget's portrait?

Rowena trotted out, but Kezzie stayed. She and Lark moved on to the next picture together.

"They're beautiful, aren't they?" Lark murmured.

Kezzie didn't answer, and Lark turned. The maid wasn't looking at the portrait of the mustachioed man in the cavalier's hat that reminded Lark of her husband. Kezzie's sharp black eyes were on Lark.

Yes, miss," Kezzie said. "I've been wondering, miss... I suppose you've heard about the dog?"

Lark nodded. Unanimous, since Ben had told his mother.

"Did you hear—anything else, miss?" Kezzie asked.

"What do you mean—*anything else?*" Lark asked.

Kezzie glanced up and down the long room where a few straight chairs on the narrow rug offered the only cover.

"Eileen had a story last night," she said.

"Yes," Lark said. "I heard it."

Kezzie's eyes brightened. "Miss Paget says it's a dog," she said. "Don't tell anyone, will you, miss, if I tell you something?"

Before Lark could even shake her head, Kezzie whispered, "Last night—all night, miss—Mister Rollin sat at the front door, and Mister Hildreth at the back, and Adam at the door to the conservatory. But this morning when Yep went to fix breakfast, half of last night's chicken was missing, and a loaf of bread, and all the bananas!"

Lark tried to keep a tight hold on herself. Dogs didn't eat bananas.

"Where was that food kept, Kezzie?" she asked.

"The bread was in the bread box, and the rest in the icebox, miss—latched tight!" Kezzie said.

Dogs didn't open iceboxes.

Lark wet her lips.

"The guards," she said. "They must have eaten it."

"Where'd the banana skins go, then, miss?" Kezzie said. "And the chicken bones? They weren't in the garbage."

Lark swallowed. "Why did you tell me this, Kezzie?"

"So you can get away, miss," Kezzie said. "The rest of us have to stay."

Thank God for that pass, Lark thought. Then she gasped. She'd forgotten to pick up her handbag from the chair where she'd dropped it to shut the windows. But the door was locked, the key still in her hand. If she hadn't been so busy every minute since she'd left her room... fingers tightening on the key, she forced herself to wait a few more seconds.

"Miss Paget ought to know about that food, Kezzie, and Mister Drew," Lark said.

"Miss Paget does, but she'd bound the others shan't," Kezzie said. "If you tell, I'll have to say you made it up, miss. And Yep will, too. It means our jobs, miss. Don't you see?"

Lark saw. And she was getting out. Whoever was here—dogs didn't open iceboxes—was already in the house.

She began to hurry toward the door.

"Th-thank you for telling me, Kezzie," Lark said. "When I get out, I'll send the police."

"Oh, no," Kezzie said sharply. "There won't be anything for them to look for—just a dog. You leave it to us. Adam and Mister Ben and Leo will find him—sometime."

If that was how they wanted it, there was nothing she could do. Miss Paget had them all jumping through hoops. Lark could imagine how they'd handle the police. As for herself, she was going down to the stable and wait until Adam came back. Better be with the horses and the good clean horse smell—than here in this haunted house.

Yep was gone from the hall, thank goodness. She wouldn't have to pass the butcher knife.

Lark was running upstairs. Fumbling with the key. Unlocking the door. Locking it behind her. Running for the chair where she'd tossed her bag.

There it was, beside the first window. Just one peek inside for reassurance...

The bag dropped. She fell to her knees beside it. Dumped out the things it held. Pawed through...

She straightened and let the bag slide off her lap.

The pass was gone. Someone else had a key to her room.

Chapter Eight

Lark ran from her room straight to Miss Paget's boudoir. But no matter how she pounded on the door to Miss Paget's bedroom, Julia didn't appear. She didn't come down to lunch. Then at teatime, Lark was sent for.

Tea was served in the boudoir this afternoon with her hostess at the window, the spyglass on the table beside her. Lark waited until Eileen had passed the cups and cakes, then she leaned forward, hands tight on the edge of her chair.

"Before Missus Drew comes, I must ask you for another pass," she said.

"Aren't you ever going to accept us for relatives, child?" Julia asked. "*Cousin* Rowena won't be having tea with us. Putting up with her three meals a day is enough. Now what's all this about a pass?"

"I have to get another pass," Lark said. "Someone took the one you gave me."

"You mean you lost it?" Julia asked.

"Someone took it," Lark insisted. "I put it in my handbag and locked it in my room, and when I unlocked the door an hour later, the pass was gone. Who else has a key to my room?"

"Why, no one, child," Julia said. "The housekeeper used to have a pass key, but I have no housekeeper now."

"Where's the pass key?" Lark asked.

"Goodness knows, I have too many important things on my mind to bother with trifles," Julia said. "As for taking your pass, that's your imagination again, child. You must have mislaid it."

"But I didn't—truly I didn't," Lark said. "I know exactly what I did with it, Miss Paget. What I don't know is who has it now. So you see why I must ask you for another."

"Then I shall have to say that I can't give you another," Julia said. "I never issue two to one person until the first is accounted for."

"But, Miss Paget—" Lark began.

"There's no 'but Aunt Julia' about it," Miss Paget said. How like her simply to ignore the things that didn't suit her, even little things, like not saying *Aunt Julia*. "I gave you one. I cannot give you two."

"Wouldn't you ever break a precedent?" Lark asked. "After all, under these circumstances—"

"You're as stubborn as your grandfather, Lark," Julia said, but the heavy face looked pleased. "... if Ulysses was your grandfather."

Julia sat drumming on the table, her diamonds sparkling in the gas flame she had ordered lighted because now the sun was on the other side of the house.

Lark's mouth opened again, but Julia spoke first.

"I get too accustomed to dealing with the servants and Rowena instead of persons of intelligence," she said. "It's not simply a matter of precedent, child. Experience has shown that people will alter the name on a pass and use it for themselves. The servants have done it several times, and—well, if you must know—Rowena has too."

Lark kept from asking, "Do you think that shows lack of intelligence?"

"I don't like to say anything," Julia continued, "because, after all, she married my mother's youngest brother. But Rowena—poor thing, she's not..." Her words hung in the air.

The gas flame overhead hissed softly.

Julia sighed. "So, you see why I can't give you another pass, as much as I'd like to please you."

"I can see why you won't," Lark amended.

Julia panted in silent laughter. "You're so much like Ulysses in some ways, it's too bad you're afraid of a dog!"

Lark leaned forward again.

"It's not a dog," she said. "Listen, Miss Paget, did Kezzie tell you—?"

"So it's Kezzie who's been talking now—about the chicken and bananas in the icebox?" Julia said.

Lark nodded.

"With all those men around last night, no food would be safe," Julia said. "I should think your common sense would have told you that. But even if it didn't—if you have no common sense, as it happened, Kezzie was lying."

"But how—why—?" Lark stammered.

"She's a bully." *Like mistress, like maid,* Lark thought involuntarily. "She likes to get people upset. To feel she has power…" The hands were out like claws again on the chair arms. Then the fingers relaxed. "She's too useful to discharge. Besides, she amuses me."

"But the missing food, Miss Paget," Lark insisted. "If it's gone—"

"It isn't," Julia said. "I looked in the icebox myself, last night, and I was up before Yep this morning. The food was there, child. Kezzie made up a story."

Lark drew a helpless breath. Someone was lying, certainly, but she had no way of telling whether it was Kezzie, Yep, or Miss Paget.

Julia's "Now let's hear no more about it" ended the conversation. Lark knew when she was beaten.

Walking dispiritedly back to her room, she knew she couldn't get out of Dune House—"Yet!" she added fiercely, aloud. Sometime she'd manage it. Somehow. Perhaps when Adam opened the gate for someone else… the way Miss Paget said the dog had come in.

But she could no more make herself believe that she could actually get out on that split-second chance than she could believe that a dog had come in.

She couldn't call Aubrey to come and get her, because Miss Paget's father hadn't had a telephone to the city in the Eighties. But she could write. Even Papa had patronized the U.S. mail.

There was stationary in the desk in her room, with DUNE HOUSE engraved at the top. Too bad she couldn't mail letters herself instead of having to rely on someone in this household. Lark couldn't even stop a car and hand a note through the fence. Anything that attracted attention to herself and Aubrey was out.

She sighed and began to write, remembering to start, *Dear Mr. Hildreth,* and write as impersonally as she would to Mr. Rollin—no more than a few conventional lines asking if Aubrey could make it convenient to pick her up. If, by any chance, this letter found its way to a steaming kettle before her mailbox, their relationship would remain a secret.

When Aubrey came for her—Lark's thoughts abruptly stumbled. Her mind hadn't said *when*; it said *if*. She was hearing echoes, remembering his words: "even if we can't announce our marriage for ten years more… Rollin *said* he'd retire in four years… thinking how it would be if he didn't." Aubrey had taken an unfair advantage of her that day she'd told him how frightened she was. No, it was she who was being unfair. Aubrey hated to have her unhappy but, knowing she was in no actual danger, he'd adopted the long-term view: better a few days or weeks of unhappiness now and be able to announce their marriage at the end of it, than limp along four years waiting for his partner to retire.

Aubrey was right. If he'd take her away for a few days until they found the man who came in last night… Aubrey had said he'd take her away if she wanted to go, and this would only be for a day or two…

When Kezzie came to help Lark dress for dinner, she said to lay the letter on the vestibule table. Leo picked up the mail once a day.

Finding other letters there when she went down gave Lark a chance to slip her own underneath and hope that it would be picked up unnoticed with the others. Then she crossed the hall to the Maple Parlor.

It was empty. She couldn't stay there alone, with curtained doorways on three sides, all the maple eyes watching—and someone loose in the house!

She hurried back into the hall, reminding herself that, if Kezzie had lied about food being missing, there wasn't anyone loose in the house. The trouble was that everything Miss Paget said was so plausible—and so hard to believe.

The hall was more open, larger than the other rooms; and there were no pianos or bookcases or embroidered screens to hide behind. If she had to scream, surely someone on the other side of one of the eleven pairs of portières or in one of the rooms off the balconies would hear her.

It shouldn't be hard to find a hiding place in a house like this… a thought that until now hadn't entered her head came in with a rush. The hall was round; the rooms opening off it were oblong. Anyone knew that curves and straight lines didn't fit. Making the rooms rectangular would leave a lot of space, particularly at the front and back of the house. Too many of Uncle Thad's historical romances, Lark told herself. She'd been steeped in secret passages and cupboards ever since she was old enough to climb the chinaberry trees and hide from Aunt Sophie with a book down her flat little front.

Nevertheless, her eyes turned to the vestibule. The coatrooms took care of the extra space there, one coatroom on each side.

At the back—she crossed the hall—from the library door to the servants' wing, and from there to the Moorish Room, were the two longest stretches without doors.

Lark pulled out the edge of a huge blue tapestry and peered behind it. She flattened her cheek against the plaster to look behind a framed landscape.

In Uncle Thad's novels the heroes always checked for secret rooms by knocking on the walls. Lark raised her knuckles and brought them down a few times smartly on the plaster. It sounded like anyone knocking, and she tried again.

"Come in," a voice said behind her.

She whirled. Benson, dressed for dinner, was holding back the portières to the library.

"Don't be so formal," he said politely. "Walk right in… but why not knock nearer the door?"

Disregarding his comment, she hurried by him into the library. "But there is—there is!" she exulted. "A bookcase on the north wall! I saw a movie once where a bookcase turned back like a door, and—"

"I saw it too, Cousin Lark," Benson said. "Only trouble with this bookcase is that it doesn't."

"How do you know?" Lark said. "This house was built long before you were born, and this bookcase fastens to the wall. It's not a piece of furniture."

"But I happen to have seen the other side of that wall, and there's nothing there but a couple of chimneys and nail points sticking through boards," Benson said. "A little whim of the architect, I suppose—that bookcase. The forerunner of built-ins, perhaps."

"How did you ever see the inside of that wall?" Lark asked.

The down curve of Ben's mouth straightened in a grin.

"The kind that pins you down, I see?" he said. "Okay... there's a space back there between the walls, as I take it you guessed, and there used to be an elevator in it. Cousin Julia's mother was an invalid—the poor thing was a Drew, you know, not a Paget—and the old Captain had an elevator put in for her when he built the house. Well, to make a long story short, Pearl Harbor came along, and elevators weren't something you could pick up downtown with the groceries. Gremlins got into the elevator in one of Cousin Julia's friends' apartments—if she can be said to have friends. The friend's building was old, and the elevator the same type as this. So—for the sake of the two bits offered, she had this one taken out and installed downtown. No one used it here, of course, except Mother—who isn't supposed to climb stairs." His mouth was back in those bitter lines again.

Lark waited.

"And that, my charming cousin, was how, before the gap in the hall was covered up and plastered over, I saw the unbeautiful backs of the walls not intended for Paget eyes."

"Lucky for me you happened to be home on leave then," Lark said, "or however it was, or I'd be knocking on those walls whenever the hall was empty."

"I wasn't in the service... and now," he said briskly, "about that space on the other side of the servant's entrance... I know what's in it, too. I had the same idea you did, once—that there might be a secret passage, or something. It's all in what you read, I guess. You were fond of Dumas, too? Anyway, I was brought up here, so I had a chance to poke into things. The phone closet takes up most of the space, and the clothes chute and another chimney the rest. Dune House has everything to offer but secret passages. By the way, if it's not being too nosy, may I ask what your interest is in them?"

"You comb the dunes all day—and ask that?" Lark asked. "I suppose *you* say it's a dog you've been looking for, too."

Ben's green eyes examined her more closely. Then he grinned. "Of course I do," he said. "That's what Cousin Julia says, and Cousin Julia always knows. But look, you're not scared, are you? There's no one—nothing in the house, you know. The doors have all been locked or guarded ever since Mister Rollin arrived, and Leo and I could handle—even a mad dog, if we had to. But in case he should be mad, or there was a slip-up of any kind, why not lock your door when you go to bed?"

So now she, too, had been warned. Ben probably knew about the missing food. If Aubrey had known—but of course he thought it was a dog—he'd have stayed here, or taken her away. He couldn't get her letter before tomorrow, even if Leo mailed it tonight. She'd have to stay this one more night, get through it somehow.

"My door's locked now," she said briefly. Someone else in the house had a key, but her lock ought to keep out a stranger. *Stop shivering,* she commanded herself. Maybe it really was a dog. Anyway, before she went to bed, she'd go over every inch of her room and the dressing room and bath, and she'd prop a chair under the knob as well as lock the door.

But if anyone had come in shouldn't there be some indication...? "What about tracks?" She looked up at Ben, remembering the straggle of tadpoles she'd left between the dunes, herself, yesterday morning.

"The wind took care of that," Benson said. "It's been blowing great guns for over twenty-four hours, and wherever there aren't any bushes or grass, the dunes are as clean as Yep's kitchen. My own tracks are covered up almost as soon as I make them, and the—dog came in last night."

Lark sighed and walked over to a window in the seaward wall. She pulled aside the drawn curtains and opened the shutters, but the night on the other side of the glass simply gave her reflections of the room she was in.

The muffled boom of the breakers was louder. How often she'd lain in bed listening to that rhythm from her room above this. "I suppose," she said over her shoulder to Ben, "this house was built facing the dunes for convenience to the road and all, but it seems odd that Miss Paget lives so much on the inland side. You'd think she'd want her bedroom and boudoir to overlook the ocean."

In the window she saw Ben coming toward her, his face more bitter than ever. He stopped a few inches away, staring at the glass that neither could see through. Perhaps he, too, was listening to the *boom... boom... boom...*

What was he thinking about? Suddenly she was shivering. If she could imagine his mother, sociable Rowena, hating her, how much more reason there was for Ben...

Lark's hands clenched. One of the things that made life here so hard was not knowing whom to look out for, not knowing for sure where danger lay. Not that there was danger for her, she reminded herself quickly. No one would want to do her any harm. Surely no one...

Ben spoke at last. "We have to spare Cousin Julia's tender feelings, but this ought to be far enough from the portières. Old Captain Paget's jammed-lock phobia kept sliding doors from going in behind them, and it's too convenient for eavesdroppers. I'll tell you why she avoids the ocean, Lark Williams, if you want to know. She can ban modern inventions from the house and hold back the city with a fence, but the ocean is stronger than Cousin Julia. The ocean's a constant reminder that there's still one thing she can't lick—and, maybe, it's the only one.

Chapter Nine

Morning found Lark still alive and embarrassingly hungry. It had been a long night, with Julia insisting on going to bed early, and Lark getting up every few minutes to put her ear against the door to the hall, locked and braced with a chair, or the bolted door in her bathroom.

Last night before going upstairs she had looked at the table in the vestibule and seen that the letters were gone. Sometime today, perhaps this morning, her appeal would reach Aubrey.

That thought warmed her enough to make her tolerant even of Julia. The poor woman had had something to put up with last night in Lark's whist. They'd been partners, and Lark had played as badly as Rowena. No wonder Julia had wanted to go to bed early. And she'd tried, as they separated at the stair landing, to assure Lark a good night's sleep… or was it just to get in the last word? She'd said, too low for the Drews going up the right-hand fork to hear, "By the way, I forgot to mention that the dog was seen—if that makes you feel any better. Adam *saw* him come in."

Anyway, morning had come—the morning of the day Aubrey should get her letter. And the sun was shining. She ran downstairs through a cylinder of gold from the Chinese hat above her.

Miss Paget and the Drews were already at breakfast.

"You're looking better this morning, child," Julia remarked.

Lark's smile included them all, as warm for Miss Paget and Ben as for pathetic little Rowena. Not much longer now to put up with any of them… "When Leo takes the letters at night, does he mail them then or in the morning, Aunt Julia?"

"Usually morning—isn't it, Benson?—unless he goes out in the evening or the letters are important," Julia said. "Incidentally, child, I hope you had nothing important in yesterday's outgoing mail."

Lark set down her grapefruit spoon so abruptly that in *pinggged* on her plate.

"What—do you mean?" she asked.

"Something—ah—rather unfortunate happened to the mail last night." Julia paused, and Lark's breath paused too. "Leo has the bad habit of smoking when he's alone, and he put the mail into one of those cardboard cartons on the back seat of the victoria. Yes, I see you've guessed it, but don't look so anxious, child. You can always write another letter. He *will* flip the matches over his shoulder, though he's been told not to time and again—and it fell into the box of letters. By the time he discovered the fire, it had burned up the letters and most of the box, and even scorched the upholstery."

For a moment Lark thought she'd have to leave the table and be sick. That letter on which so much depended... it couldn't be true... then anger like a hypodermic straightened her drooping shoulders. Probably it *wasn't* true. Another of those fishy coincidences... though, as usual, nothing could be proved. But now suddenly all her terror and apprehension were not there—gone up in smoke, like letters. In fact, gone up in smoke *with* the letters. Burning them had been the last straw. Now Lark was ready to fight.

She dug her spoon into the grapefruit so hard that juice spurted, and she didn't look up to apologize or see if it had hit Julia.

"That's the right attitude, child," her hostess commended. "You're learning to take things philosophically."

Lark almost laughed. If Julia could read her mind! Right now it was on Paget money. She'd stick out these phony accidents and phonier explanations—barricade herself in her room if necessary—until her mother's share of the Paget money was legally hers, as it was rightfully hers even now. And after that—if what Julia wanted was a Paget heir, a stooge of the sacred blood to hang around at her command like poor Rowena, she wouldn't find it in Lark. What if Julia did have millions of dollars, and the trust fund was only two? Two million would keep Lark and Aubrey nicely. Let Julia give the rest to Ben. He must have earned it—living at Dune House all his life, taking her insults and seeing his mother take them, even to the removal of the elevator she needed.

Across the table Rowena asked curiously, "Who were your letters to, Lark—the ones that were burned?"

"Mother!" Ben expostulated.

Lark said quietly, "There was only one—to Mister Hildreth."

"Oh, well, you'll be seeing him soon," Rowena soothed. "Unless, of course, there were enclosures you can't replace?"

"Mother," Ben objected again, "do let the girl—"

"It's all right, Cousin Rowena," Lark smiled. "There was nothing private about that letter"—she had seen to that—"and there was nothing that can't be brought up again, either."

"You see, Ben?" his mother nodded. "I knew Lark wouldn't mind. Anything like this is so exciting. I didn't have any letters in last night's mail, myself." She didn't ask Julia about her, Lark noticed. Rowena must remember too many snubs.

As they left the dining room, Julia said to Lark, "Come to my boudoir a minute, will you?"

A rhetorical question, of course, but Lark couldn't help wondering what Julia would say if she refused.

This time Julia closed her own door and stood with her lorgnette turned on Lark. Stood with that look of crocodile power that Lark was too angry now to be scared of.

"There's something I must mention, child," Julia said. "You've seen a lot of Aubrey in the five years you worked for his firm. He's attractive, too—unusually attractive. But you're meeting him now in a different way—a social way, in a sense. Remember this: No Hildreth is good enough for a Paget. Decayed old family like the Drews. No money, no power... I don't want you getting interested in Aubrey Hildreth."

Not get interested in Aubrey... not *get* interested! Lark wasn't capable of speech.

"Another thing that puts him beneath a Paget's notice, child: his mother was no better than the woman Ulysses ran away with," Julia continued. "Friends in the same burlesque show! That's how Aubrey's father and Ulysses—great friends, too—got involved with them. But that Georgette creature who bamboozled my brother was smarter than Aubrey's mother. Georgette got a marriage certificate."

"You mean—?" Lark began.

"Certainly I mean that Aubrey's father didn't marry his mother," Julia said. "Aubrey was born out of wedlock."

Lark was speechless again, speechless this time with fury. As if Aubrey could help it!

"So you see"—Julia gave a conclusive nod—"why I don't want you building up romantic ideas. You may run along now, child."

The interview was over. Lark returned to her room to seethe for the rest of the morning, except the times she thought of Aubrey. It was strange that, in a sense, he too had been tied in with the Pagets. She knew that his father and Ulysses had been friends, but not that his mother and Georgette had. No wonder Lark and Aubrey had taken to each other, and no wonder the poor darling didn't say much about his early life. He wouldn't enjoy telling her he was illegitimate. Something she'd never understood before was clear now—why his grandmother had legally adopted him when he was eight. He must have been fond of his mother, though. After all the years they'd been apart, when she fell ill after he was discharged from the army, he'd gone East to be with her, and stayed with her until she died almost a month later. Those burlesque queens must have had something. It made having one for a grandmother more agreeable and gave Lark and Aubrey more in common.

Lunch passed without excitement for anyone but Rowena, who exclaimed all over again about the dog and the burning of the letters. Ben wasn't there. Still combing the dunes, his mother said. What loyal adherents Julia had—relatives and hirelings, all out to prevent her discomfort! "Hay fever can make you so wretched, you know," Rowena finished.

Lark was alone until Eileen called her for tea, served today in the music room, with Ben, back from the dunes, playing the piano. Rowena was there, too; evidently Julia was rewarding the Drews for loyalty.

Music filled the room to the sixteen-foot ceiling. Up there, appropriately enough, the ever-present cupids were blowing trumpets among sheet pelt clouds against a blue never seen in the sky. In one curved corner of the cove ceiling, St. Cecilia accompanied Ben, and kitty-corner from her Beethoven made it a trio. A stained-glass window made a church-colored spot on the grand piano and streaked the embroidered fire screen that hid an empty grate. There were as many tassels and fringes in the music room as any of the others, and the patent rocker next to a great gold harp had a tidy pinned to its back.

As Ben came to a crashing chord, Eileen hurried in, giving Lark an odd glance as she passed. She murmured something to Miss Paget.

Julia's hands came down on the arms of her chair and spread out like claws. She sat without speaking while Eileen waited.

Finally Julia said, "Have Leo bring her up." Her hands dropped to her lap and she picked up her lorgnette. "The rest of you, particularly Lark, will be interested to know—" she paused, head up, a malicious gleam in the eyes behind the lorgnette—"that another aspirant to the trust fund has arrived."

"I thought there were hundreds," Ben murmured.

"This one's different." Julia's eyes were still on Lark. "Adam says this one has a picture exactly like the one in the paper."

Lark gasped.

"They won't be long," Julia said. "Leo has the team already harnessed."

But it seemed long. Ben's playing had washed away Lark's anger, and her fear had not yet returned. For half an hour she had been almost peaceful. Now, with her heart beating faster, harder, she could only refuse the frosted cakes Miss Paget kept pressing on her, and wait for the crunch of wheels on the gravel.

It came at the same moment Kezzie arrived with the matching baby pictures from upstairs—the one Lark had brought and the one Miss Paget already had.

At the door Eileen announced, "Missus Seymour, madam."

A slender, golden-haired woman in dramatic black came through the portières.

"I'm Ulysses Paget's daughter—Juliette Paget Seymour. I have her—the photograph." She whipped it out of her handbag. The white-tipped tails of a double silver-fox scarf toe-danced as she neared the tea tray. She held up the picture.

"The baby on brocade—the hand in the corner—see? And here—" pulling off a black glove—"the sea horse on the amethyst—the Paget ring!"

Chapter Ten

Lark, Ben, and Rowena hung over Julia to see the three photographs in her lap. All were identical; the one Mrs. Seymour produced looked as genuine as the others.

"Well, Lark"—Miss Paget's lorgnette came up—"how do you account for this?"

"I—can't," she said. "Someone else must have had a copy…"

"*Someone else* evidently did." Julia's tone said as plainly as words that Lark's mother could have been the someone else.

"But, Miss Paget—" Lark began.

The blond stranger pounced. "*You* are Julia Paget! Ah—my long lost Tante Zhulee!"

Julia drew back. All the other woman was able to clasp was one pudgy, ringed hand.

"Miss Paget, if you please," she said.

"Forgive me," Mrs. Seymour said. "I call you what the good French friend who reared me always called you—Tante Zhulee."

The slim newcomer, still bending over Julia, sent a charming smile toward Lark and the Drews. "And these are relatives too—these others?"

No one answered.

Lark stepped forward, looking at Julia beyond the foxtails swinging almost in her lap.

"All I know is that that picture was in Mother's—" she said.

"That picture!" Foxtails fanned as the woman who called herself Julia Paget Seymour dropped Julia's hand and whirled on Lark. "You mean to say someone else has *my* baby picture?"

"It's the other way around," Lark said spiritedly. "My mother—"

"Do you dare claim that picture is of you?" Mrs. Seymour said. The older woman's look slashed Lark from hair to heels.

Then suddenly the bright eyes softened to a pansy blue-purple.

"A charming girl," she said sweetly to Miss Paget, "but much too young to be your brother's daughter."

"Miss Williams," Ben remarked quietly, "says that photograph was taken of her mother."

"Then Miss Williams is mistaken," Mrs. Seymour said. The voice that had been so sweet was now crisp. "It was taken of me at six months—the daughter of Ulysses and Georgette Paget. Turn it over and read on the back."

They all craned again. In sprawling, faded ink were the words, "Juliette. Age six months. Looks like Ulysses, *n'est-ce pas?*"

Julia reversed the two other pictures. The one Lark had brought was blank. The other revealed the same words, written in the same hand.

"They look okay," Ben said. "But of course both writing and photograph would have to be tested."

Lark had never expected to be grateful of Benson Drew—and for the all-but-identical words that had once made her boil.

Apparently, they didn't anger Mrs. Seymour. She reached again, in a businesslike way, into her handbag and brought out another paper. "I do not yet have my birth certificate, but I have cabled France—here is a copy of the message sent to the American Consul at Nice. I was born in the consulate, you know, so I did not have to be naturalized when I came to this country."

"This story came out in the paper five days ago," Julia said coldly. "Where have you been all this time, Missus Seymour?"

"Why, New York! Didn't you get my telegram?" Mrs. Seymour asked. "I sent it as soon as I saw the paper over my *café au lait* in the morning. It was such a surprise—as you can imagine—my own baby picture right on the front page!"

"I'll bet," Ben said dryly.

"Think how you'd feel if it happened to you, Ben!" his mother cried. "Your own picture, and a trust fund for two million! But, Lark, my dear, what about you?"

"Suppose *I* do the talking, Rowena," Julia broke in. "What's this about a telegram, Missus Seymour?"

"I sent one right away to say I'd come as soon as I could get a seat on the plane," she responded. "You know what transportation is. You didn't get my wire?"

"I had so many," Julia said. "I don't remember yours."

"Mine was signed Juliette Paget Seymour," Mrs. Seymour said.

"I had messages signed Juliette, and Georgette, and even Ulysses," Miss Paget said. She rose, standing inches above the slim stranger, with that air of leashed power that always sent shivers through Lark. But no tremor blurred the smart outline of Juliette Paget Seymour. Erect and confident, she stared back, not even the foxtails quivering before the crocodile look.

"I shall check on your telegram, Missus Seymour, and have your photograph tested" Julia said. "In the meantime..."

The newcomer smiled. "I have the ring, you remember—the sea horse ring of the Pagets."

"Yes," Julia said slowly, "you do have that ring... let me think a moment." She walked around the piano to a window overlooking the dunes and stood behind the harp.

The room grew very still.

It was still for so long that Rowena began to fidget. "You—uh—I trust you had a pleasant trip, Missus Seymour? On the plane, I mean."

Mrs. Seymour, without taking her eyes off the thick-shouldered woman at the window, said, "Very pleasant, thank you."

The room was still again.

Rowena did some more fidgeting. "I—I've never been on a plane. How long does it take to cross the continent now?"

The blond stranger's exquisitely curved breast rose in a not-quite-stifled sigh. She turned her pansy purple eyes toward the group by the tea table, distributing again her charming smile. "You must forgive me. After all these years to see my father's sister..."

Not her father's sister, Lark corrected silently, *my mother's father's sister.*

The other woman's fuchsia lips were still moving. "The emotion... it brings out my French background. My own Tante Zhulee..."

A loud twang of harp strings interrupted.

"Sorry," Julia said, coming toward them. "I caught my heel and my hand struck the harp. You are registered at one of the downtown hotels, Missus Seymour?"

"The St. Francis," she replied.

"Let me send my coachman for your bags, and you can stay with us," Julia said. "It's not right that Ulysses' daughter should be anywhere in San Francisco but at Dune House."

Ulysses' daughter—the same routine she had gone through before. Was Julia actually insane, Lark asked herself, or was she just soft-headed, believing first one, then another? At least Lark had been vouched for by Aubrey and Mr. Rollin, but this claimant from New York... no telling how she had acquired the sea horse ring. Or was Mrs. Seymour, as well as Lark, intended to play a part in some scheme that Miss Paget was hatching?

"I can't call you Juliette, my dear," Miss Paget was saying. "It makes too many Julias in the house. Don't you have another name?"

"Ah, Tante Zhulee—"

"Aunt Julia." The correction was sharp, but Miss Paget smiled as if to take out any sting.

"Aunt Julia, of course," Mrs. Seymour said. "As I was telling the others, emotion always brings out my French. I do have another name—Marianne. Not Marian or Mary Anne, you understand—but Mari*anne*—the French way, you know."

"I've lived in France," Julia said.

"Of course," Mrs. Seymour said quickly. "And of course you speak—?"

"I know French, but I prefer English," Julia said. "I've traveled on four continents without speaking anything else."

"How wise you are," Mrs. Seymour said. "There is always someone to speak English. For myself, I have lost my French. With my mother an American, and coming to America when I was small... you know how it is."

"But you still drink *café au lait*," Ben observed, "and say *Tante Zhulee*, and the way you move and dress…"

Marianne Seymour laughed with a French lift of the hands. "But it wouldn't be natural to lose it all," she said. "I was born in France, you know, and the kind friend with whom I lived in New York was French. It was through her that I kept—what I have."

"Of course you'll give us her name and ad—" Benson began.

Julia interrupted him. "Benson, will you pull the bell cord?"

Eileen came in with suspicious quickness.

"Tell Kezzie to prepare Miss Venetia's room for Missus Seymour," Julia directed, "and have Leo get the car out and await instructions."

As the portières dropped behind Eileen, Miss Paget said, "Come up to my boudoir, Marianne. We must get acquainted."

The curtains dropped behind them, too.

"Just one big happy family," Ben murmured. "Getting bigger by the week."

The music room was quiet. Rowena's faded lips were parted, her eyes blinking fast as they rested on Lark. Ben's eyes were on her too.

"You—you don't believe that woman, do you, Ben?" Lark cried. "Do you, Cousin Rowena?"

"If it were simply a matter of her word against yours…" Ben looked thoughtful. "Unfortunately for you, she has that ring."

The room was still again.

But for only a minute. "Don't you know," Lark burst out, "that I'd never—" But how could Ben and Rowena be expected to know that she wasn't a climber, a fortune hunter?

"Don't take it to heart," Ben said lightly. "With two million bucks at stake, it's a wonder the house isn't crawling with heirs."

"But I'm—" Lark broke off again, sighing. "I wonder if it would show that I'm not trying to chisel in on anything I have no right to, if I stood on my dignity? If I went away and left Missus Seymour here, would that show Miss Paget that I wasn't trying to influence her, that I was so confident—?"

"How're you going to leave?" Ben asked bluntly. He was looking at the scratches on her hands.

114

"Perhaps, my dear," Rowena said, "leaving *would* be best—that is, if you can get away. With this woman here, you may come in for quite a little unpleasantness, you know."

"I know what I'd do." Ben leaned back in his chair, long legs spread out, arms folded. "If I had a chance at that trust fund, I'd sit tight until I got thrown out—the way I'm sure Marianne Juliette Paget Seymour is going to do."

Lark laughed, and then was amazed at herself. Here she was treating the Drews like real cousins, asking their advice—the Drews who, only yesterday, she had feared.

At the moment Rowena's counsel was more appealing than Ben's—to withdraw in chilly dignity (providing she'd be permitted to withdraw), no stooping to squabble over millions. But, after all, it *was* millions. If Lark gave them up to a phony... she stiffened her already straight backbone. She'd take Ben's advice, even though she had to take a barbed wire fence, a singing ghost, and an uncaught lurker with it.

She had her regrets later on—when she went upstairs to dress and found Marianne sharing her bath. So the empty room next door had been Venetia's. But all that it meant now was that Lark could no longer bolt the door out of the bathroom. She'd have to prop a chair under one more knob every night if she wanted to make sure of being alone. And certainly she did, as long as who—or whatever—had come in Thursday night remained at large.

She had more regrets at dinner, with Marianne sitting on Miss Paget's right, and Lark moved down a chair. It was Marianne who was made much of now, and Lark who felt like an intruder.

Only twice was the duet that excluded Lark and the Drews broken up. When coffee was brought to the dining alcove with cream puffs that were bigger than baseballs, Marianne took out her cigarette case and Julia's neck began to arch.

"Oh, my dear," Rowena gasped across the table, "Julia won't let anyone smoke cigarettes at Dune House!"

Miss Paget's neck came back to normal but her eyes remained cold. "Call it odd if you like, my dear Marianne, but I like things to be the way my father

115

left them. He was a great man, you know, and those were great days. I want to keep them here at Dune House. No lady ever smoked then, and cigarettes were—"

"Coffin nails," Ben finished with that bent-down grin.

"Pardon me," Marianne murmured.

The second time was at the card table after dinner. Lark kept finding Marianne's eyes on her face.

"What's the matter," she asked finally. "You stare at me so."

"Forgive me, *cherie,* I was only thinking," Marianne said. "All those little cuts and scratches... you have been in an accident—no?"

"No," Lark said briefly, telling herself with a spite that surprised her that someday Marianne Juliette Paget Seymour, if she stayed here, with her little French airs and all her charm, might get scratched too—the same way.

After Kezzie had taken Lark's dress off that night and turned down the bed, she went to help Marianne, leaving the connecting doors open. Through her dressing room and Marianne's beyond the bath, Lark could hear the sound of their voices. If the woman must be here, why did she have to be so close? Another enemy in Dune House, one more to lock the doors against...

Lark had turned the key and was propping a chair beneath the hall doorknob for added reinforcement when a voice spoke behind.

"How about a cigarette now that—what on earth are you doing, *cherie?*"

Marianne stood in Lark's dressing room doorway. Without makeup or figure adjustments, she looked distinctly less young and charming.

Lark knew a moment's panic before she reminded herself that this woman might be a threat to her claims but was surely no threat to her person. In fact—Lark suddenly felt much better—if there was someone hiding in the house, wouldn't Marianne be in as much danger as Lark herself?

"I'm getting back for the night, Missus Seymour," Lark said briskly. "Do you mind stepping back into the bathroom so I can prop my dressing room door shut too? Since we're sharing the bath, I can't bolt the door into your room."

Marianne gave an unpleasant smile. "I admit we're both after the same thing, *cherie*—two million now and more when the old lady dies. But murdering you in your sleep's not the way I plan to get."

"Oh, it's not you I'm afraid of, Missus Seymour," Lark said sweetly. "It's the man Adam let in night before last—the man they haven't found yet."

She had the satisfaction of seeing Marianne Seymour's cheeks beneath their glaze of cold cream turn white.

Chapter Eleven

L ark's native honesty also made her tell Marianne about the dog, though she didn't neglect to mention Kezzie's story of the missing food and invite Marianne to draw her own conclusions. That they were the same as Lark's was evident when the door on the other side of the bathroom was shut with an almost breathless firmness, followed by the sound of wood scraping wood and the rattle of the knob.

But morning brought no changes to Dune House. No one, nothing—two-legged or four—had been found, and Marianne was still the favorite. At breakfast she sat on Julia's right, receiving all the Paget asides and pats on the arm that Lark had been receiving.

When they all left empty coffee cups and rose, Ben whispered to Lark to wait.

"Look," he said as the two stiff skirts and the undulating soft one swayed through the portières, "don't mind Cousin Julia. Remember how she treated me when *you* came. Some people get a kick out of that sort of thing... the wind's not so wild this morning, how'd you like to go out on the dunes with me and fly kites?"

"Fly kites?" Lark asked. "For heaven's sake, Ben, don't you have something more important to do? What about the—dog you've been searching for?"

"He must have gotten out by now," Ben said. "I told Cousin Julia so. Suppose he hid in the stable near the garage door—when Leo opens it and goes around to get into the car... of course that takes only a few seconds, but if someone was ready to slip out right then—"

"With Adam underfoot all the time?" Lark objected. "It's too nip and tuck.

It's also a cinch that no one went over the fence."

"It wouldn't be any easier to jump than climb, would it—in case he turned out to be a greyhound?" Ben said. "But he might have dug under."

"And filled up the hole, I suppose!" Lark said. "Or did you find a hole?"

"You'll never let a fellow make you feel good, will you, Lark?" Ben said. "Anyway, I admit that fence would be hard to dig under. Cousin Julia remembered that sand's easy to scoop out when she had the fence put up, and made them sink as much netting under the ground as there is on top. But the dog might have sneaked out sometime when Adam opened the gate or Leo drove the car out—"

Lark made a sound of disbelief.

"—or," finished Ben, "he might have gone over the cliff."

"Like Venetia," Lark said. Only she wasn't thinking of a dog.

"It's time you got out and flew kites," Ben snorted. "Some of that wind off the dunes will be good for you."

"Wait until I change my shoes," Lark said.

When she came down in slacks and low heels, she saw Ben through the open front door, standing on the porch.

Eileen and Kezzie were in the hall near the vestibule, arguing across a small table. Lark caught the word *Thursday* and turned her head. Thursday was the day "the dog" had come in.

"But I tell you," Kezzie said, "it was there Thursday morning. It had a smear across the nose, and you hadn't dusted the lower lip for a week. I was going to speak to you about it, but—"

"Dusted the lower lip..." Lark stopped. "Smear across the nose... what on earth are you talking about?"

Eileen giggled.

Kezzie gave her a subduing look and turned to Lark. "I don't see how anyone, even Eileen, could lose a marble bust as big as a real baby's head and shoulders, do you?"

"Oh," Lark relaxed. "It's one of those busts. The way you spoke of lips and noses... there're so many busts around the house, I should think you could lose a few and never know it. Who was this one supposed to be?"

Kezzie looked offended. "It happened to be a bust of Napoleon and was made of Italian marble. Of course *you* wouldn't know—" She stopped and finished obsequiously. "None of the young folks your age, miss, care about such things, but it was an expensive piece in its day, and Miss Paget won't like Eileen's losing it a bit."

"Don't tell her, then," Lark suggested. "It probably got moved to another table. Give Eileen a chance to find it and Miss Paget won't be upset." Lark smiled at them both and went out to join Ben.

He had two large kites, one under each arm like folded wings.

"This ought to please Cousin Julia," he said as they crossed the lawn. "Two cousins getting together..."

"Then maybe you should have brought Marianne," Lark said.

"You'll do better for kite flying," Ben said. "Twenty years makes a difference in wind and limb. It must have come hard for her to admit to forty-two. But I suppose two million would be worth it. Do you know, if she hadn't shown up, I wouldn't have known things weren't already settled between you and Cousin Julia."

"But—"

"Yes, I see now," Ben said. "But I didn't know then there was any but."

"I guess Miss Paget—likes to keep people in the dark," Lark said.

"That's putting it mildly, sister," Ben said.

They had left the road and began to climb a dune.

"I'm glad I wore sneakers," Lark said. "When I think of the other time I plowed through the sand..."

"I know how it is—not the heels part, of course," Ben said. "But that feeling of being locked in... you have to get out, even if you have to climb an eight-foot fence. Once when I was a kid I tried to tunnel under. But by the time you get down eight feet, and then start digging up the other side... man isn't built for burrowing, I found out the same day Adam discovered the hole. Cousin Julia started him patrolling the fence while Venetia was alive—so she couldn't dig out either."

Poor, poor Venetia, Lark thought, with sudden desperate kinship.

"The patrol still goes on because of reporters, though Leo does it now,"

Ben said. "Think the top of this dune's good to start our kites from?"

The wind tried to wrest away the one he gave her.

"Hang onto the string," Ben yelled, plunging forward with his own kite.

Lark followed, tearing through beach grass and bushes. Her feet sank in the sand while the great kite jerked at her arms. Dune House was forgotten—Julie—Venetia—raided iceboxes and prowlers. All she was conscious of was the salty wind in her face and keeping the kite in the air.

She caught up with Ben finally sprawled between two dunes with his back on the sand, the bunched red papers of the tail of his kite like a string of chili peppers grafted on a lupin.

Lark hauled in her kite and sank down beside him. "You certainly can build them," she panted. "I thought I was going to take off, myself, for a while."

"Don't blame me, blame Leo," Ben said. "He grew up on these dunes a few years before I did. He made my first kite and taught me the manly art of self-defense—and, incidentally, offense; showed me how to bat balls and play marbles, and all the things a kid has to learn. It was a lucky break for me to have him here, with Cousin Julia running things, and no father or brothers of my own."

"Leo must have been a real hero to you," Lark said.

"He's a hero to more than me now," Ben said. "Ask any man in his company who didn't get killed in the war."

"Eileen says the war's changed him," Lark said.

"Could a fellow go all the way through it—a lot of time at the front—without changing?" Ben asked. "He was even in Germany with the occupation troops for a year. He's harder, all right. A lot harder. I guess it's not easy for Eileen."

Lark sat looking at the bright tail of Ben's kite.

Ben's eyes were on the nearest dune horizon. "When your world has just a few inhabitants," he said, "the way it is at Dune House, it makes ever motion and emotion of those inhabitants loom twice as large—ten times maybe. Leo and Eileen are finding that out. When Mother first used to visit here before she was married, it was Adam and Kezzie."

"Adam and *Kezzie!*" Lark said. "Was she ever human enough to be in love?"

"Head over heels, Mother says," Ben said. "Of course, Adam had all his hair then. She told me once she never did understand why Kezzie stayed on when Cousin Julia wouldn't let them get married."

"Miss Paget wouldn't *let* them?" Lark said.

"You know Cousin Julia," Ben said. "Or you will if you're here long enough. She interfered, and after a while Adam began to court the downstairs maid. For some reason Cousin Julia let that alone, and when they wanted to get married, she let Adam take his wife to his quarters over the stable. That's where Leo was born. She's a strange woman—Cousin Julia."

"I agree with you there," Lark said firmly.

"What do you say we climb a dune for another takeoff?" Ben said. "The kites must be rested by now."

Lark laughed. "It's good you didn't bring Marianne. She'd never have been able to take it."

"Not at her age," Ben agreed.

"I was thinking of her silhouette," Lark said quickly. "The trouble she goes to keep it. Forty-two's not old." Aubrey was forty-one.

"Not young, either," Ben said. He got up and they started to climb. "Maybe I'm working against myself when I tell you this, but her accent's as phony as her hair. If that's not bleached, I never saw a real blonde."

"Oh, I *know* she's phony, Ben, but I didn't know about the accent, not speaking French myself," Lark said.

"Cousin Julia made me learn it the first time she took me to Europe," Ben said. "Yes, I get off the reservation now and then. She likes to have a male relative along on her trips. It's only been because of the war and the run-down state of Europe since that she's stuck so close to San Francisco. She'd never go to the Orient or South America or Alaska; Europe's the only fit place for a Paget. She put me in a French school once, and I spent a season on the Riviera with her. So this morning before you came downstairs I rattled off a bunch of French, and Marianne was stymied. She went all big-eyed about being a child when she came over and her mother not being French.

Cousin Julia was there. She should have seen for herself."

"But Marianne said yesterday that she'd lost her French, you know, Ben," Lark said.

"Lost it!" Ben exclaimed. "If she ever had it—why, if she knew one word of what I said this morning, I know all the dialects in China! You can't help remembering some things, especially if you live with a woman with an accent thick enough to give Marianne hers."

"It certainly is decent of you to tell me," Lark said gratefully. "After all, I'm trying for the same thing she is, and I suppose you feel all the money should be yours."

"Mother does," Ben said. "But there's more where the trust fund comes from, and Ulysses Paget got a dirty deal. Anyway—" Ben paused, then grinned. "Oh, well, there're ways and ways—like marrying money, for instance."

"No doubt the Paget millions give you plenty of opportunities," Lark said stiffly.

Ben's grin widened. "It was the Paget millions I was thinking of, to keep them in the family. Neither you nor Marianne would be hard to take—whichever way the cat jumps."

"Thanks, pal," Lark said. "Wish you'd make that threat to Marianne. Maybe she'd withdraw her claim."

"Are you withdrawing yours?" Ben asked. He was looking at her sideways, not quite laughing, while the wind jerked his kite.

Lark parted her lips to make the kind of reply she thought she ought to make, when something he'd said the moment before made a sudden sharp picture in her mind—*whichever way the cat jumps...*

"She *is* a cat!" Lark burst out. "A great, big, cruel cat playing with a lot of helpless mice—before she kills them!"

Ben's face changed. "You're not letting Cousin Julia get you down, are you? She's only another woman, after all."

"Sometimes I wonder if she is," Lark said, "if she could be another human being like the rest of us. Sometimes she seems like a monster... and it scares me."

"Don't think for a minute that she'd do anything physical to you, Lark," Ben said. "Although, in her family greed, her Paget-worship, she *has* become a sort of monster. She wants to take you over—you or Marianne, force you into the Paget mold…"

"Swallow us up," Lark shivered.

"Whichever one of you's a Paget," Ben said.

Venetia. Lark couldn't keep her thoughts away from the slim, gentle girl with the voice like a bell—Venetia had been swallowed up.

They had reached the top of the dune. Ben looked back at the house with its many roofs and chimneys and towers. Lark looked too, and remembered her thought the day she arrived that each tower was a lighthouse—to warn her away.

"Let's go!" Ben cried. "Forget all this monster stuff."

They were off again—lunging, tripping, jumping bushes. Feet found landings somehow, with faces turned up toward the kites. Lark felt like a little girl on the chicken ranch again. Julia might have been Aunt Sophie.

Ben, in the lead, was the first one down. He took a wild plunge, tripped on the long dune grass, and landed face down in a patch of sand. His kite sailed off—a flat sting ray swimming in air instead of water, trailing a string of chili peppers.

Lark reeled in and sat down panting. "Well, that settles that," she said, "unless you want to take turns with mine."

"Too lazy," Ben said. "I'd rather lie here and stare at the sky."

He had turned over on his back. His profile was good, she decided. You didn't get the effect of bitterness so often apparent full face.

The mouth she was looking at opened. "You know, sometimes I wish I didn't expect Cousin Julia to leave me anything," Ben said. "Then I'd have to get out and work, instead of moaning at not having the guts to break away and do what I want to."

"What's that?" Lark asked.

"Iron work," Ben said. "If I'd lived in grandpa's time and hadn't been the cousin of a Paget, I'd have been a blacksmith. As it is, Cousin Julia won't even let me shoe the grays. Although I suppose it would be screwy bringing horses down into the basement."

"The basement of *Dune House?*" Lark asked.

He nodded. "It does seem a little incongruous, but that's where my amateur forge is," Ben said. "Cousin Julia doesn't care if I make flower stands and ornamental grilles, as long as I don't turn professional." The hands Lark had noticed the first evening, the muscular hands of a man of great strength on one who had nothing to do, clenched and relaxed again. "I know it sounds crazy—reaction, I guess—but I'd like to have a job in a foundry and carry a tin dinner pail." The hands gouged sand.

"Why don't you, Ben?" Lark asked.

He turned his head. Down-bent mouth and greenish eyes mocked her. "And leave Julia's millions for you—or Marianne? Besides, there's Mother."

"I don't think your mother leads any life to rave about," Lark said.

"But I couldn't give her even four walls and a roof for a while," Ben said. "Here she has all the comforts of—"

"Dune House," Lark finished.

The green eyes swung toward her again; the mouth turned farther down.

"Okay, of Dune House—where all you have to do to get early morning coffee served in bed is ring for Kezzie," Ben said. "I must say I enjoy that extra cup before breakfast. If what Cousin Julia prepared me for had even been something I wanted to do. Can you imagine anything worse than studying law, when you hate it?"

"Law's a wonderful profession," Lark said warmly, thinking of Aubrey again. "But of course..."

"But of course," Ben said. "That says it all. Cousin Julia wants a lawyer in the family. Keep the fees at home, and so forth."

Aubrey's best client—exactly what she might expect of Julia Paget!

"As soon as I pass the bar examinations, I'm slated to go into Rollin's office," Ben said. "Of, well, you know the old saw: you can lead a horse to water, but you can't make him drink. I've got everything done, up to taking the actual examinations, but so far I've always managed to be out of town or sick or something each time they've come up. Cousin Julia's fit to be tied. She says she never should have taken me junketing. Gave me too much taste for the nose off the grindstone… as it looks like you're thinking now."

"Well…" Lark began.

"Okay, she should have taken me," Ben said, "because she should have taken Mother. Mother would have enjoyed Europe."

"Didn't she ever take your mother?" Lark asked.

Ben shook his head. "Left her in charge of Kezzie."

What a life that must have been! "Why didn't you get away long ago, Ben, and take your mother with you? I'm sure she'd have been happier, no matter how you had to live."

The green eyes slewed around again. "Why aren't *you* on your job at Rollin, Rollin & Hildreth right now? You didn't have to come to Dune House, Lark. Now you're here, which do you like better—luxury, and the monster; or two third-floor walk-up rooms on Lombard Street?"

"You know where I live?" Lark's voice went up in amazement.

"Cousin Julia sent me after Oscar once, and while I was looking for his name, I saw yours. Lark's not a name you forget."

It was funny how the Paget household knew so much about Aubrey's office, even down to herself and Oscar. Perhaps Red and Dizz had been checked on too. Ben had never mentioned that he'd seen Lark's name before or looked up Oscar out of office hours. Ben did lots of things for his Cousin Julia that he didn't talk about.

For that matter, why was he being so nice now? Lark sighed; living at Dune House was enough to turn even a trusting soul like herself suspicious, and Marianne's claim made her feel uncomfortable and insecure. Certainly Ben had never suggested flying kites or been so friendly before. Was it all supposed, in some way she couldn't understand, to reflect to her discredit? He might feel as friendly now as he acted, or he might, as Uncle Thad used to say, have other fish to fry. Ben Drew's life had been different from most men's.

Lark picked up the tail of her kite and ran the Joseph's-coat papers, cut from comic strips, through her fingers. She didn't look at the man beside her. "Too bad you weren't in the war. I think it would have been good for you in some ways."

"I was 4-F," he said briefly.

Then she did look at him—at the brown cheek and throat, the wide shoulders and chest, the lean look of strength—and those muscular hands.

In the silence they heard a sharp pop.

Ben sat up.

"Was that a backfire?" Lark asked.

"We're not close to the highway here; we're near the ocean—and the house," Ben said. "Hand me your kite, Lark."

He was climbing the dune where the dents of their plunging down-tracks still remained. Lark scrambled up behind him. Before she reached the top, she saw him start to run.

When her own head was high enough to see what he had seen, she began to run too. Three or four dunes nearer the house, Leo and Miss Paget were bending over a lupin bush.

By the time Lark reached them she was too breathless to ask what had happened. But she didn't need to ask, or even follow Ben's pointing finger. All the faces were centered on something lying in the shade of the lupin.

For a moment Lark was conscious of a strange sense of flatness, of letdown. She didn't know what she expected to see, but it hadn't been a dog—a brindled bull terrier shot through the head.

"Now you'll believe me, won't you, child?" Julia said.

Lark's eyes came up, and for the first time she saw the old-fashioned revolver in Miss Paget's hand.

"I shot him," Julia said. "Not with this, though. This was in case I hadn't killed him. I was up in Papa's pilothouse and saw him cross the road. He'd dodged around Leo somehow and was going in the other direction; so I used Papa's rifle. I couldn't let him get away..."

Ben shifted the kite under his arm and glanced at Lark.

"Better look out for your hay fever, Cousin Julia," he said. "Or don't dogs give it to you when they're dead?"

Julia turned toward him, and Lark couldn't see her face. She heard a strange sound—the Paget equivalent of a sneeze?—and saw Julia reach up her sleeve for a handkerchief.

"That's thoughtful of you, Benson," his cousin said, "even if you weren't so thoughtful this morning—going off to fly kites while that dog was still at large! You and Leo will see to burying him, of course."

It was hard to imagine anyone moving majestically through sand and beach grass, but Julia managed it. Lark watched her glide down one dune and up another.

"Why don't you catch up with her?" Ben suggested. "Leo and I have our orders or I'd take you back."

Surely she could cross a few dunes in broad daylight unescorted, Lark thought. Then she saw how, the minute she started away, Ben and Leo's heads came together. For a few yards she could hear the sound of their voices. Did it take that much talking to bury a dog, and such earnest talking?

Even after she could no longer hear them, she could see the two men on the skyline still absorbed. She found herself walking faster, fighting the suck of sand and the tentacle clutch of the grass. By the time she reached the road she was almost running.

Miss Paget was going out of sight through the hedge and Ben and Leo were hidden by the dunes. The hollow that Lark had come into was something she had to get out of quickly, before it was too late.

She began to run, and a voice behind her cried, "What's the matter? Wait for me."

Marianne was coming up the road, a slender, panting figure in dusty black carrying her big black hat and silver foxes. Her voice came faster, high and shrill. "What are you running for, Lark? What's happened?"

"They shot a dog." Lark noticed even as she spoke that she didn't say "*the* dog." "I don't know why I was running. I got nervous, I guess."

"Who wouldn't be nervous?" Marianne had caught up now. Her face was as strained as her voice. "I'd like to know who these people think they are! You can't smoke—you can't phone—you can't get out of her without a pass!"

"I know," Lark said briefly.

"How do they send out mail?" Marianne demanded.

Lark told her.

"Anyway, they'd know who every letter was to—and probably a damn

128

sight more than that."

"You can always stop a car, Marianne, and pass a letter through the fence," Lark said.

"If you don't care how it looks," Marianne said.

So Marianne didn't want to be conspicuous either! That was something more to tell Ben and Aubrey.

Chapter Twelve

That afternoon in her boudoir, Julia told Aubrey about Marianne. His head gave a startled jerk toward Lark, but by the time he spoke only the muscles around his mouth showed strain. "You're actually going to let her stay here, Miss Paget—a stranger you know nothing of? Why, the Santa Barbara sale alone... it'll come through any day, you know—a hundred thousand in cash. I don't suppose you'd let us bank it?"

"Put Paget money in a bank?" Julia asked. "Not while Asa Paget's daughter is alive! But don't think for a minute, Aubrey, that I don't know what my guests have brought with them. There are neither explosives nor safe-cracking tools among their lingerie and dresses."

"But sometimes when you're opening the safe or Kezzie's getting out your jewels..." Aubrey said.

"My guests brought no weapons either, Aubrey—nothing with which to stage a hold-up," Julia said. "Anyway, no one could climb those spiral stairs without my hearing them. Or, if they did, there's always my ace of trumps, you know—Papa's revolver."

Aubrey shrugged. "Well, you can't say I haven't warned you. If you'll let me have the photograph that woman brought I'll take it right down to be tested."

"Thank you, Aubrey." Julia smiled while her fingers moved on the chair arms and her diamonds sprayed drops of rainbow. "I've already attended to that. I sent the photograph yesterday to the man who tested the others. He promised to telephone the stable as soon as he was sure of the results. But I'm willing to wager it's genuine. And she has Ulysses' ring."

Aubrey's face looked harder than Lark had ever seen it. "I've got a man checking Lark's mother, but I'll put on a couple more if necessary and get a check-up started on this—Marianne Seymour." He sat staring at the fire in the grate beneath a mustard yellow lambrequin and a bee-swarm of framed photographs.

Lark got up and held her cold palms toward the flames. "Wait until you meet her—Mister Hildreth. You'll see—" She stopped. She couldn't say, *You'll see that veneer of charm and find out what's beneath it. You'll see that air of sweetness and deference and something entirely different when you talk with her alone.* She couldn't say, *She's hard as nails and her hair's bleached, and the only way she keeps her figure—*

"Now, now child." Julia broke into Lark's thoughts as if she read them. "Youth must be generous. Don't forget she's as old as your mother."

"My mother wouldn't have been like this if she lived to be a hundred," Lark said.

Aubrey's sudden smile was a flash of white in his outdoor-brown face. "That's what I like about Lark. One look at her would tell the world *she'd* never try to put anything over."

"You'll find Missus Seymour quite attractive, Aubrey," his hostess said. "You'll see for yourself in a minute. I told Eileen to call her when she brings the tea."

Aubrey leaned forward. "Does she have her birth certificate from the consul at Nice? Not that that's any proof. Anyone could send for a copy."

"She cabled the consulate there right away," he said, "but she says if her mother brought one from France it's been lost. That Georgette creature's dead now, it seems." Julia's fingertips patted damask upholstery while she savored the burlesque queen's death.

"Too bad the child was born in the consulate," Aubrey added. "If she'd only been French, there'd be so many more things to check when they came over—passports, visas, perhaps citizenship papers. Well, we'll simply have to work on other things." His jaw tensed.

"I know there's some mistake, Mister Hildreth," Lark insisted. "This woman, trying to take my mother's place..."

The set jaw relaxed and he came over to the hearth beside her. "Can't you ever learn to call me Aubrey, Lark? Everyone else here does; it shouldn't be too hard."

Julia cleared her throat.

"There's one thing I don't understand, Aubrey," she said. "Marianne says she was too small to remember when they came over, but she's sure she was under six, as her first school was American. She says her mother went back to France when she was ten, leaving her in the care of a friend in New York. I took down the friend's name, of course. Georgette wrote infrequently (no wonder, with her education!), and after she'd been gone about a year, Marianne had a letter from a man in Paris saying her mother had died in the south of France. He sent Marianne the ring with the Paget crest and some trinkets of her mother's, but didn't give the date of Georgette's death, or the place, or his own address."

"No wonder you don't understand," Aubrey said dryly. "Can't you see how everything's carefully calculated so you won't?"

"I haven't finished, Aubrey." Julia sat straighter. "The thing I don't understand is how Georgette could be in America four years without trying to get money from me. She never once communicated with me or asked me for a dollar."

"Incredible," Aubrey said, "in view of the appeals she made when your brother was killed and the baby born. It looks to me—"

Eileen knocked and came in with the tea tray.

She was only an animated table to Miss Paget, who picked up the conversation where Aubrey had left it. "It's unfortunate there are so few facts to check, I admit. But the main facts speak for themselves—the photograph and the ring."

"Lark has the photograph too, you know," Aubrey reminded her.

Lark smiled up at him. Her back toward Julia, she could let her eyes say that she loved him.

But he was facing Julia. He could only smile back in a pleasant way without even moving closer.

"If you'll give me the data on that friend in New York, Miss Paget," Aubrey said, "the one this woman says her mother left her with when she went back to France—"

"She died years ago, Marianne says," Julia said.

"There're a lot of deaths in this case, Miss Paget," Aubrey said. "A peculiar number of deaths."

"Oh, Aubrey"—Lark spoke his name self-consciously, but it was good to say it in public at last—"that reminds me, is Oscar all right? Mister Rollin said he came to for a few minutes, then relapsed again."

"Why, Oscar left the hospital two or three days ago," Aubrey said.

"Did he say who pushed him?" Lark asked. "Or does he still say he was pushed?"

"Mum as an oyster now, far as I know," Aubrey said. "He must have been out of his head when he said that in the first place."

Julia cut in. "Did you call Missus Seymour, Eileen?"

"Yes, madam," Eileen said. "Here she is now."

She opened the hall door as Marianne's fist was poised to knock again. The pansy-purple eyes discovered Aubrey—and approved.

"Missus Seymour," Julia murmured, "my attorney, Mister Hildreth. He brought Lark to us, Marianne."

"Oh, dear"—the slim blonde, in a gray dress that somehow looked both nunlike and seductive, added a dash of appeal to her recipe for charm—"then he won't be on my side."

"I'm on Miss Paget's side," Aubrey said. "Her attorneys must protect her interests."

Did he have to smile like that? Lark knew it was best to be politic. But, standing by her husband on the hearth, she felt sudden loneliness.

Eileen passed cups and cakes as varicolored as the sparks from Julia's diamonds, and while spoons rang faint porcelain bells, Aubrey bent toward Marianne, murmured, laughed, and kept his eyes on her constantly as if she were the only person there. Lark told herself that he had to know what he was up against, the kind of person with whom he had to deal. But it was sickening the way that woman accepted his attention, took it as her due.

Lark had a chance to speak with him alone only once, while Julia was

133

asking Marianne a question. "Missus Seymour's afraid of publicity, Aubrey," Lark whispered. "She tried to get out this morning, but Adam wouldn't let her leave without a pass or use the phone. I told her to poke a letter through the fence, but she didn't want to be that conspicuous. She practically said so."

"Must have a confederate outside, but I wonder why she'd try to get in touch with him on the day after she arrived," Aubrey said.

"I don't know," Lark shrugged, "unless—"

"Come here, child," Julia ordered before Lark could say that last night she had told Marianne about the dog, bearing down on the fact that it wasn't a dog.

"There"—Julia waved toward the window, while Marianne, with smiles and lash-veiled glances, resumed her chat with Aubrey—"That's where I saw the dog first. You and Benson—silly children—were flying kites over there to the left, and as I turned the glass toward the stable, I saw the dog run across the road. I picked up Papa's rifle and—Aubrey, did I tell you I shot the dog this morning?"

Lark had no chance to talk further with Aubrey. When Eileen came back for the tea things, he rose to leave.

"I have to get a lot of things going," he said, and she knew that he meant he'd put detectives on Marianne. Trace her back to New York, find the French friend she had lived with...

Lark couldn't tell him about the letter he didn't get, or her missing pass, or the food that wasn't in the icebox... now he'd be sure it was a dog, and the dog dead.

"How attractive!" Marianne exclaimed as soon as Aubrey shut the door. "That black mustache"—she pantomimed with hands that were very French—"those wings of white in hair so black, and such a presence! I don't know when I've seen anyone who attracted me more—except for you, of course, Tante Zhulee."

"Aunt Julia," Miss Paget corrected.

An urge to claim her own swept through Lark.

Miss Paget said briefly, "He's divorced."

Lark felt the pull of eyes, and looked up to meet Julia's lorgnette.

Julia turned back to Marianne. "You seemed to hit it off. I haven't mentioned it before, but you're *Missus* Seymour. What about Mister Seymour, my dear?"

"He was interested too—your handsome Mister Hildreth," Marianne said. "Mister Seymour and I aren't living together, but we're not divorced. However, there are always grounds."

Providing, said her eyes, one finds a good reason.

If Marianne only knew, Lark thought. The only reason Aubrey had been nice to her was to get information. Marriage, divorce, death records were things that could be looked up.

"Girls are such fools, aren't they?" Marianne rippled on. "Madly in love at seventeen—and at twenty-seven they can't bear the man. And at thirty-seven..." She palmed-up both hands and raised her shoulders. "I married my seventeen-year-old love. We ran away, and I didn't even give my right name on the license."

So that settled that. If Aubrey had the marriage license checked, there would be only the name she gave. No death records. No divorce. Would there be so many blind alleys in anyone's life unless they'd been planned?

Then Lark thought of all the blind alleys in her mother's life, and in her own. Those hadn't been planned. For the first time doubt edged into her mind. Marianne seemed so certain, so sure of herself, and Lark had often thought how strange it was for her quiet mother to be the daughter of that wild young blade Ulysses Paget and his burlesque queen Georgette. What if the blind alleys in Lark's mother's life led to other places, and Marianne's to the Paget gate?

Lark shook her head firmly. Her mother never would have kept that picture in their many moves, without family association. She'd disposed of everything else. If only something could be proved...

But the first thing proved was not in Lark's favor. At the pre-dinner gathering that evening—this time in the French Salon—Miss Paget announced, with a smile for Marianne and a side glance at Lark, that the photograph Marianne brought had been pronounced genuine. All three pictures had been made at the same time and placed around forty years ago; the words on the back of Miss Paget's and Marianne's had been written by the same hand.

Ben looked more skeptical than ever, while Rowena exclaimed, "But isn't that funny? You'd think—"

"Yes, Rowena," her hostess interrupted, "it is indeed 'funny.'" She looked at Lark and flexed claws on the chair arms. "Benson, will you pull the bell cord?"

Eileen was sent off with a message to Kezzie to bring Miss Venetia's pearls.

Lark glanced down at her long, graceful skirt. Pearls would be as lovely with turquoise as they had been the other night with Venetia's dress of moonbeams. Poor, gentle Venetia who had hated to argue and quarrel.

Kezzie came in with the blue velvet box and gave it to Miss Paget, who opened it and sat looking inside. At last she took out the pearls. As she returned the box, they dangled like cold, strung hail from her hand.

"Come here, my dear," she said.

Lark started to rise. But Julia's face turned toward Marianne. It was Marianne who bent forward tonight while Julia fastened the clasp about her neck, as five nights ago she had fastened it about Lark's.

Whichever way the cat jumps. Tonight the cat had jumped at Marianne. Tomorrow... what a real cat she was—this Julia Paget who played so heartlessly with unimportant mice.

Marianne now sat touching the pearls, a satisfied smile on her newly shaped mouth. What did Julia have in mind that she must keep both Lark and Marianne at Dune House? Why hadn't she let them go their own ways and simply be notified of her final decision? Or why hadn't she kept only one? Something prickled at the back of Lark's neck—what if their hostess wasn't sane?

Lark sat looking dully at Venetia's pearls on Marianne's white neck. Once Venetia Paget had been young and beautiful—and disappeared. Marianne wasn't young, but she was beautiful and young looking. Lark herself was young...

She ate little of Yep's rich cooking that night and was glad to go upstairs—one mouse temporarily escaping from the cat.

Marianne received Kezzie's ministrations first tonight. Lark was getting into bed when Kezzie came in.

Her small black eyes were bright. "Miss Venetia's pearls were lovely on Missus Seymour, weren't they, miss?"

"Miss Venetia's pearls are lovely, period," Lark smiled. Marianne hadn't been left with them overnight any more than she had. Kezzie had the blue velvet box in her hand.

"You know, miss," she said suddenly, "there are folks who think Miss Venetia's still alive."

Lark, with both feet up to slide them under the covers, dropped them to the carpet. "But how—?"

"That's what I say, miss," Kezzie said. "I saw Miss Julia's face that night after she came in, and the downstairs maid heard Miss Venetia scream—and then stop. But there are folks that say it, all the same."

"How can they, Kezzie?" Lark asked. "The men who recovered her body—"

"That's just it, miss," Kezzie said. "There wasn't any body."

Lark's body went dry.

"The tide was high when she went over, miss, and some folks think the fall didn't kill her," Kezzie said. "It was the night before the earthquake, you know, the big Nineteen Six earthquake and fire; so, with all the excitement and confusion, the search wasn't any too thorough." Kezzie paused. "Of course I think she'd dead, all right. Even if..." She paused again while Lark tried to swallow. "Even if—the other night—you did hear that singing."

They stared at each other—the tall, thin woman in black with a maid's white apron, and the girl in shivering peach satin on the edge of the bed.

"By the way, miss, I thought I ought to tell you there was more food missing from the icebox this morning," Kezzie said.

Lark moistened her lips. "You knew, didn't you, Kezzie, that Miss Paget shot a dog this morning inside the fence?"

"Does that make you feel better, miss?" Kezzie said goodnight and left.

Marianne's voice from the dressing room door at last focused Lark's whirling thoughts. "Well, *cherie*, why don't you either turn out the light and go to bed, or get up and lock the door?"

"I'll lock the door... do you want something, Marianne?" Lark said.

"So, shooting the dog doesn't make any difference when it comes to locking up!" Marianne said. "I saw your light and thought I might as well ask you a question now as later. That maid says the old lady bought you all those clothes. Is that true?"

"How do you know I have 'all those clothes,' Marianne?" Lark said. "I don't know what clothes you have."

Without their usual confinements, the other's contours were not so svelte. Now they shook with laughter. "There's no lock on my dressing room, any more than on yours. Well, *cherie*, did she give them to you or not?"

"I don't go snooping through other people's things, and I expect them to keep out of mine," Lark said. "What if Miss Paget did give them to me? I don't see—"

"Then she's going to buy that many for me!" Her lax muscles tightened. "I knew no stenographer's salary would cover those clothes, but of course, with that good-looking boss..."

Lark sprang off the bed, and Marianne ran out laughing. Tomorrow, Lark told herself furiously, slamming a chair beneath the door knob, she'd ask for another lock.

In the morning, her request flew across the landing as Julia was coming down the right-hand fork of the stairs.

"Marianne will want a lock, then, I suppose," Julia sighed. "I'll have Leo attend to them both. I suppose she'll be offended if I don't take her on a shopping tour, too, but I haven't time now."

Nor did she have time that day. Before breakfast was over, Eileen scurried in with cheeks flaming. "M-Miss Paget," she gasped, "Adam's on the phone. There's a *policeman* down there who wants in!"

Julia's hand closed around her fragile silver egg cup. When it came away, Lark saw a dent in the silver. The breathing of the maid and Rowena made the only sounds while Julia and Ben stared at each other.

The man finally nodded. "Guess you'll have to—eventually," he said.

"Tell Leo to bring him up, Eileen," Julia said coldly. She returned to her egg.

Was it something about the dog that was shot? Perhaps the owner... Lark looked across the table. Had Ben taken her to fly kites yesterday to get her out of the way while Julia and Leo staged the act with the dog? And here she'd been thinking...

"Eat your breakfast, Lark," Julia ordered. "That policeman's not here to see you."

When the last crumb of her own breakfast had been methodically swallowed, Julia said, "Come along, Benson. I want you with me." She tinkled the silver bell, and Eileen came in, still big-eyed. "Show the policeman into the library when he comes, Eileen—and stay away from the portières."

Lark, Rowena, and Marianne remained at the table until the sound of wheels and hooves on gravel came in through the window. They waited another minute or two, and then, as one woman, rose.

The state dining room beyond the alcove was quiet. They strolled, almost stopping, past the portières to the library, but no sound came from the next room.

Then they heard it, right as Eileen dashed through the hall curtains, met the three pairs of eyes, and stopped short.

"Miss Paget?" came a heavy masculine voice. "Sorry to disturb you, ma'am, but we've traced a missing man to your gate. Left the hospital Thursday afternoon and was seen out here Thursday night. That was the last time he was seen, ma'am. A lady in one of the little houses across the street saw him let in at your gate. His name's Oscar Fry."

Chapter Thirteen

Rowena repeated, "Oscar Fry?"

"Shh," Marianne said, and Rowena finished in a whisper. "Isn't he the law clerk Aubrey was talking about the other day—the one who said someone pushed him out a window?"

Eileen murmured confusedly, "I thought I left my dust cloth here," and hurried out.

Lark urged the others after her. What if Julia should look through the portières.

In the hall Rowena persisted, "Isn't he the one?"

Lark nodded absently. Thursday night—when "the dog" got in. If Oscar was the man Eileen had been talking about, would Mister Rollin sit up all night with a gun and Aubrey and Adam guard the other doors—to keep out *Oscar Fry?*

From the library, the voice of the policeman was an indistinguishable rumble. Eileen, looking slowly about the hall for her dust cloth, had gone back to the servants' quarters.

"I think," Rowena said gently, "I'll step into the music room. Ben couldn't find that Grieg sonata..." The portières dropped behind her.

The music room overlooked the drive. But it wasn't the only room that did. "If anyone should want me," Lark murmured, "I'll be in the French Salon."

Marianne gestured toward the doorway between the French Salon and the vestibule. "What's in there?"

"We'd call it a powder room now," Lark said. "A place to leave coats and freshen up when the Pagets used to give balls."

"Exactly what I'm looking for." Marianne's charming smile mocked her.

Lark stepped through the bottle-green curtains of the Salon. Now she and Rowena and Marianne all had front windows and access to the hall—if they didn't meet each other or Eileen there.

Why had Oscar come to Dune House? If he was "the dog"... missing, the policeman had said, since Thursday night. But why come here? That was hardest to understand. Oscar had no family to go home to, but he might have wanted to see someone at the office. If he telephoned there before closing time and learned that Aubrey was at Dune House and Mr. Rollin was coming in the evening...

The rumble of the policeman's voice came in through the hall portières. Did that mean he was leaving?

In a moment it was more than a rumble. She heard him say, "Sounds like you found the answer, ma'am, but since no one saw him go and you've invited me to search the place, I'd better do it."

"It's a large home," came Julia's voice. "Large enough for anyone to keep out of sight for days. Then, when he got the keys, it was night. He could climb out a window, in spite of the guards at the doors, and walk on through the gate."

"The key was in the lock, you say?" the heavy voice asked.

"He left it there," Julia said. "Or someone did. The ring with the five keys I always carry. That's another thing that makes me think he's all right now, or was when he left. He knew I'd want my keys."

"That was Saturday night, though, ma'am, and here it's Monday, and he hasn't shown up yet. Well..."—the policeman's voice was louder, as if he felt more sure of himself—"may as well start on this side of the door."

"You stay with him, Benson, and show him around," Julia directed. "I'll wait in my boudoir and send Leo back for Aubrey. He said he'd be here by nine."

Then Lark would catch him first. She'd wait right here.

The next sounds she heard were at the door of the room she was in. A blue-sleeved arm pulled aside the portières, and a large, uniformed man said

over his shoulder, "This won't be another washroom, will it, with a lady—"
The red ear and cheek turned to full face, and a pair of marble blue eyes met
Lark's. "Excuse me, ma'am; I've got to search this room, too."

Ben appeared in the doorway now. The curve of his mouth was turned
up. "We ran into Marianne in the coatroom, and I take it, by the feminine
hand that came through the portières to the music room, that Mother or
Eileen's in there. So there's no need, is there, for me to explain the presence
of the police?"

"Is it true, Ben, that Oscar Fry's missing, and he came out here?" Lark
asked.

"You know Fry, lady?" the policeman asked.

"Why, yes—"

"This is Miss Williams, Officer," Ben broke in. "She's a guest here, too. We
all know Oscar—except Missus Seymour, I suppose—the lady you saw in
the washroom. She only came Saturday, from the East. But the rest of us all
knew him slightly. Rollin, Rollin & Hildreth are Miss Paget's attorneys, you
know, and Oscar's been here any number of times on their errands." The
eyelid next to Lark, away from the policeman, came down as Ben's eyes met
hers.

Lark's lips, still parted to talk about Oscar, closed. Ben was right, of course.
If she said that until last week she'd been working with Oscar, the policeman
might ask why she was now Miss Paget's guest, and then the cat would be
out of the bag. She mustn't have publicity—with another contender in the
next room and, the first thing she knew, someone digging up that Arizona
marriage license. No publicity until everything was settled.

Marianne wasn't courting publicity, either. But what about Ben? Was he
trying to give Lark protection, or frying those other fish again?

"Say," the policeman said suddenly, "did the old—uh—Queen Victoria back
there"—he jerked his head toward the hall—"ever find her brother's missing
kid—the one written up in the papers?"

"Not yet," Ben said. "The picture gallery's on through here. There's no
place to hide in it, but I guess you'll want to see for yourself."

They moved down the room, the policeman's sturdy neck turning from side to side as if he were looking at everything.

Ben pulled back the gallery portières. "Want to see the pictures?"

The other shook his head. "I'm no connasewer. Fry's not in there, I can tell from here."

As they came back toward her, Lark saw him glance at a large cabinet heavily carved with plumes and French fleur-de-lis.

"Look into anything you want to," Ben said promptly. "If it's locked, I'll get the key."

The cabinet was opened. So was its mate's on the other side of the portières in the long inner wall to the west.

"The two rooms between here and the smoking room at the back of the house aren't in use," Ben explained. "We'll have to lift off dust sheets."

He pulled apart the side portières, and Lark followed him to the doorway to look into the only one of the Paget parlors she hadn't seen—the Japanese Room, she'd heard someone call it. Captain Paget had filled it as full of covered furniture bumps as the occidental rooms. The fireplace looked like a heathen altar, and Lark blinked at three giant dragonflies on a bamboo trellis against the wall. The policeman was staring at them, too.

"Jeweled imitations," Ben grinned. "But don't they almost make you want to reach for a fly swatter?"

Lifted sheets revealed waist-high vases and teakwood stands and cabinets of carved ebony inlaid with mother-of-pearl that the policeman wanted unlocked.

He and Ben moved on to the Egyptian Parlor, and Lark returned to her window overlooking the dunes. Leo had trotted the grays down the drive while Ben had been telling the policeman how well they all knew Oscar. Aubrey was due any minute.

If she'd known that Oscar was the man who came in Thursday night, she wouldn't have been afraid. Poor, hang-dog Oscar, with his proffers of dates and that air of knowing things he could tell if he wanted to that he tried to cultivate. All he'd have to tell would be that Red or Dizz had refused to go to the movies with him or that Lark herself said she'd seen the new night club on Columbus and was going to be busy that night anyway, thank you. All the more reason to be shocked that a man like Oscar, even delirious, should say that someone pushed him out a window, and be reported missing, with police on his trail.

Julia's talk a while ago in the hall sounded as if Oscar might have gotten out with her keys. But how would he get Julia's keys?

Lark leaned there, tapping the glass, until at last she heard wheels. Leo drove up with his usual flourish, and Aubrey sprang out of the victoria—alert, brown-faced, alive-looking.

Unluckily for Lark, Marianne was one room closer to the vestibule. She opened the front door as Lark reached the hall.

But that was her husband, that tall man in navy blue tweed whose smile, flashing white in the sun-brown of his face, was directed at the blonde so possessively taking his arm. Lark's husband, who didn't even see his wife standing in the doorway.

They stayed a few minutes in the vestibule, murmuring, smiling, arm in arm. Then, still arm in arm, Marianne propelled Aubrey into the hall, as they started toward the Maple Parlor.

Lark's grip on the portières relaxed and her feet involuntarily began to cross the red hall carpet. Then she stopped. She had to see Aubrey. No silly pique must prevent her telling him about Oscar. Aubrey said yesterday that Oscar had left the hospital. Maybe Aubrey knew something the police didn't.

"Aubrey," she called, beginning to run across the hall.

He turned quickly at one of the red marble pillars that held up the galleries, where the skylight gilded Marianne's hair to bright gold.

"Excuse me, Marianne," Lark said firmly. "I have to see Mister Hildreth a minute."

"Oh, dear." The other woman smiled; she had the good sense not to pout. "I can see Lark thinks it's important. Perhaps later…?"

"Definitely later," Aubrey promised. He wasn't missing the brightened hair or any svelte line.

Marianne moved away, and Aubrey's gaze returned to Lark.

They were in the center of the hall, yards from all doorways. She said softly, as quickly as she could before anyone else interrupted, "There's a policeman here looking for Oscar. Someone saw him let in the gate Thursday night. He says Oscar's *missing!*"

Aubrey looked more alert than ever. She could see that thoughts were racing behind those slate-grey eyes of his. Then he gave her the smile that was only for her—tender, instead of quick and flashing like those he had given Marianne. "Knowing you, dear, I couldn't tell you he was missing."

"You knew it?" Lark asked. "Why, you told me—"

"I know, Lark," Aubrey whispered. "But I know your warm heart. If I'd told you the hospital reported him missing, you'd have worried until you made yourself sick. I wasn't having that—for my wife. That's why I had to act as if he was well. He must be well by now. He'll probably turn up in an hour or so, apologizing for giving us trouble."

"But, Aubrey—" Then another thought brought her head up. "You didn't know it Thursday night, did you? That it was Oscar who came in, not a dog? Didn't you think it was a dog?"

"Why, darling—" Aubrey broke off and raised his voice. "Ben, come here a minute, will you?"

Dropping the Egyptian Parlor portières Ben waved the policeman toward the next doorway. "Go on in. I'll be right back."

He walked toward them—not so alert looking as Aubrey, but certainly as healthy looking, not at all like a 4-F. By the time he reached them, his mouth had begun to turn down.

"Lark's in a tizzy," Aubrey said, smiling—his quick, public smile, she noticed—"because we didn't tell her it was Oscar who came in Thursday night. She thinks—"

"Ben, did you know it was Oscar?" Lark interrupted. "Did you know it wasn't a dog?"

He looked from one to the other. "Well…"

"What *is* this?" Lark cried. "A conspiracy?"

Ben's mount was more cynical. "The gentlemanly kind where the men all get together to keep the ladies from being frightened."

"Talk about the Eighties!" Lark said. "You men are as bad as Miss Paget!

But if you all knew it was Oscar, why would Mister Rollin sit up all night with a gun? No one would need to be afraid of Oscar!"

"But, Lark," Aubrey began, "if he was—"

"Why would he come here, anyway," she rushed on, "and then not make himself known?"

"Cousin Julia's theory," Ben said, "all neatly tied up and handed to the police, is that Oscar was delirious when he left the hospital and thought he was on an errand for the office. Leo was driving Mister Rollin to the house when Adam let Oscar in; so he started to walk, and Cousin Julia says he must have come to, either on the way up here or after he got in the house, and was too embarrassed to show up. She thinks he kept hiding, always one jump ahead of the searchers, until Saturday night. I'll tell you her theory of how he escaped another time; I've got to herd the cop; no telling what sacred Paget treasures he's prying hinges off of now. See you later." He hurried away.

"We were only trying to save you a fright," Aubrey said gently. "Oscar was out of his head in the hospital, you know, and if he came here in the same shape..."

"But surely he'd never be violent, even if he was stark, raving mad," Lark said. "I wouldn't have been scared at all, Aubrey, if I'd known it was Oscar."

"I'm sorry if our judgment was wrong—for you, dear," Aubrey said. "I'm sure it was right for Rowena and the maids. Miss Paget said—"

"I might have known she was behind it!" Lark said. "I'm sorry, Aubrey; I shouldn't have flown off the handle. I wonder if Oscar has gone out again. Ben spoke of Saturday night..."

"I don't know what Julia's idea is about Saturday night, but I'm sure neither Oscar nor anyone else could be inside the fence after all the fine-tooth-combing Ben and Leo have given the place," Aubrey said. "Look, darling, I want you to know I've been out here every night, taking my turn guarding the doors. We do it in rotation: sleep a couple of hours, guard a couple, and so on. If there was anyone lurking around, you've been well protected, my lovely little girl."

Up most of the night, and still he looked fresh and alert. She should have known he'd protect her. *Anyone lurking...*

"Aubrey"—she caught his arm—"Kezzie told me last night Venetia's body was never found. What if she didn't drown? What if she's still here—locked in one of those towers. Or maybe not locked in; there was that singing the other night, and the missing food... what if it's not Oscar? He might have gotten right out again some way, after he got in. What if the prowler's *Venetia?*"

"Oh, nonsense, Lark," Aubrey said. "Venetia's been in Davy Jones' locker forty years. Even if they didn't find her bod—"

"Well, Aubrey—" Lark said.

Lark's head jerked up, and even Aubrey started. At the foot of the stairs, level with the gold-washed statue, Julia stood looking at them.

"—so this is the way you attend to my business!"

"I stopped him," Lark said quickly. "I saw him come, and wanted to—"

"Oscar was a friend of hers, you know," Aubrey said. "Everyone she works with is her friend, no matter how unprepossessing. So Lark, of course, thinks she has to find him herself."

"Suppose you leave it to the police," Julia said dryly. "And if you're quite through with Mister Hildreth, we have some business to discuss."

Lark drifted into the art gallery, wandering up and down the long, skylighted room until Eileen announced lunch. As she passed the windows of the French Salon on her way to the dining room, Lark saw Ben and the policeman poking among the shrubs in front of the house. She felt suddenly as if Dune House were swarming with policemen.

Neither the officer nor Ben appeared at lunch. Aubrey was there, with Marianne beside him, looking particularly charming in pansy-blue wool the shade of her eyes; and Lark, beside Rowena, unable to catch what they said over Rowena's constant chatter about Oscar.

"I see," Julia remarked, the down-curve of her mouth almost like Ben's as she looked at Rowena, "that all of you know why the long arm of the law is among us. The grapevine grows luxuriantly at Dune House."

She carried Aubrey off again after lunch, and Lark went slowly up to her room. Since Ben and the policeman were now outdoors, they must have finished searching the house, and she could have her room to herself. Really to herself, she found, as she went through her dressing room to the bath—Leo had put on a lock. Though without doubt someone else had a key, as someone else had a key to the hall door.

Walking to a window overlooking the sea, Lark stiffened. One hand flew to her mouth. But how silly she would be to cry out. They couldn't hear her, with the ocean booming at their feet. Anyway, Ben and the policeman were surely not so near the brink as they looked from this angle. Just because there'd been one accident on that cliff... and Oscar had said someone pushed...

Oscar... Venetia... Lark's hand caught the sill. The other search of Dune House had been made by Ben and Leo; this policeman was not a member of the household, dependent on Julia.

Then Lark's hand was on the door knob. Her key in the lock. She was running down the stairs, into the library, dodging about plants in the conservatory until she found the door...

She felt wind on her face, the taste of salt stronger...

"What's the matter?" Ben cried.

"Good gosh, ma'am," the policeman said, "you shouldn't make a fellow jump like that, so near the edge."

"I—I—" Lark wet her lips. She mustn't make a wrong impression. Smiling—this stranger wouldn't know what her natural smile was like—she said, "You mustn't think I'm crazy, Officer, because I live behind a fence, but I've been wondering..."

The sea crashed, and the wind blew, and Lark tried frantically to think how she could put her question.

"Yes, ma'am?" the officer prodded.

"It's funny how people get notions." She smiled again, that too-bright smile. "This house is so big. Have you gone through it yet?"

He nodded, watching with vivid blue eyes.

"My notion—I suppose it's silly—is that there might be someone in one of those towers—I don't mean Oscar Fry—I mean a hangover from fairy tales, I guess: enchanted prisoners in towers... but Miss Paget doesn't like her

148

guests to poke around. Did you—did you find anyone else here—another woman perhaps?"

The house at her back seemed incredibly closer—looming right at her shoulder—crowding…

The policeman caught her elbow. "Don't go so close, ma'am, that's a nasty cliff. Let's see, all the women I found were two maids and yourself, and Queen Victoria, of course, and the little lady with glasses who was all in a twitter—beg pardon, sir: she's your mother?—and that smooth looking dame with blond hair."

"No one else?" Lark asked.

"No other women, if it's enchanted princesses you're after," the policeman said.

Down at the foot of the cliff a seal barked, and Lark drew in salt air on a long, quivering breath. "Then I guess it's a question of too many fairy tales." She tried to smile again.

"Wouldn't be surprised if it was the house, ma'am," the officer said. "There's something about a great pile like that—the long life it's had, and the things it's seen, and all those empty rooms… that's how stories start that old houses are haunted." The policeman's smile, too, was a little self-conscious.

"You're very—understanding," Lark said softly. "I'll try not to bother you again. I hope you find Oscar soon."

She had to turn toward the house to reach the door. But she didn't have to look up. She didn't have to give that great, dark, solid cloud another chance to blow nearer, to crowd her toward the cliff.

At last the knob of the conservatory door was in her hand. She could turn it—step in—lift her head.

Inside, the house was only a house, instead of a solid cloud. Stuffed clouds, the aviators called them, when planes crashed into mountains. Inside, the house had rooms with lots of air, even if the light here in the conservatory was grotto-green—she hurried through it… and the library was too full of furniture—she bumped her hip against a chair… and the hall—she pulled aside the portières—had listening doorways and a colosseum core.

It did look like a colosseum—Lark crossed to a red marble pillar—with the two rows of arched galleries above the stairs, and light spilling into the arena. The golden statue in jeweled belt and headband might be a Christian Martyr. Lark had no wish to be another for a lion to maul, roaring out from behind one of the eleven pairs of green curtains.

A sound like a lion's roar burst through them. Mutely she cried out to the golden woman, before her heart tumbled down the centuries, back to the Eighties that enclosed her and the modern present that lay outside the fence, with a caged, flea-ridden lion roaring in a zoo.

But even with realization, Lark didn't want to step into that circle of light. She went back to the picture gallery, instead of up to her room.

There, too, she had her first moments whenever clouds passed in front of the sun. The first time the long skylight darkened, she found herself pressed up to the wall, hands raised and shoulders hunched to hide from something peering in—something with a flowing robe that covered the glass, with eyes that searched her out...

From below another eye stared up—catlike, shining green...

Then the sun came out, and she saw that the eye staring up was Venetia's opal ring, and the thing peering down had been a cloud.

No matter how often she asked the old question—who would want to hurt her?—each time the sun vanished, Lark found herself starting to crouch. She turned the ring inward on her finger, her hand closing over it as if it were something to throw.

What had happened to Aubrey? Was he still with Miss Paget, or had Marianne...? Lark bent determinedly nearer the great dark canvas of an Eighteen Eighties' revel and tried to make out the detail.

Teatime passed without a summons from Julia, the first time Lark hadn't been called. "Putting up with her three meals a day is enough." The words seemed to echo down the gallery, though Miss Paget had been speaking of Rowena.

It was nearly time to dress for dinner before the grind of wheels on gravel sent her running to the French Salon windows.

But the voice in the hall wasn't Aubrey's. "Okay, Leo, thanks," Ben called. "I'll find your passenger for you."

Lark ran down the pastel-flowered carpet. She wanted to catch Ben anyway and ask a lot of questions. But when she pulled aside the portières, he was halfway upstairs.

"I want to see you," she cried.

"Be right down, Lark," Ben said.

It was hard to remember that perhaps she shouldn't trust Ben. He seemed so friendly that she couldn't help responding.

It was barely a minute before he was back, dropping the curtains behind him. "Don't mind if I seem to drip sand," Ben said. "Now tell old Doc Drew where the pain is."

"Has he gone—the policeman?" Lark asked.

Ben nodded. "He left a few minutes ago," he said. "That's why I'm still dripping sand. We've been up and down every dune on the place."

"He didn't—?"

"No, he didn't find Oscar," Ben said, "or any other outsider, whoever you were gabbing about out there by the cliff this afternoon."

"I was thinking of Venetia and no, I'm not being silly," Lark insisted. "I heard yesterday that they never found her body. That singing the other night, and all…"

"Listen, honeypie: no ghost did that singing," Ben said. "You can take it from Uncle Benson. If there are any ghosts, and they can sing, I'm telling you there aren't, and they can't, at Dune House. I know."

Lark wished she did. Then she heard the carriage start, and forgot everything else. She saw it move off—first the grays, as the drive turned away from the house, then Leo on the box of the victoria, then Aubrey on its cushions.

She'd missed him. But someone else was seeing him off, someone at whom he was waving as she'd never seen him wave at Miss Paget. Lark turned quickly back to Ben and asked what the policeman had said about the dog.

"Nothing. Why bring up something he didn't know?" Ben asked.

"You've been living here too long," Lark scolded. "You sound like Miss Paget! Didn't he ask about the grave? Or did you and Leo dump the poor dog in the ocean?"

Ben's grin turned down again. "No, we gave him a decent burial. But that was yesterday, and you know what the wind does. There's nothing to show now that any grave was ever dug in the sand. I didn't treat our friend the cop to the story of Cousin Julia's hay fever."

"I suppose all those tracks we made where he was shot were gone too?" Lark asked.

"With the wind," Ben nodded.

Lark sighed. "You said this morning that Julia had a theory about Oscar getting out. Something about Saturday..."

"Yes," Ben said. "It seems Cousin Julia always pins a few keys to her underwear. Don't ask me which piece; she didn't say. But the keys are the ones to the front door and the gate and the inner doors of both safes and the money compartment in the one upstairs. At night Kezzie always takes them off the underwear and pins them to the Paget nightie. Saturday night, according to Julia, Kezzie was rattled because of Marianne's showing up with that picture and ring, and forgot to change the keys."

"That's right," Lark said. "Kezzie *was* in the room when Marianne—"

Ben grinned. "Not that that would make any difference; as Cousin Julia says, the grapevine grows luxuriantly here. There're too many doorways and not enough doors in this house for anything else." He glanced over his shoulder at the portières in the middle of the long inside wall. "Maybe someone's back of those curtains right now, in the Japanese Room."

Lark tried not to shiver.

"Anyway," Ben said, "Cousin Julia claims those keys were dropped down the laundry chute Saturday night still pinned to her shorts—or whatever. Don't know why she didn't notice they weren't on her nightie. Guess she was rattled herself. To make a long story short, as they say when they're not going to do it, she woke up early Sunday morning and found she didn't have the keys. She's a light sleeper and has the habit of early morning prowling, so as soon as she thought of her day's-before underwear, she popped down to the basement to look and found the pin there but not the keys. That was all Cousin Julia needed to make her trot right down to the gate. She's strong as a horse, you know, and she knew Adam wouldn't be up yet. Anyway, she claims she found the keys sticking in the padlock."

"But she could have made that up, Ben, the same as those other stories," Lark said.

"The trouble is, such screwy things do happen around her, that you can't tell what she's making up and what she isn't," Ben said. "Leo bears her out to some extent. He says he thought he heard someone monkeying with the gate and got up to look, and met Cousin Julia coming around the corner of the stable looking queer. She said good morning and had him hitch up the horses and take her back to the house. Kezzie insists she changed the keys Saturday just like every other night, but the action's become so automatic by now that she can't remember for sure, and Cousin Julia swears she didn't."

"Then I suppose that means that Oscar—or someone—could have found them," Lark said. "But what would he be grubbing through the soiled laundry for?"

"Cousin Julia had an answer for that one, too," Ben said. "She says Oscar must have some dimwitted idea of disguising himself, perhaps even as a woman; so if anyone caught a glimpse of him before he could get out, at least he wouldn't be recognized."

"Trust Miss Paget!" Lark said. "She has an answer for everything, doesn't she?"

"Cousin Julia always has an answer." Ben's voice had a hollow ring. "It'll take a lot more than one flatfoot to get anything on Julia Paget."

Chapter Fourteen

Ben's "It'll take a lot more than one flatfoot to get anything on Julia Paget" haunted Lark all the next day. If Oscar hadn't left Dune House... if something had happened to him here... but why should it? Just because something had happened to Venetia...

Kezzie said the day before yesterday that food had been missing again Sunday morning. It was the night before that, the Saturday Marianne came, that Miss Paget said she didn't have her keys. If Oscar had let himself out Saturday night, would food be missing Sunday morning? Of course he could have taken it with him. He might have, too, if he'd left the hospital without money. Julia would certainly bring that up if Lark went to her, or say again that Kezzie was lying.

More than one flatfoot... if anything had happened to Oscar inside the Paget fence, there'd be a lot more than one flatfoot at Dune House. Even if the dog was traced here, the real brindled bull terrier she had seen Sunday morning, there'd be at least one more policeman. People didn't like to have their dogs shot.

Through the window—she was standing in the library, looking out toward the ocean—she saw Leo cutting the grass. At least he could set her right about the dog. Since everyone knew about Oscar now, Leo should be willing to talk.

The whir of the lawn mower was louder outside, mixed with the crash of breakers, and newly cut grass smelled as green here as it used to at Aunt Sophie's.

She was almost in the path of the mower before Leo stopped. He fingered

154

the handle, waiting, with his face turned away.

Lark wasted no time. "Did you buy that dog Sunday, Leo, or pick him up on the street?"

His head jerked up, and for an instant he looked straight at her. "Why? What difference would it make?" His eyes were dark and intelligent. This was the first time she'd seen them.

"I wondered if we'll have another visit from the police," Lark said.

Leo looked down again at the handle of his mower. "I paid for him, all right, miss," he said at last. "Good Paget money. The police won't come—for that."

"'For—that'? What else would they come for?" Was he thinking what she was—about Oscar?

"I sometimes wonder, miss..." He glanced toward the house, and his voice dropped a note lower. She could barely hear him above the sea roar. "She pays me so well I stay away, but I'm a man, used to looking out for myself."

"What are you getting at, Leo?" Lark asked.

"Haven't you guessed, miss?" Leo asked. "When a woman pays good money for a dog—to shoot him—what does that suggest?"

"What—what do you mean?" Lark asked.

"I'd rather not say, miss... but if I weren't a man and didn't make such good money, I wouldn't stay here."

"There's—the matter of money with me, too, you know," Lark said.

"But you're a kid, and a girl at that," Leo said. "Money's not worth—everything." Did Leo randomly happen to look out to sea then, out over the cliff where Venetia had gone? Or did he do it with intention?

"Leo"—Lark's voice shook—"are you trying to tell me I ought to be afraid for my life?"

"I never said that, miss." He glanced briefly up at the house again. "You heard about—Miss Venetia?"

The slim girl who used to sing in this garden, who made it a garden then, with herb-sharp lavender and roses, instead of unrelieved green. "Yes, I—heard about Venetia." Lark didn't look at the cliff.

"You can't tell, miss—with a woman like Miss Paget," Leo said. He paused.

"Then there's the fellow that came in last week. Mister Benson says…" He paused again. "Not that she's responsible, poor thing."

"Not responsible… are you trying to tell me that Miss Paget's insane?" Lark asked.

"I wouldn't say that, miss," Leo said. "Of course I wouldn't say it—working for her." He gave the handle of the lawn mower a shake. "But if I were you, miss—I'd get out."

The blades began to whir again with the boom of the sea, and Lark looked up at Dune House. At the towers, the windows, the great, dark bulk of it. What did Leo know of insanity? But he'd been through the war. Men saw things then…

All evening she watched. At the card table, Julia said crossly, "For heaven's sake, child, you'd play a better hand of whist if you kept your eyes on the cards instead of on me."

Perhaps, thought Lark, she'd play a better hand of marriage if she kept her eyes on Aubrey instead of Julia, too. Surely he must have all the information he needed from Marianne, but every time he came through the bronze doors he seemed to move toward Marianne as naturally as water runs downhill.

On Sunday they had been introduced. On Monday she had hurried to meet him in the morning and seen him off in the afternoon. On Tuesday, when Lark came in from the back lawn shivering after her talk with Leo, she had found Aubrey and Marianne sitting close together on an ornate sofa in the French Salon, the blonde in her demure black looking more seductive than any naked cupid on the ceiling. Aubrey had inched away a little when Lark appeared.

That was the difference between Tuesday and Thursday. Whenever Aubrey and Marianne were in the same room, they were on the same sofa, murmuring, shoulders touching—only, now that it was Thursday, he no longer moved away.

Did he come here to see Miss Paget or Marianne? Lark asked herself tartly, and barely kept from asking it aloud. Marianne's possessive, almost intimate ways, were disgusting. And even Aubrey… for the first time since their wedding—that strictly business formula in an Arizona justice's office—Lark

156

thought of Ninon's evidence at the Hildreth divorce trial. Aubrey said the evidence was faked, but what if it wasn't? She thought of all the evenings between the few weekends he'd spent with her, of the debutante phone calls that still kept Rollin, Rollin & Hildreth's lines busy, and the time that Dizz said Red's lipstick was smeared after she'd come out of Aubrey's office.

Lark had been so sure of herself and so sure of Aubrey—then. She'd simply told herself that he wasn't like that and refused to admit that he could be. She told herself now that he wasn't like that, and another thought, almost worse tonight, sprang up like a jumping jack. Suppose Marianne was declared Ulysses Paget's heir… Ben Drew might joke about keeping the Paget money in the family, whichever way the cat jumped, but Aubrey had been a practicing lawyer for years. What if he thought—if he could see—that Marianne's chances were better?

Then Lark felt sick with shame for being so disloyal to her husband. She returned to watching Julia. It was Thursday at tea when Lark discovered that Marianne was watching Julia too.

Thursday again. Oscar had been missing a week. Tea was served in the music room that day, and it was while Ben was playing the Moonlight Sonata that Lark saw Marianne's expression. Julia was leaning back, eyes closed, hands going through their claw routine on the chair arms. Marianne's own fingers were rigid, her eyes fixed on Julia's hands.

The music stopped, and Julia opened her eyes. Marianne averted hers—and meet Lark's. Both looked away. But now Lark saw that Marianne's gaze hardly left her hostess. It wasn't simply a stare of curiosity. There was horror and something like fear in it, too.

Julia stood up abruptly as Eileen began to collect the cups and saucers. "The way you two girls stare is enough to make a wooden image fidget. In my day, we were taught not to make others uncomfortable. But, of course, that Georgette creature…"

She glided out of the room on small, offended feet.

"What's the matter with Julia?" Rowena complained. "If you girls are doing something to fuss her, I do wish you'd stop. She's so hard to live with when she's cross… have you seen my smelling salts, Ben? I haven't been able to find them all day."

"Did you look in the library, Mother?" Ben said. "Why don't you, while I run up to your room?"

The Drews went out the hall door, Eileen took the tea things away, and Lark and Marianne were left alone.

"What's the matter, Marianne?" Lark asked softly.

"If they'd only serve cocktails instead of this everlasting tea," Marianne grumbled. "But all we'll get that's alcoholic is burgundy or sauterne or claret at dinner. Or maybe if we said pretty please, we'd get mulled wine at bedtime like the Great One herself—Tante Zhulee!"

Lark sat watching Marianne, who watched the portières into the hall where Julia had gone.

"What's the matter?" Lark repeated. "Have you been talking to Leo?"

Marianne's planned slenderness straightened, and her eyebrows went up. "Do you think I hold conversations with the servants?"

Lark laughed. "Of course, I'm up from the ranks myself. But you'd be surprised what they tell me." Then she sobered. "Leo said something the other day about Miss Paget…"

As Lark hesitated, Marianne shivered. "If I could only have a cigarette, but the old devil'd know it, sure as fate. This place gives me the creeps. Did Leo tell you she bought that dog to shoot him, and about—what happened to that sister of hers?"

Lark nodded, shivering too.

The other's voice sank to a whisper. "My God, do you think Julia's crazy?"

"I don't know."

For a moment, the two contestants drew together.

Marianne gave a little shake and stood up. "If she is… you came here five days before I did, Lark Williams, and nothing's happened to you. If you can take it, so can I." She walked dramatically into the hall.

Lark had a strange feeling as they sat talking, a pull at the back of the head, as if someone were watching. Now, with her eyes on the portières still swaying behind Marianne, the feeling came again.

She turned quickly. The portières to the Maple Parlor were swaying too.

Would the draft from the hall…?

Lark made a sudden lunge toward them. But on the other side she saw only crowding furniture, blue silk walls, and pale maple eyes.

But weren't the curtains into the dining room swaying?

Silent on the flowered carpet, she flew across the Maple Parlor.

No one in the dining room crouching under the long table…

But were the curtains into the library swaying now?

For an instant she paused. You could draw a straight line through all these middle doorways, from the music room at the front of the house to the library at the back. If a draft went through one, would it go through all, make all the curtains stir?

The portières into the hall were still, those into the library stilling. Detouring around the table, with only a glance at the alcove curtains, Lark dashed into the library.

There the hall portières hung straight and still. Too bad there was no way of telling if a bookcase had recently been moved. Did the stillness of the portières mean that the draft was exhausted? Or that she'd been too long in the dining room? If someone was actually one jump ahead…

It would only be someone she knew, Lark reminded herself, someone who'd been eavesdropping. Things were different, now that she knew who'd come in the gate a week ago. Even if Oscar were still here, it would only be Oscar Fry. She'd rather meet him, even out of his head, than Yep with that butcher knife. It was the unknown that was terrifying… or was that something she'd read?

Her choice now lay between the doorway into the hall at one end of the room and the conservatory at the other. She chose the hall.

Within its great circle, none of the eleven pairs of motionless curtains gave her any clue. She had never been in the servants' wing. She crossed to the smoking room with its Moorish carved wood and grained leather.

Which way now—through the double glass doors to the balcony where she'd gone the first evening with Ben, or the portières to the Egyptian Parlor? There were connecting doorways started again, through the empty rooms with their white dust-hoods to the French Salon.

Slowly she turned toward the unused rooms and parted the green plush curtains. Here was no familiar clutter of tables and chairs. Here pale shapes crouched, with the bird-headed statue watching. Crouching pale shapes whose sheets quivered in the draft from an open window—whose sheets might cover something that was not furniture.

The curtain slid from Lark's hand, and she ran for the hall. Rushed up the stairs to her room.

Kezzie came to dress her for dinner, and Lark had to go down again. But she opened her door and stood waiting for someone else to go first. Across the gallery she saw the flutter of girlish pink ruffles on the right-hand fork of the stairs. Rowena was passing the lamp statue by the time Lark turned her key and started downstairs, going into the Maple Parlor when Lark, herself, reached the bottom.

As she followed Rowena, the front door opened and Ben came in.

He shook his head solemnly. "Lark, you're as jumpy as Mother. Want a whiff of smelling salts?" He produced a squat green bottle from his pocket.

Lark tried to laugh. "Have you taken to smelling salts?"

"I'll have to if the pace keeps up at Dune House," Ben said. "Or settle for a strait jacket. But the salts are Mother's. I've been to the drugstore to get them."

"Do you mean to say, Ben Drew, that Miss Paget gave you a pass to get a bottle of smelling salts?" Lark asked.

He glanced around the great hall—cautiously, she noticed. "Between us, Lark—and only between us—Leo sometimes lets me out without a pass."

"But Miss Paget—"

"Hasn't caught us yet," Ben said. "We use discretion, of course. Leo has a key to the garage door and always tells Adam I gave him a pass. Smelling salts are as important to Mother as food, and she lost her last bottle."

Smelling salts belonged here as much as the furniture Captain Paget bought in the Eighties, as much as gaslight and brooms and victorias. Sometimes it was hard to remember that across the empty Paget dunes, only on the other side of the fence, were electricity and automobiles and Twentieth Century living.

"What's it like, Ben," Lark asked wistfully, "out there in the world?"

His hands closed for an instant on her shoulders, and he gave her a little shake. "Don't let it get you, Lark. You've been such a hundred percenter in the face of eight-foot fences, and dictatorships, and competitors, and prowlers. If you cracked up now, I'd lose my faith in womankind. A faith, I might add, that wasn't particularly strong until you came."

Warmth spread through Lark. Her fingers, meshed as tightly together as gears, relaxed and separated.

"You're a real woman," Ben said softly. "Now I know why the Forty-Niners brought their wives."

"Thank you, Ben." If Aubrey would only treat her like an equal, too, instead of a child to be humored and doled out peppermint sticks of praise. He couldn't help his age, of course. Compared to it, she *was* a child. But would that feeling of his ever change?

When they had a chance at a proper marriage, things would be different—everything, from his reaction to her youth to the time he spent with women like Marianne. It was Lark's job now to understand, and here she was contrasting his attitude with Ben's. Perhaps she was seeing too much of Ben. For the first time she realized that she was taking him her questions almost as she used to take questions to Aubrey. She wasn't being fair. Besides, she reminded herself as she turned quickly toward the Maple Parlor, Ben might not actually be as friendly as he seemed.

"Hey, don't rush off," Ben said. "I was going to tell you the guard's been removed."

"Really? When?" Lark asked.

"Monday," Ben said. "When my friend the flatfoot left, Cousin Julia said that there couldn't be anyone here. Guess she finally realized if she wanted people to believe her story about Saturday night, she'd better make like she believed it herself."

"It's not as if she cared!" Lark cried. "She doesn't give a hoot about Oscar—what may have happened to him. All she cares about is not getting herself involved in anything unpleasant." She paused, then added more quietly, "Anyway, I still lock my doors."

"Sensible move, in this joint," Ben said. "With all these connecting doorways, it'd take an army to corner anyone. Though I doubt Oscar's a menace, even if he's still here and still out of his head. It was Ed Rollin and Aubrey who thought he might be dangerous. The hospital called them, you know. Cousin Julia backed them up. Her native instinct to keep things to herself had made her jump at the chance. Bet that's behind her hatred of publicity, too. Mother says all the Pagets were secretive, even the gentle Venetia."

"She'd have to be, Ben—with Julia in the house," Lark said.

"You heard about Venetia's episode with the coachman that made her father change his will?" Ben asked.

Lark nodded. "Don't you think the poor thing was starved for love—any kind of love?"

"Cousin Julia called it 'low taste.'" Ben said.

"Ben—" Lark's fingers meshed again—*like an anxious child's*, Aubrey said. She pulled them apart and dropped her hands. "Ben, do you think it's possible for Venetia to be alive?"

"Whatever put that into your head?" Ben asked.

"Well, Kezzie says—" Lark began.

"Kezzie!" Ben said. "If that old witch thought she could get your goat, she'd say she was Dracula."

"But she said it was high tide when Venetia went over the cliff, and the search wasn't thorough on account of—" Lark said.

"The earthquake, I suppose," Ben finished. "The things that are blamed on that earthquake! But of course what Kezzie said about the search could be true. And if Venetia actually got out of the water alive, with most of San Francisco running around half-dressed and half-crazy, who'd notice one more homeless waif?"

"But the fall, Ben," Lark said. "Those two big rocks... could she fall from such a height right above them—and live?"

"If she missed those two rocks, I think she could," Ben said. "They don't spread out much on the landward side, and all the other rocks are pretty deeply submerged. I used to swim around them when I was a kid and picture

Venetia coming over the cliff. Adam said nothing was found on the rocks above the water line to indicate she hit them."

"Then do you think—?" Lark asked.

"Well, she could swim," Ben said. "Mother says Captain Paget made all his children learn."

"It was night," Lark added, "and Dune House wouldn't have high-powered electric searchlights to turn on the water, either."

"I guess she could have made it," Ben admitted, "with luck."

For a moment the hall was still, the great round hall of the house in which Venetia had been born, in which she had spent so many months of her helpless youth as a prisoner. Lark could almost see her coming down the stairs, one light hand on the plush-covered railing, the other at her heart, while her head, with hair as gold as the lamp-bearing statue, turned quickly from side to side to find Julia before Julia found her.

"Poor girl," Lark said softly. "What if she did get out alive? Do you think she'd ever come back?"

"Come back where she'd have Cousin Julia to deal with?" Ben shook his head. "Her father's will gave her a home here, but she wouldn't get any money until her sister died. Personally, I don't think the poor kid ever came out of the ocean, but if she did—since you want to play that way—I'd say that from all I've heard about how Venetia hated quarrels and how scared she was of Cousin Julia—and she'd have more reason to be than ever, if Julia pushed her off the cliff—I think she'd wait until Julia died, and then cash in without having to buck her."

"Everything would be hers, then," Lark mused, "since Miss Paget didn't have children."

"Cousin Julia'd get her Paget heir"—Ben gave his wry grin—"and never know it."

"Ben, what if Venetia—got tired of waiting for Julia to die? Kezzie said—"

"Kezzie!" he snorted again. "She's trying to make you jittery. She loves that sort of thing. In all probability, Venetia's been dead forty years. Look here, Lark—this Paget money deal—I hate to have you mixed up in it. You're too fine for the vulture class. To flap in slow, wide circles—waiting for someone to die. It's not decent. But it's what all of us here have been doing, and are doing, and will go on doing—until Cousin Julia dies."

"But you've been in school!" Lark said. "You haven't stood by, waiting."

"I'm through school now," Ben said. "If I don't pass those bar examinations and start to practice—or get out and shift for myself... if anyone can make a man of me, Lark, it's you. And there are times when I almost begin to think you're doing it."

She smiled up at him wholeheartedly, for the moment at least, all reservations gone. "You know, one of the things I'm going to like especially about proving I'm a Paget is that you'll be my cousin."

"A very pretty speech, my lass, but... still, you'd only be a first cousin twice removed. You see I've got it all figured out." He stood looking down at her, not a foot away, his green eyes startlingly gentle.

Warmth surged through Lark again. Good heavens, who was she to get all fussed over a young man's expression of—interest? She, a married woman. She must be seeing too much of Ben. Quickly, she started for the Maple Parlor.

"Lark," he called softly behind her, "if you ever hear Venetia sing again, come up and wake me. Mine's the room on the third floor that corresponds to the Moorish Room. I'll settle her hash."

Lark felt oddly buoyant all through dinner, no matter what Miss Paget said or how many times the pudgy, ringed fingers rested on Marianne's arm. Until Julia said, "I'm not sending for Venetia's pearls tonight," Lark didn't even remember to wonder who would receive the royal nod to wear them for the evening.

The card session passed in the same queer daze. She climbed the stairs, undressed—with Kezzie's taciturn assistance—and, after locking the doors, slipped between the cool sheets.

She lay waiting for sleep, when every nerve and muscle went taut.

Through the open window, mingled with the crash of waves, came the sound of singing. The high, clear notes of her favorite aria from *Aida*.

Chapter Fifteen

L ark was jerking at the lock of her door before her dressing gown was on. Running up the third-floor stairs without slippers. Hunting for Ben's door. Pounding… pounding…

"V-Venetia!" she gasped when he opened it. "She's singing down there by the ocean!"

Ben ran past her, not stopping for a bathrobe. "Don't be scared," he called back. "You know it's no ghost. I'll fix—" The word sounded like *her*.

Leaning over the gallery railing, Lark saw him run down the main stairs, past the statue whose lamp was turned low and disappear beyond the red pillars. Lark was suddenly alone up on the third-floor gallery.

She began to run, too—down the stairs to the gallery below, through its light-and-shade arch patterns to her door. Then it was locked behind her, and she was leaning out the window.

The voice was still singing—those lonely silver notes above the sea.

She heard a door bang, and a gray shadow tore out on the lawn. It looked like a man in pajamas.

The singing stopped—broke off as suddenly as if fingers had closed on a throat.

"Hey!" Ben's voice—sharp, peremptory.

Lark gripped the sill. If anyone answered… but no other voice came up through the dark.

Ben's rose again. "Come on! I've got you covered."

No figure joined his on the lawn. No one spoke.

She could see Ben, dim in the starlight, begin to poke among the shrubs

165

by the house.

"Lark, are you up there?" he called softly.

Her voice quavered a little as she answered.

"Where did the sound come from?" he asked. "Could you tell?"

"Down there on the lawn," Lark said. "It must have been between the servants' wing and conservatory or I couldn't have heard it so plainly."

Somewhere in the dark on the wet rocks a seal barked, and the light patch of shadow moved on along the jut of the servants' wing. Then the shadow left the house and went out toward the cliff.

The cliff... Venetia... he mustn't... Lark gripped the sill again.

He seemed to go to the brink—to bend out... Lark beat clenched hands on the sill. Then he straightened and came back toward the house. While Lark was still exhaling, he returned to poking among the shrubs, and presently the conservatory door opened and shut behind him.

In a minute she heard a soft knock on her door.

"Who is it?" she asked, her hand on the key.

"Me—Ben. I wanted to say—"

She turned the lock and he came in, bare feet slapping down like a frustrated small boy's. "Whoever was there must have scrammed. That wind blew the conservatory door right out of my hand. And of course that was all the warning anyone'd need."

"The singing stopped right after the door banged," Lark agreed, "and I couldn't hear anything else but the ocean."

"There wasn't even a window open," he grumbled. "You say you didn't—" He broke off and looked at her sharply. "Lark! Why, Lark, you're shaking!"

All at once she was in his arms. She had no idea how long she stayed there. Her first conscious thought was of how happy she was, and her second of the fact that her own arms were coming up to Ben's shoulders.

She gasped and pulled away.

Ben shook his head as if he were coming out of water. "Excuse me if I seem to sweep you off your feet, Miss Williams. Incidentally, my intentions are strictly honorable, you know. I didn't get myself asked in to see your etchings."

"But, Ben—" Lark stopped. She couldn't say, *But Ben, I have a husband; it must have slipped my mind for a minute.*

"Somehow—for a second or two—I had the impression that my attentions weren't too hard to take," Ben said. "Was I mistaken, Lark?" He reached out again.

This time she was ready and drew back.

"I'm so impulsive," he murmured. "Look, Lark, I'm not trying to be funny. The fact is I love you. I—well, I want you to be Missus Benson Drew, if you don't mind sounding like the butler's wife." He stood there trying to grin, then suddenly burst out, "Damn it, Lark, I've spent so many years trying to cover up any feelings I might have that I can't make them sound convincing now!"

"I—I'm sorry, Ben." Her hands gripped each other. "I was scared, that's all, and you felt so safe."

"And you found that good old Uncle Benson wasn't so safe after all?"

"Don't say that, Ben," Lark said. "Don't look like that. If I'd known this was going to happen, I never would have called you tonight!"

"You'd have let Venetia go on singing until you died of fright, I suppose," Ben said. "Am I that repulsive, Lark?"

"You know you're not repulsive," Lark said. "You said yourself—" She stopped. She must forget how it felt to be in Ben's arms—she, who had been censuring Aubrey for seeking out Marianne.

"You don't have the Paget money yet, you know," Ben reminded her. "Marianne's got as good a chance of holding the winning ticket—so look at the risk I'm running." His habit of making fun of emotion was too strong to break all at once. "Anyway, Lark, you can see it's not money I'm after, whatever fool crack I may have made the other day about getting back the Paget millions by marriage."

"I know, Ben, I wasn't thinking of that—now," Lark said. "I was only thinking—well, I let myself be carried away—what with being so scared when I heard the singing and thought of Venetia and all… and then you ran out to the cliff down there tonight."

"Okay, Lark," Ben said. He spoke gently. "I'm glad you cared enough to want me to stay away from the cliff, but say no more about it. When a girl doesn't want to be rushed, she doesn't want to be rushed. There's a good old saying out of something or other: 'If at first you don't succeed, try, try again'—as they used to point out to us in the third grade. So perhaps some other time..."

Ben was grand. He did everything to help her, and she—she was the kind of married woman who fell into other men's arms, who hadn't the faithfulness not to enjoy it, who—

Ben put his hand on the doorknob. "I don't seem to have brought my hat, but I know when it's time to get it and go. Listen, Lark, you don't need to be scared of that singing. If it was supernatural we'd still be getting a few little numbers from *Rigoletto* and *Carmen*; a thing like slamming a door wouldn't stop a ghost. It's not supernatural, and we'll track it down of these days."

"Th-thank you, Ben; you're such a help," Lark said.

"But not enough to qualify for a permanent job as mama's little helper," Ben said. He grinned again, wryly. "Goodnight, Lark. First thing in the morning, Detective Drew will be out looking for tracks in the shrubbery." The door closed behind him.

But it was hours before Lark went to sleep, even though no more silver notes blew in through the window with the boom and kelp smell of the sea. If she hadn't been so frightened, she kept telling herself, Ben wouldn't have put his arms around her like that. It wouldn't have changed his loving her, of course, but if she hadn't been upset, she'd have seen what was coming in time to ward it off. It was only because she'd been so frightened that she'd felt happy in Ben's arms. That hadn't been real happiness, but rather a sense of security and protection, not the sort of happiness she felt with Aubrey. Perhaps if she'd spent more time worrying about her marriage—trying, for instance, to keep Marianne and Aubrey apart—she wouldn't have had enough time to give Ben to encourage him. After all, Marianne didn't look the forty-two she said she was. And even if she was in her forties, Aubrey was in his forties, too. Sometimes a more sophisticated woman appealed to older men. When a marriage was secret... how was the world to see a "no trespassing" sign that wasn't posted? Marianne didn't know she was poaching—not that that would make any difference to her. But men like Ben...

Oh, wouldn't this Paget money tangle ever get straightened out? Once Ulysses Paget's inheritance let her and Aubrey live together openly as man and wife, things would be all right.

Across the breakfast table the next morning, Ben's face had a look so different from its usual skepticism that she wondered why the others didn't ask him what had happened. But no one commented. And no one mentioned any singing. Perhaps she and Ben and the woman who had sung were the only ones who heard it.

Breakfast at Dune House was almost as formal as dinner. A stated time—eight o'clock, and until Julia gave the signal to rise, everyone was expected to wait. Ben held back the portières to the main dining room, and the ladies started down the long Persian rug beside the long table.

Ben caught up with Lark, and she found herself being maneuvered away from the others and stranded beneath Julia's portrait over the mantel as neatly as Uncle Thad used to mark down fryers for Aunt Sophie's skillet.

"Lark," Ben said softly, "come out on the lawn. I want to talk a minute. We won't be out of sight of the house—I promise."

"But—"

"Don't worry," Ben said. "I won't kiss you right under Cousin Julia's spyglass—much as I'd like to. But I want to talk with you before I go downtown."

Rowena and Marianne glanced back curiously at Lark and Ben. Julia's portrait stared from the wall above them as if it were listening, and Julia herself, going through the hall portières, turned to look back too.

"If you don't say you'll come, I'll kiss you right now," Ben declared. "I'll make your face so red in front of Cousin Julia and Mother and Marianne—"

"All right, all right," Lark said quickly. "But I haven't time—there're some things I ought to do..."

He laughed. "With all the breakfast dishes to wash, and the beds to make, and a cake to throw together for lunch, I know you haven't time for idle chatter. But this isn't idle chatter. All right, don't look so worried. I'll only—do this—now the others have left."

"This"—Lark's face was stinging hot—was a faint, light touch on her cheek, his big hand as gentle as the drop of an eyelid.

Her heart was going much too fast as she stepped through the front door beside him. She tried not to look at the hand that had touched her so lightly.

He led her across the lawn opposite the long blunt finger of the art gallery. "We'll make Cousin Julia crane her neck," he said when he finally stopped at the hedge. "I don't want anyone listening behind curtains this morning, but I knew I couldn't decoy you out of sight of your kind. Not that there is anything else quite your kind."

They stood gazing over the Paget dunes at the blocks of new houses beyond the fence and the uneven line of hills. It was all waves, she thought: waves of water down there in the ocean, waves of sand on the dunes, waves of hills, waves of houses…

"You love it, don't you, Lark," he said quietly, "the world out there you're shut away from?"

"It's the world I'm used to—those bright, cheap, little share-a-wall-with-your-neighbor stucco cottages—not this nineteenth century magnificence."

"It's the world I'm going to get used to, Lark," Ben said.

"What do you mean?" Lark asked.

"A stucco cottage is going to be my speed from now on," Ben said. "So you may as well get used to them again. Forget this morning-coffee-in-bed sort of thing. Or am I the only one with that habit? Anyway, forget it, and think about packing a dinner pail to send off in the morning with the man of the house—and running down the street to meet him at night—and—"

"Oh, Ben, I've got to go in!" she cried.

"All right, Lark—for now," Ben said. "I can't detain you, with Cousin Julia's spyglass at the window. But that's your destiny. That's what you were born for—so saith old Rabbi Ben Drew. Wait a shake; I haven't told all."

"Is there more?" Lark asked.

Ben laughed. "I've pretty well outlined the complete life, haven't I? But it all hinges on my getting a job. I'm going to look for one today—something snappy in iron."

"Oh, Ben, are you actually going to break away from Dune House and Julia Paget?" Lark asked.

"If I can find the right job, and it'll have me," Ben said. "Wish me luck?"

"So much luck!" Lark said. "It's the best thing that could happen to you. But I've got to go back to the house now."

He was still standing at the hedge when she reached the front door.

The day was long. Lark found herself hovering about the front windows again—watching for Aubrey, of course. But he came soon after lunch. She heard Marianne greet him in the hall, heard the murmur of their voices fade together, and Lark stayed on in the French Salon. She had *The Last Days of Pompeii* in her lap and had to sit by a window for good light. The fact that all the windows in that room were in the front of the house and that she read at the rate of three pages an hour was no one's business but her own.

She and *The Last Days of Pompeii* sat without interruption until teatime when Eileen called her to the music room. The others were all there except Ben: Julia, queen of the great silver service; Aubrey next to Marianne on a satin-covered settee, Rowena fidgeting with a teacup at one of the front windows.

Marianne was particularly ravishing in a two-piece dress of the black she affected so much, with a froth of white at her throat and a peplum almost like a bustle. With that well-planned figure and fairy-book yellow hair, she looked like a costume piece. Aubrey seemed well aware of it, too, yet Lark, to her own amazement, took her teacup over to a chair beside Rowena at the window.

Julia's fingers were tapping, sparks leaping from her diamonds. "I don't see what's keeping Benson. He can't be off the grounds; he has no pass. But it's so thoughtless of him to go someplace where he can't be found. I wanted him to play for us this afternoon."

"Oh, well, Aunt Julia, we're happy." Marianne's coo and the glance she gave Aubrey would have made a pig gag, thought Lark, and then told herself not to be catty.

On her other side, Rowena leaned suddenly toward the window.

"Is Ben coming?" Lark asked quickly.

His mother sighed. "It's only Leo. I hate to have Ben upset Julia like this."

But Julia's fuming wasn't even a preview of the way she'd act if Ben got his job. Then belatedly Lark remembered that she'd turned away before she saw how Aubrey reacted to Marianne's ogling.

Why should she care when Ben came back? It was Aubrey she was interested in—Aubrey Hildreth, her husband. At that moment his right hand, only an inch from Marianne's left, was settling on his knee. Had he put down his teacup, or what had his right hand been doing?

Before she had decided, Lark found her attention straying to the window again.

That was how she spent the afternoon: with her head turning back and forth between settee and window—like an old woman with palsy, she jeered at herself.

Ben still hadn't returned by the time Eileen announced dinner. But as Miss Paget led her guests—all but Aubrey now in evening clothes—across the hall from the French Salon to the dining room, Ben came in the front door.

He raised a hand while his eyes sought out Lark. She lagged behind the others.

"I got it," he murmured.

"Oh, Ben, how wonderful!" Lark said. "A dinner pail job?"

He nodded. "I'll whip into other clothes and tell you all about it after dinner." He ran for the stairs.

"Coming, Lark?" Aubrey was waiting with Marianne beside him.

Ben was in his chair next to Lark in the dining room alcove before Eileen had finished taking off the soup plates. Now that Marianne was here, when Aubrey stayed to a meal he was put beside her, with Lark by the Drews.

"Don't you hope there's fried chicken tonight?" Lark asked Ben softly. "It would pack so well in a dinner pail." Imagine a dinner pail going through the great bronze doors of Dune House!

Ben laughed. How different he looked since the night she'd seen him first with his mouth turned down and his eyes hostile green. They were bright with laughter now, and something more, as gentle as the touch of his hand.

At the head of the table his hostess spoke sharply. "Well, Benson, you didn't come to lunch. You even saw fit to absent yourself from tea when my guests would have enjoyed some music. May I ask where you have been all day?"

"I was going to tell you after dinner, Cousin Julia—in private," Ben said. "Shan't we wait till then?"

Her diamonds sparkled in the gaslight. "I see no reason to wait, Benson."

Across the table Aubrey and Marianne's perpetual murmuring had stopped. Lark could hear Rowena breathing on the other side of Ben.

Flecks of rainbow jumped from Julia's impatient fingers.

"All right, Cousin Julia," Ben said, "if you want it now." Lark could fell that he was bracing himself. "I've been looking for a job."

"On the Dune House grounds, Benson?"

"Well, no, Cousin Julia," Ben said. "I managed to get off them."

"We'll take that matter up later," his cousin warned him. "In the meantime, if you're looking for a position in the city, may I remind you that you haven't passed the bar examinations yet?"

"I don't need to—for my kind of work," Ben said.

"And what kind is that?" Julia asked.

Ben returned her straight look. "A laborer's job—in an iron foundry."

"Ben!" his mother gasped.

Julia's neck began to straighten and her chin came down. "Do you consider yourself amusing, Benson?"

"It's no joke, Cousin Julia," Ben said. "My job starts tomorrow morning. Whoops... I should have bought an alarm clock! Incidentally, children, I'm about to join the union."

"But, Ben!" Rowena cried. "Ben, dear, *iron*... it won't be like your flower pots and pretty grilles. This kind of iron will be heavy."

He smiled. "My muscle's good."

"It's not your muscle I'm thinking of, dear; it's your heart," Rowena said. "Remember what the army doctors—"

"The doctor who checks the foundry applicants says it's okay, Mother," Ben said. "Whatever was the matter before must have been corrected."

Julia Paget cleared her throat. Her neck was so straight that it almost arched, and she had three chins instead of one. "That's easy to explain, Rowena—though you'll find it distasteful."

She looked so much like a crocodile that had snapped off a human hand that the alcove curtains were like hanging moss and the burgundy and water were swamp slime.

She lashed out again. "We were at war, Rowena, and Benson was about to be drafted," Julia continued. "You can make your heart do a lot, you know—if you help it along a little."

Beside Lark, Ben went rigid. "What do you mean by that, Cousin Julia?"

"Yes, what do you mean, Julia?" Rowena asked. "I don't see—"

"If you don't want to fight—" Julia's lorgnette circled the table. "Surely you've all read articles about the men who took drugs?"

"So they wouldn't pass their physicals?" Marianne cried. "You don't think Ben—" She stopped, and for once looked embarrassed.

Each word of Julia's answer dropped hail-sharp and hail-cold. "A favorite trick was taking drugs that affected the heart."

Ben's face was white. "If I didn't know you—didn't know how furious you are because I'm getting out from under—"

"Naturally you say it's pique." Julia Paget smiled, and the smile was more chilling than the crocodile look. "But I know better. I thought it was odd that a boy who could do everything you've always done should have a bad heart. The second time you were called, I peeked in your room after Kezzie left your early-morning coffee."

"For the love of mud, Cousin Julia, what—?" Ben said.

"There's no use bluffing, Benson," Julia said. "I saw you take the tablets myself."

Every face at the table was still.

"You sat up in bed with the bottle right beside you as bold as you please, and washed the stuff down with your coffee."

"Wh-what stuff?" his mother quavered.

Julia swept on. "The bottle was one of those big ones druggists fill prescriptions from; you made sure you'd have enough for the duration.

I got it out of your closet as soon as you left and had a private detective check on it for me. He found out it was thyroid and—"

"Thyroid!" Rowena's tortured brow smoothed. "Why, Julia, thyroid tablets are nothing! I know at least four people—Eileen's mother and Adam's wife before she died, and—"

"Nothing!" Julia interrupted. "Do you know that this bottle was stolen from our local druggist on the beach only two weeks before Benson took his first physical examination? Nothing, indeed! Benson had time to experiment in advance and find out how much it took to give the reaction he wanted. The detective told me that doctors say some people are so affected by thyroid medication that even a few large doses will make their hearts race and hands tremble, and give them every symptom of a condition no army would want." Suddenly she began to laugh, that panting-dog laughter. "You thought you were clever, Benson. You may have fooled the U.S. Army, but you didn't fool me."

Eileen came in with a tray, and Ben rose. "Under the circumstances, Cousin Julia, you'll excuse me if I don't stay to dinner?"

He bowed slightly, and all the heads but Julia's followed his black back through the alcove portières.

"Miss Paget," Lark cried as they dropped, "there must be some mistake! Ben would never—"

"That will do, child." The reptilian eyes turned on her. "Do you think I'd make a statement like that—without proof?"

"You might if—"

"That wasn't a question," Julia snapped.

Across the table, Lark met Aubrey's warning gaze. He picked up his fork and moved it toward her, looking down at his plate, then at hers. Telling her she ought to eat, she supposed. Eat—when what she wanted to do was to take up her huge crystal water goblet and throw it at the thick-shouldered dictator at the end of the table!

Aubrey shook his head slightly and gestured with his fork again. Something in his slate-gray eyes—could it be compassion?—rang the first alarm bell within Lark. Miss Paget had talked about proof; but Miss Paget had also talked about a dog getting in, when all the time it had been a man. Ben might be fond of luxury, he might be a waster, but surely—surely he'd never... then why was Aubrey looking sorry for her?

It took another signal from him to show Lark that Eileen was holding out a platter of fried chicken. A wishbone for a dinner pail...

The next time Eileen came around, with hearts of artichoke dripping butter, she said softly, "Miss Lark." Between them, they got Lark through dinner. She remembered, herself, to move the food around on her plate.

As soon as they rose from the table she felt Aubrey's hand beneath her elbow. The long trip through the dining room... then, in the round hall, she saw Ben standing by the stairs.

He said, "Cousin Julia, may I speak with you a moment in the library?" and Lark felt Aubrey's hand propelling her toward the front of the hall.

"We'll join you in the Maple Parlor," Aubrey said to a curious-looking Marianne and a frightened-looking Rowena. "There's a picture I want to show Lark."

But he didn't go on to the picture gallery. As soon as the French Salon portières dropped behind them, he took Lark's hand and said gently, "Darling, I've been afraid of this. He's a handsome kid and so much younger than I am, and here in the house all the time. But I thought you loved me enough... I can't tell you how it hurt to see you so upset about another man."

"But, Aubrey, I simply can't believe that Ben—" Lark began.

"A lot of rich young fellows, Lark, have been brought up to think the world is theirs, instead of vice versa," Aubrey said. "Not that they did what Ben did; they won the war as much as the garbage man's sons. But sometimes too much money—"

"He doesn't have a cent—only what Miss Paget gives him!" Lark said.

"I drew up a will in his favor several months ago, Lark, but Julia hasn't signed it yet," Aubrey said. "She brought him up to expect the Paget millions. With expectations like that—and her philosophy, what could you hope for Ben?"

"Don't talk that way, Aubrey—as if you believed her," Lark said.

"Listen, dear, I hate to tell you; you're so loyal, and I know it'll hurt," Aubrey said. "But it's not fair for you to go on accusing Miss Paget. You see, I know her story's true."

Lark's breath came in sharply, and Aubrey went on, "She wanted to find out how Ben got the stuff and didn't want to put too much information in the way of that shady private detective of hers; so she came to me. Oscar and I did the job together. We found out about the local drugstore burglary of the year before and located the night-watchman. A couple of fifties got him to talk. Seems he'd already had a hundred dollars from Ben to keep him from talking, but that had been the year before. The old fellow came around the back corner of the drugstore right as Ben was climbing the window. Ben gave him the hundred then to keep still."

"That makes me sick, Aubrey," Lark said. "Don't you think there could be some mistake?" Maybe someone who looked like Ben—"

"Sorry, darling," Aubrey said. "The night watchman knows him and they talked together quite a while. It was Ben, all right."

"Oh, Aubrey, I can't—" Lark began.

"I know it's hard to take, dear, but I saw the man who caught him at it," Aubrey said. "I'll get you his name and address as soon as I got to the office. I never would have told you this if Julia hadn't brought it up. No matter how burnt I've been, seeing you watch for Ben and drink in every word and—oh, well, skip it. You know how I've been trying to get you back."

"How you've been—?" Lark said.

"Don't tell me you haven't even noticed," Aubrey said. "I've been doing my damnedest to make you think I was falling for Marianne. I thought if I could make you jealous—"

"It's not right," Lark broke in. "Ben doesn't seem like the sort of man who—"

"Oh, God," her husband groaned, "you're not even listening. Don't tell me Ben means so much that—he's not worth it, Lark! This draft evasion thing's not all. Don't you know he's been doing Julia's dirty work for years—the things Rollin, Rollin & Hildreth won't touch, things she can't even give to that shady detective of hers?"

Lark was fighting back nausea—and the memory of that day on the dunes flying kites when Ben told her he'd gone to Oscar's apartment on an errand for Julia, the day he saw Lark's name on the mailbox. She should have kept on remembering not to trust him.

Suddenly she was fighting back tears. She pressed her face quickly into Aubrey's tweed jacket that smelled comfortingly of tobacco. "He—doesn't seem—like that kind of—man!"

Aubrey's arms were around her now—like a shelter. "They never do, darling—that plausible, well-set-up type."

The French Salon was very still.

"Wait until we're properly married," Aubrey murmured, "openly, before the world. I'm going to take up so much of your time you won't have any to spare for other men. Not for any other men, Missus Hildreth, let alone good-looking young rascals who leave fighting the wars up to broken-down old crocks like your husband."

"You're no broken-down crock, Aubrey Hildreth!" Lark said. Aubrey had shouldered one of the guns that Ben hadn't. Aubrey hadn't used even his age or his marriage (he was Ninon's husband then) to try to get out of service. Aubrey did no one's dirty work.

Her arms came up beneath his, and she pressed herself closer. "I married you," she whispered. "I love you—of course." Of course she loved her husband. Why should she be so upset about a man she'd known only eleven days?

"Why do you say *of course*, Lark?" Aubrey said. "Let me look at you."

She bent her neck backward and raised her face. Aubrey's gray eyes, his firm lips beneath the black mustache... what if there were lines in the smooth brown skin? They were lines of character, of a man who did his duty...

"Lovely little girl," he said softly. His arms tightened, and when his lips came down, hers were ready.

A sound whirled Lark and Aubrey apart, the sound of glass breaking.

Behind them, inside the portières, was Ben. Pieces of a vase lay on the carpet at his feet. His back was almost turned, but the half of his face that she saw was sick white.

Chapter Sixteen

B en did not appear at breakfast. His mother's eyes were red and puffy. Like Leo, she kept her face turned away. Once she met Lark's gaze across the table, and Rowena's bloodshot eyes looked baleful. Julia, as majestic as an ocean liner at a river wharf, paid no attention to Lark and Rowena. Julia's breakfast hour was spent ordering Eileen about and sending for Kezzie to issue more orders. The few Paget conversational pronouncements were addressed to Marianne.

After breakfast Julia took the stairs as a ship does a swell, and Rowena toiled up behind her. From the lower hall Lark saw Julia, on the second-floor gallery, turn toward her boudoir and Rowena toward the third-floor flight. Ben wouldn't like to have his mother climb all those stairs. If he'd inherited her heart... but the doctor for the foundry said Ben's heart was all right.

"You should have heard the row last night before the whist game," Marianne murmured. "Missus Drew and I cramped each other's style too much to listen at the door. But the sound of the voices was something. I'd be scared to stand up to that woman the way Ben seemed to be doing. Lord, I'll be glad when I can get out of here. When even a nice-looking young fellow likes that turns out to be a draft-dodger... this place gives me the willies."

"Me too," Lark said.

In silence, both women stared up at the second-floor gallery where the boudoir door had closed.

The gilding from the skylight tinged Marianne's lineless face yellow. She was looking at Lark again. "What did you and Aubrey do to the boy last night? The row with Julia only lasted a few minutes. He came out of the library with his face brick red and those green eyes shooting sparks and demanded to know where you were. But after he came out of the French Salon he looked sick. He said to his mother, 'I'm clearing out of Dune House,' and picked up his suitcase and left."

So he'd gone—without every carrying a dinner pail through the bronze doors. Ben, who should have had the Paget money, who flew kites and bought smelling salts and had a forge in the basement, whose big hands were as gentle as eyelids...

"Well," Marianne said, "did you bite him?"

Lark blinked.

"Come down to earth, *cherie*," Marianne said. "What did you do to Ben that upset him so much more than his row with Julia?"

"Why—nothing," Lark said. "Nothing at all. We didn't even speak to him."

"Then he must have stumbled on a body. He hardly went in before he walked right out again. If it wasn't your fault that he looked so white, he certainly must have thought of something hard to take. I wonder..."

Lark gripped the lamp statue's gold foot. "I'm going upstairs."

Marianne came a step closer. "Did you hear about Kezzie?"

"What about her?" Lark asked.

"Old lady Paget went on one of those early morning prowls of hers and caught Kezzie sneaking food out of the icebox."

Lark's grip on the statue's foot tightened. "When? *This* morning?"

Marianne nodded. "She dragged you in, too. When Julia gave her hell, Kezzie said she was trying to make you think there was someone in the house. Then Julia gave her several more kinds of hell; so you'd better look out, *cherie*. Kezzie's a dangerous gal to rile."

Kezzie had never exactly loved Lark, but she must hate her now. Rowena hated her, too, because of Ben's leaving; she must think Lark responsible. Ben hated her because he'd seen her in Aubrey's arms. Marianne hated her because they were both after the same thing. Julia hated her because she was "that Georgette creature's" granddaughter, or because she wasn't, or just on principle; and—

"I've got to go upstairs." Lark's voice, even to herself, sounded desperate.

Dune House was a house of hate. She began to run up the carpeted treads.

"When's Aubrey coming out?" Marianne called.

"I don't know," Lark said.

At least he didn't hate her, Lark reminded herself. Though she'd made him unhappy. He didn't hate her. But Aubrey wasn't here.

In her room, with both doors locked, her thoughts returned to Kezzie and the food. All those times Kezzie had said food was missing—had she taken it herself, to give reality to her stories? Or was Oscar still here and Kezzie feeding him?

But why would Oscar still be here?

In the back of her mind, an answer glimmered and then blazed. It had come out last night at that nightmare game of whist demanded by Julia. Marianne, watching Aubrey devote himself to Lark, had played her cards stiffly, while poor Rowena, choking back sobs, had played hers so shakily that they'd fallen to the table instead of being laid there. Lark herself had hardly known one card from another. But no one had been released until midnight, cutting in and out glumly at the end of each rubber.

As she added up the evening's score, Julia had grumbled, "You wouldn't think anyone who'd finesse a seven the way Aubrey did would be such a timid Tabitha about money."

"Aubrey—timid?" There was something too knowing in Marianne's voice.

Julia snapped her pencil point. "When you have to put up a fight to get your own money... anyhow, I got it, and it's a lot better off in my safe than in a bank, or in a fancy apartment house in Santa Barbara."

So Lark knew that the Santa Barbara sale had been completed. Oscar had worked in the office too. He knew that the sale was pending and he knew about the Paget allergy to banks. He might not be out of his head after all. If he'd hung around Dune House waiting for that hundred thousand to be delivered in cash... what if the money *was* in the pilothouse safe? It was unlocked sometimes to get out jewels and for this and that, as Aubrey had pointed out, warning Julia against Marianne, and Julia never locked the door when she entered her bedroom. If Oscar took his shoes off, would his steps be heard on the iron stairs? Leo and Adam slept in the stable, and the only

181

man in the house was Yep, aging away in the basement...

Oh, why did Ben have to leave? And leave hating her, too. Why—? She stood straighter. She wasn't going to think about Ben. Or of why so many people hated her. Anyone living in this terrible house would find hate. It began way back with Venetia. Or even farther, when Julia and Captain Paget hated the woman Ulysses was in love with. Julia hated Georgette. And Venetia hated Julia.

Venetia... it might not be Oscar who'd been eating the food that had vanished. Kezzie and Ben both admitted that Venetia could have survived. If she came out of the water alive—and Kezzie found her... but Kezzie couldn't go on hiding and feeding her for forty years! Suppose Julia found her... she might report Venetia drowned, and then... Lark swallowed. Was Julia Paget sane? She might have locked up her sister again, this time in one of the towers where no one ever went, where maybe no one else even knew there was a room; or perhaps in the cellar among the storage catacombs: the wine rooms, the furnace room, the gas and elevator plants, the jam closets, fruit closets, and great bins of apples and potatoes and onions. The policeman said that there were no other women in Dune House, and Ben insisted there were no secret rooms or passages... but the policeman would have missed her—if Ben was wrong.

Ben again.

With a shock, she found herself wondering what would have happened if she'd met him before she married Aubrey. How much was her marriage due to those years of having Aubrey for a boss, of being exposed to his vitality and exciting good looks and the competition of other women?

She ought to be ashamed, she told herself. She'd married Aubrey and he loved her. She loved him too, of course. Ben wasn't worth a second thought—not after what Aubrey had told her last night. She wouldn't have believed it if Aubrey hadn't said it, hadn't seen the druggist, himself.

Lark straightened again and pulled apart interlocked fingers. It was like Aubrey said: as soon as they could openly acknowledge their marriage, everything would be different.

Lunch time came at last. But Aubrey wasn't there. Miss Paget said, when

Marianne asked her, that he might come that afternoon. Lark needed him to help her tear out of her private album the pages that held the pictures of Ben.

She waited, after lunch, at her old post in the French Salon where Ben had found her last night with Aubrey. She wasn't going to think of Ben, though, only of her husband. Remind herself that he was her husband and the most brilliant, the finest man she'd ever known. How could she have so let him down that he thought he had to make her jealous to get her back? It was hard on Marianne, too, with Aubrey as attractive as he was. She didn't know he was married—any more than Ben knew Lark was. That embrace he saw last night could have given him a lot of wrong ideas—for how could she explain that she and Aubrey were married? But she wasn't going to think about Ben anymore.

She got up and stood at a window. From the first floor she couldn't see the lupin-speckled dunes beyond the hedge, only the hills, slatted with lines of houses, as if the hedge walling off the Paget lawn walled off Dune House from the world. The hedge—instead of a half mile of dunes, and an eight-foot fence, and a woman's will.

Inside, the house was hushed—that hush of deep-napped carpets and closed shutters, of velvet and plush and padding. If there were other people about, they made no sound that Lark could hear.

Something seemed to pull at the back of her head, urged her to turn.

She stood as board-and-plaster still as the house itself. Behind her on the inside wall was the curtained door to the Japanese Room. Once Ben had said, on this exact spot, "Someone may be back of those curtains now, listening."

And someone might be back of them—watching.

Lark whirled. But the curtains were down: deep green and seemingly as still as stagnant water.

No one behind them could hear her move on this carpet...

She began to run—softly, swiftly...

Jerked the portières back—and saw no one.

This place was getting her down. Next time there'd be someone there.

Next time she'd be seeing things.

Dune House might be in another world from the one she had left, but these closed-off rooms were in still another world—eerie, ghostlike… in the shuttered gloom where dragonflies glinted, she seemed to be peering into a witch wood of monster mushrooms and toadstools and hunched, hiding gnomes.

Lark shivered. She was letting her imagination run away again. Those whitish lumps were only sheet-covered tables and chairs. Except for being Asian, they were like the things she used every day, covered to keep clean.

But by now her shivering was so violent that she took a step forward to steady herself and reached out a hand to what looked like a sheeted table.

Her unsteadiness shook the sheet too, seemed even to shake the table. She groped along the edge for a firmer hold—and her hand touched something that gave… moved…

Then suddenly the sheet was jerked through her fingers. It was standing up—taller than Lark. Standing—then running away.

Chapter Seventeen

Lark ran faster than the sheet—in the other direction. Lark ran for the hall. For the vestibule and the out-of-doors. For the lawn and the road to the stable.

Ben was no longer in Dune House. But if Leo would call him, show him he was needed... no matter how he hated Miss Paget—or despised Lark—if Ben knew there was someone loose in the house, surely he would come to protect them.

Leo would know where he was working, how to find him...

She stumbled in the sand, recovered, and ran on. If she couldn't get hold of Ben, she'd wait for Aubrey. He was coming out this afternoon. She couldn't stay in that house. She twisted for a backward glance and stumbled again. Once more the towered bulk behind the hedge looked like a storm cloud blowing toward her.

At last she jerked at the stable door—jerked, fumbled. By the time she got it open Leo was hurrying across the mats down the polished aisle.

He didn't try to hide his scar. He asked sharply, "What is it? What's happened?"

Lark tried to speak and could only gasp. In a minute she stuttered, "B-B-Ben—can you get him?"

What's the matter?" he asked more sharply.

His tone steadied her. "Ben must come back. We need him—up there. I saw—" She swallowed. "There's someone in the house."

Beneath the olive-green livery, Leo's muscles tensed.

"I—I don't know who it is. The sheet got up and—" She swallowed again.

"I was looking in the Japanese Room and touched something I thought was a table. There—must have been someone under it, because the sheet was snatched off and ran away."

"What run away? Who?" Leo said.

"I d-don't know," Lark said. "The sheet was wrapped around him. It wasn't like a person at all. It was like a—ghost."

"Okay, miss," Leo said briskly. "Don't get excited. There's another angle, you know. It may not be 'someone in the house' like you think, at all. It could be—Miss Paget herself. I told you she was..." He let the words hang.

"I—May I stay down here? I don't want to go back." Lark tried not to let her teeth chatter.

"Guess you'll have to, miss—go back, I mean," Leo said. "It'll be a good three hours before Ben arrives. Miss Paget'll be sending for you."

The chattering won. "B-b-b-but—"

He held up his hand. "Now, wait a minute. I can't do anything until Ben comes. It'll take two of us to go through these rooms—one from each direction—and Dad in the hall."

"Isn't Mister Hildreth coming out?" Lark said. "He could help you now..."

"Phoned he'd be delayed, miss..." Leo said. "This may not be anything new, you know—just Miss Paget, like I said—so we can't make Mister Ben risk losing his job by calling him away the first day. I'll phone him now and go get him at five—"

"And what'll I do?"

"Go back to the house, miss, and I'll go with you," Leo said. "I'll work in the conservatory and leave the library door open. You stay in there where I can see. Don't let anyone coax you out. I won't have an excuse to go anyplace else. And by the way, miss, don't mention this to anyone. Miss Paget won't like a story like this getting about—not even to the folks in the house."

As Lark, with Leo a respectful five yards behind, stepped into the shadow of Dune House darkening the drive, she tried to keep her eyes down, but the great, stone-colored mass pulled them toward it. She kept reminding herself that Leo was with her.

"I'll have to go in the back way, miss," Leo said quietly. "But I'll look over the shrubs in front of the house until Eileen lets you in. She'll be with you in the hall. You needn't think it was Eileen you saw in the sheet."

No, Eileen could be found near any doorway, even in the closed-off rooms, without having to hide behind a sheet. Lark hadn't thought of that trip through the hall, but the granddaughter of the house could hardly sneak in the back way with the coachman.

She walked, shaking, up the marble steps.

But it wasn't Eileen who opened the door. Kezzie stood there, angular and yellow-faced. "Been out getting air, miss?" she asked with that insolent respect.

"Out-out—for a walk," Lark stammered.

"I see Leo came up from the stable, miss," Kezzie said.

"Yes, he—walked up with me," Lark said.

"Oh, so Leo brought you back?" Kezzie asked. Like someone escaping from a keeper.

Lark was inside now, and the doors were closed behind her—the double bronze doors of Dune House.

She started swiftly toward the library, when Kezzie's hand closed on her arm. "You're chilly, miss. It's not so warm out, for all the sun. There's a fire in the Maple Parlor. Go in there and warm up."

Goose flesh rose on Lark's arms. "Not—not now. I have to—" She stopped.

Kezzie's hand still held her. "Then come into the French Salon, miss, where you go so much. I'll light a fire there."

"Will you walk into my parlor?" said the spider to the fly...

"I'm going to the library, Kezzie," Lark said. "I have to—"

"What do you have to do, miss?" Kezzie asked.

The library—her haven... what did people do in libraries? "Why"—in a flood of relief—"I have to look something up!"

"The Pagets have never been what you'd call the intellectual type," Kezzie said. "If you're a Paget, miss—"

"They can read," Lark said tartly.

"Very well, miss. I'll light a fire there," Kezzie said.

"D-don't bother, Kezzie," Lark said.

"But you're chilly, miss." Kezzie walked beside her.

As they went through the library curtains, Leo appeared at the door of the conservatory.

"Shut that door, Leo," Kezzie said sharply. "Miss Lark's cold."

"No, don't!" Lark's voice cracked. "I need air."

"Do you feel faint?" Kezzie demanded.

"No, I—well, yes, maybe, a little," Lark stammered.

"Then that door must be shut," Kezzie said firmly. "That air's steamy. I'll open a window."

At least it was glass, Lark thought desperately, as Kezzie shut the conservatory door. But the air, she'd said, was steamy. If the glass became steamed...

"Oh, for heaven's sake, Kezzie," Lark cried, "go away and leave me alone! Or I'll tell Miss Paget you've been impertinent."

Kezzie gave her a look that scorched and stalked out. Lark ran to the conservatory door.

"Kezzie seemed quite determined, miss," Leo said dryly.

"I wonder if it was Kezzie under that sheet?" Lark asked.

"I wouldn't think she'd need one any more than Eileen," Leo said.

He was right, of course. Neither of the maids would need a disguise. "You—you'll work where I can see you?" Lark begged.

Leo nodded, and she reluctantly went back to the red-walled room and the claw-legged table that reminded her of a crouching lion. She'd better take out an encyclopedia to make her story convincing. She chose one at random and placed a chair where she could see Leo.

Her watch ticked off almost an hour and a half before the hall curtains parted again.

Eileen came in. "Aunt Kezzie said I'd find you here, miss. Did you know it's teatime?" Her glance strayed to Leo bending over a yellow begonia.

"I'm not hungry," Lark said.

The maid moved closer to the open glass doors. "I'm surprised to see you gardening in your best livery, Leo."

The man shrugged his shoulders.

Eileen looked back at Lark. "Miss Paget'll be asking for you, miss."

"Tell her I'm sorry I can't come today, will you, Eileen?" Lark said. "I'm looking something up and don't feel like eating now."

Eileen's head turned toward Leo. She stood uncertainly, and then went out.

Lark hurried into the conservatory. "Do you think Ben got the message all right?"

Leo nodded. "Sure. I said it was important and I'd be there to pick him up. You don't need to worry, miss."

"Don't you think it's time to start?" Lark asked.

"Not yet, miss," Leo said. "It's best for me to be here as long as I can. Then you won't have to wait so long with Dad."

Lark sighed. "I think I'll stay out here with you if you don't mind. The library table seems a mile away."

"Don't worry, miss," Leo repeated, digging his fork into the soil around a large plant with a salmon pink flower.

He worked in silence while Lark stood and watched.

She didn't know how long she'd been there when she heard Eileen's voice again. The pretty maid was standing in the doorway.

"Does the thing that takes you so long to look up, miss, have something to do with begonias?" Eileen asked.

Leo went on turning over dirt with his fork, but Lark jumped.

"I didn't hear you come in!" she exclaimed.

"Does it, miss?" Eileen repeated.

"Does what, Eileen?" Lark asked.

"That thing you were looking up," Eileen said. "Does it have something to do with begonias?"

Eileen would be ushered right out the back door if Miss Paget could hear her, Lark thought, but to her Eileen was no more than another girl with something on her mind. "The thing I was looking up? Oh, yes." The story she'd told Kezzie. "Leo wanted to know something about begonias, so I said I'd try to find it."

"About some special variety, miss?" Eileen asked.

189

"Why—yes, some name I can't pronounce," Lark said.

"Then that's why the encyclopedia on the table is the M book, instead of the B, I suppose," Eileen said.

Eileen's face was as pink as the pinkest begonia. It wasn't like her to talk like this. Lark's eyes turned to Leo, who continued to dig.

"Miss Paget wants you to come to tea, miss," Eileen said firmly.

"But I said—" Lark began.

"She told me to tell you, miss," Eileen said.

"Tell Miss Paget"—Lark's tone was as firm as Eileen's—"that I'm sorry but I can't come today."

"She won't like it, miss," Eileen said.

"Then that's too bad," Lark said coldly.

Leo chuckled.

Eileen's pink face flamed. "The war certainly changed some folks I know. Gave them a lot of highfalutin' notions. No girl in his own class's good enough for plenty of ex-soldiers now. They've got to have heiresses these days." She flounced out.

"Oh," Lark gasped. "I'm sorry, Leo. I had no idea she'd think..."

"She'll get over it, miss." He was trying not to grin. But Lark could see nothing to grin at, for now Eileen hated her too.

At last Leo put down his fork. "Guess we can go now, miss, if you're ready. Don't leave the stable, will you? Stick close to Dad."

* * *

There was no danger, Lark thought as she watched Leo drive away, in a car this time instead of a carriage, of her leaving the stable. She wondered what Miss Paget must be thinking if, at the boudoir window with her spyglass, or up in the pilothouse, she had seen Lark run down to the stable, come back with Leo, and go down again. Now she wouldn't be returning for an hour. Julia was probably remembering her sister's low tastes.

It seemed like a week before the car came back, but finally Adam opened the garage door for Leo, with Ben in the front seat beside him.

190

Ben… as he stepped down she saw that he wore tweeds instead of overalls and had no dinner pail. Then she saw the streak of dirt near the hairline and thought of a small boy washing only the middle of his face. Ben… Ben…

She had to remind herself quickly that Aubrey was her husband and Ben was the corrupt product of too much money and no conscience, charming, spoiled…

He was standing beside the car like something stuck together with cement. "You wanted me, Lark?" His voice sounded queer.

"I think you're needed here." She changed the wording a little. Her own voice sounded queer, too. "Did Leo tell you about—the dust sheet that ran away?"

Ben nodded. "Of course it would be Cousin Julia. Or even Mother. It would be embarrassing, you know—to be caught peeking. But I wouldn't feel I was doing—shall we say my *duty?*"—his mouth was as bitter as she'd ever seen it—"if I didn't make another search."

So, he didn't care about her safety. And once he hadn't cared about duty.

"Leo'll start from the Moorish Room," Ben said, "and I'll start from the French Salon. If there's anyone between, we'll flush him."

"If—if Adam can't come and Eileen'll stay with me, I'll watch in the hall," Lark promised.

Leo, who had been talking with Adam, came over. "I can't take you folks up now. Mister Rollin phoned Dad twenty minutes ago that he and Mister Hildreth were on their way out. They'll be here any minute; so I'll have to wait."

Lark drew a long breath. "Then I won't have to watch in the hall."

Ben looked stiffer than ever, his mouth still bent in that bitter curve. "Aubrey'll take care of you now."

He had no right to use that tone! Though, after seeing that embrace last night… "L-let's walk on up the road," she stammered.

"Why don't you?" Leo said. "If Miss Lark can take more sand. I'll catch up with you before long."

They went through the long aisle behind the stalls with the clean horsy smell and the sound of munching. Ben closed the stable door and they walked a hundred yard without speaking.

Lark kicked up a spurt of sand. "Ben, I hope you—" She started again. "I'm sorry you came into the Salon last night. I—" She broke off lamely.

"I'm sorry, too," Ben said.

"I—don't want you to get the wrong impression," Lark said.

"The wrong impression I got was the first one," Ben said.

She stopped. "What do you mean?"

He kept on walking. She had to hurry to hear what he said. "I shouldn't say the first impression. I should have said the second. At first I thought you were a grabber like Marianne—out for the Paget fortune. Then I decided you weren't, and I thought you were sweet and—shy. Shy! I wish I couldn't laugh."

"Why should you laugh?" Lark asked.

"After what I saw in the French Salon?" Ben asked. "The way you and Aubrey were clinching wasn't shy."

"But—but—" Lark stammered.

"I've been played for a sucker, that's all," Ben said.

"Oh, Ben, no!" Lark said.

"Oh, Lark, yes!" Ben said.

What could she do? Aubrey didn't want her to tell of their marriage. It might spoil her chances with Miss Paget or get to Mr. Rollin. But Ben—that twisted, set face... she had to tell him. She couldn't let him go on thinking... "Ben, you don't understand. We're married."

That stopped him. Sand ridged up before Ben's feet. He was completely white again.

"Who's married?" he said. "Not you and Aubrey Hildreth! My God!"

"We had to keep it quiet—don't you see?—or Miss Paget would think we were trying to put something over. And we had to keep still in the first place because Mister Rollin—" She launched into her involved explanations.

In the middle he caught her arm. "Hell, the others are coming. Let's take to the dunes. I've got to hear you out."

They had come three quarters of the way. Ahead, Dune House loomed large. Back at the stable, the small victoria was leaving.

Lark went on talking unhappily while Ben trudged beside her.

"It's so damn hard to take," he muttered.

There was nothing for Lark to say.

In the silence, the wind brought the sound of a shout. The carriage was opposite them now. Aubrey was standing up, he and Mr. Rollin both beckoning with deep in-swoops of their arms.

"Let them yell," Ben growled. "We've got things to settle."

The gesturing grew wilder. They seemed to be urging her and Ben toward the house as the carriage passed.

"They—they must want us pretty badly," she faltered.

"Not the way I want you, Lark." Ben said.

She began to run. Aubrey's wife mustn't listen to that sort of talk from other men. Especially not from Ben, whom she was trying too hard to erase from her mind. Motioning the victoria on, she ran toward the house.

"Wait!" Ben called.

She ran faster. Up and down dunes... lurching... stumbling... tripping...

Down one more sand hill now to the hollow below the gap in the hedge where drive went through. She had almost reached the road when something white caught her eye. But the rocks here weren't that color. Why would anything white be out in the sand? Rounded... like a skull.

Her feet faltered. But it *was* like a skull, only smaller than a man's. And suddenly she was on her knees—bending closer...

"Oh, Ben, it looks like a face!" Lark cried. "Like a head with a nose. Oh, it is!"

Ben, yards behind her, came up. "What—?"

She pointed to the white rock.

He gave a sharp exclamation and reached for it. The part that was buried wasn't round.

"It's a bust!" Lark cried. "One of the marble busts from the house."

"Napoleon," Ben said. "What the hell's he doing here?"

"That's the one that was missing from the hall!" Lark said. "Kezzie was scolding Eileen about it. What—?"

Ben didn't answer. He was on his knees, scooping up sand like a terrier.

"What's the matter?" Lark cried. "Surely you don't think you'll find any more?"

"Hold it back, Lark—that sand I dug out," Ben said. "It keeps filling in."

Sand flew faster. Lark found her mouth strangely dry.

Then he came to the answer. Lark saw it too, before he could cover it again. There was no mistaking the brown, sand-matted filaments finer than thread or the outline appearing through the sand—both like, yet unlike, the white marble bust. For these features had once been human.

Lark recognized them. She smothered a scream.

They had found Oscar Fry.

Chapter Eighteen

L ark and Ben panted through the hedge. As they stepped into the shadow of the house, Lark shuddered.

Ben said quickly, "Keep your chin up, gal. You're doing fine."

"Think, Ben, if I hadn't happened to see that white stone and been curious..."

"It was sticking up a good eight inches, Lark—Napoleon's whole head," Ben said. "And not more than four or five yards from the road. It would have been found any minute. Horses don't go the same speed as motors, you know, and toward the house they'd be going uphill. Whoever buried the poor guy must have thrown the bust in last and not covered it enough—and the wind did the rest."

Lark pulled herself up the steps by the railing. The metal was gravestone cold. "You think he used the bust..."

Ben reached for her hand, gave it a quick squeeze, and let it drop. "Sure, he used the bust for a weapon. Perhaps to scrape sand with, too. We'll get the police... the door *would* be locked!" He gave three loud bangs with the knocker.

The bronze doors parted and Eileen's rosy face appeared. When she saw Ben, her mouth opened.

"Don't say it, Eileen," Ben said. "If Cousin Julia told you not to let me use it, you'll have to disobey orders. I've got to phone Adam to relay a message."

"The phone closet's locked, you know, Mister Ben, and this time Miss Paget's got the key instead of Kezzie," Eileen said. "She—Miss Paget—and the two lawyers and Missus Seymour are all in the library, and she said she

195

didn't want to be disturbed. She'll be glad to see Miss Lark, though. She's been asking for her."

"Asking?" Ben almost managed a grin. "That's not the way I'd put it. If Miss Paget has the key, I'll have to see her. There's no telling how she'll take it," he said to Lark. "Too bad I couldn't get the police first. I'd have gone to the stable if Leo had a key to that phone. Adam's as persnickety as Cousin Julia."

They started across the hall. Eileen's voice came doubtfully after them. "Mister Ben, you'd better not—"

"I won't deliberately rile her," he said over his shoulder, then kept on walking.

He pulled aside the library curtains for Lark. Of the four at the end of the massive table, only Julia and Aubrey looked up.

"So you've come back, Benson," Julia said.

Mister Rollin and Marianne looked up then.

"Miss Williams," Mr. Rollin began, and Aubrey said, "Lark, we found—"

Ben cut across them both in almost Paget style. "I'm not here to stay, Cousin Julia; I want to use the phone. I have to report a murder."

Marianne gave a little scream, quickly stifled with both red-nailed hands. Mr. Rollin half rose, his ruddy face purple. Aubrey, whose tan had paled to yellow, looked more alert than ever.

"Who's dead?" Julia asked sharply.

"Oscar Fry," Ben said.

The other three at the table all started talking at once, but Julia's decisive voice won. "Oh—Oscar Fry." She didn't add, *Then of course it doesn't matter*, but she might as well have. "I suppose I should report it. But first we'll get this business settled."

"Julia!" Mr. Rollin's tone was shocked. "A murder must be reported as soon as it's discovered. The law—"

"*I'm* the law at Dune House, Edward," Julia said.

They all stared at the thick-shouldered woman roped in pearls. The room was so still that Lark could hear the ocean.

"Well, Aubrey"—Julia's voice was crisp—"before Lark and Benson came in, you were saying..."

"But, Miss Paget—" Aubrey said.

"I have the key to the telephone closet, and Adam has the key to the booth in the stable," Julia said. "He unlocks it for no one without my permission, any more than he unlocks the gate. Is that quite clear to all of you? Anyway, Aubrey, you were saying..."

"A murder must be reported, Julia!" Edward Rollin's bony fist came down on the table.

But it came down only once. Julia Paget gave him the crocodile look and turned to Aubrey. "You were saying..."

"Rollin's right, of course," Aubrey said. "And quite aside from the social implications of not reporting a murder, Miss Paget, you're apt to get into all kinds of hot water."

"I'll report it when I'm ready—not before," Julia said. "Now if you'll get on with your story..."

Mister Rollin gave a strangled sputter and Aubrey shrugged. "You can't say we haven't warned you, Miss Paget—when you try to explain to the police. Well, I guess poor old Oscar won't run away. Sit down here, Lark, by me."

Ben slid into the chair on her other side.

"This is why we were wigwagging from the road, Lark," Aubrey said, "to get you in to tell you that our detectives have checked on Missus Seymour."

"But they're wrong," Marianne cried across the table. "You bribed them—so Lark would win!"

"Did I bribe the New York City officials twenty-five years ago?" Aubrey said. "Or the doctors who signed the death certificate of Missus Lamotte and her ward? Or the census takers? Or—"

"Oh, save that for the juries, Hildreth," Ben interrupted. "What did the detectives find?"

"That Juliette Marianne Seymour's name is Blanche Johnson—" Aubrey said.

"That was only the name I used on my marriage license," Marianne broke in. "I told you I gave a false one."

"It keeps turning up," Aubrey said dryly. "Remember, Lark, she said she'd been raised by a Frenchwoman? A Missus Lamotte once lived at the address Missus Seymour gave us, with a blond ward from France who used the same name. Missus Lamotte died in the flu epidemic of Nineteen-Eighteen, and the girl a few years later, but she'd moved away and dropped the name of Lamotte after her guardian's death. Missus Seymour thought that would throw us off the track. She took a lot of chances, but they might have worked."

"Blanche Johnson," Mr. Rollin added testily, "acquired her French accent and mannerisms by taking French parts in a stock company, and she couldn't resist showing them off. I suppose she thought them appropriate, with Ulysses' child born in France. She's been a cheap actress for twenty-five years. And her mother before her was an actress—in burlesque."

"That's how Marianne's mother got to know your grandmother, Lark," Aubrey added. "They were pals in burlesque, such pals that, when Georgette Paget had her baby, she sent Blanche Johnson's mother a photograph, the one Marianne—"

"Mother's baby picture?" Lark cried.

Aubrey nodded. "Marianne remembered seeing it in her mother's trunk, and when the picture of the Paget baby came out in the papers—"

"That may be how Lark got her photograph," Marianne interrupted with spirit, "by my mother sending one to someone in her family. But the ring! I have the sea horse ring!"

"Oh—do—you—Missus—Seymour?" Aubrey's tone was so strange that everyone stared as he fumbled in his coat pocket.

He brought out something and laid it in front of Julia Paget.

Lark gasped. Another big amethyst ring with a glint of gold on top... Julia turned it around, and Lark saw a sea horse inlaid in gold. No wonder Julia didn't want to stop to call the police. At moments like this, Lark could almost forget Oscar herself.

Julia held the ring in first one light, then another. "I'd forgotten," she said slowly, "but now I see it, I remember that Ulysses' amethyst was chipped. I remember—now—the day it happened. This is the one with the chip."

"You're all lying!" Marianne cried. "But her spirit was gone; only shrillness remained. "My ring's the real one. That's a fake!"

"She ought to know about fakes," Mr. Rollin observed caustically, "after getting a crooked jeweler to fake the ring she presented! Blowing up that baby picture and looking at Tiffany's Eighteen Eighty records were all he needed. That's why she was five days late getting here, not because of transportation."

"He wouldn't know about the chip, of course," Aubrey said.

"Where did the ring come from?" Ben asked.

"The Williams chicken ranch," Mr. Rollin said, "where Lark used to live with her aunt and uncle. One of our men arranged to have Missus Williams called to town and quietly searched her place. Not strictly legal, of course, but under the circumstances…"

"Don't know whether your Aunt Sophie hid the ring or your mother did, Lark," Aubrey said. "It was behind a loose board in the place where Missus Williams keeps her chicken feed."

"Chicken feed, indeed," Mr. Rollin said, his red face deepening to purple again.

Lark only said softly, "Oh." An "oh" of compassion more than exclamation. She was thinking of her mother hiding the ring in the month of her last illness and forgetting or being unable to tell where it was.

Julia's diamonds sprayed color as she reached out to pat Lark's arm. "Of course I don't owe you an apology, child, but I almost feel that I do. People with money have to be careful, and when I put two million dollars into a trust fund…" Julia lifted pale eyebrows and let it go at that. "You both had the picture, of course, and when Marianne apparently had the ring as well… you were the one I wanted all the time." She patted Lark's arm again.

Marianne stood up. "I see no reason to wait around for insults. I shall pack and leave Dune House immediately."

"You tried to once before, I believe." Julia's diamonds sprayed again as she tapped the table. "You found the padlock strong?"

Marianne flushed angrily. "Caged animals—that's what you are—all of you! You made me stay, Julia Paget, and then when I found out the first night

199

that someone else was here—someone you couldn't even find!—of course I tried to get out. Think I was going to stay in this—*zoo*, without letting anyone know what was going on?"

"You have friends in San Francisco?" Aubrey asked smoothly.

"What does it matter, Mister Hildreth, whether I have friends here or was going to wire them," Marianne asked. The purple in her pansy eyes was all fury. "Good-by, lions and tigers and—monkeys. I must say this has been—an experience."

"Sit down, Marianne," Julia commanded. "You cannot leave now."

"Oh, *can't* I!" she said. "If you think you can go on stringing me along, you're crazy... as crazy as Leo said."

Julia was the one who flushed now, until her yellowish eyebrows looked white. "Pull the bell cord, Benson. I said *sit down*, Marianne."

Marianne sank back on her chair.

Eileen came promptly, almost too promptly, and Julia began to issue orders. "Have Kezzie call Missus Drew and tell Leo to drive back to the stable for his father. Have him tell Adam to leave the telephone locked and bring me the key. When they return, I want you all here—you and Kezzie and Yep as well."

"If you phone Adam to drive himself up—" Ben began.

"I'm not taking out the key to the telephone closet," Julia returned sharply. "What difference does ten minutes make?"

"That much more to explain to the police," Edward Rollin fumed.

"Must I remind you, Edward, that Dune House is mine?" Julia sat straighter. "Now where was it that you found this—body, Benson?"

So she hadn't forgotten about Oscar after all.

"About four or five yards from the drive," Ben told her, "and maybe fifty from where it goes through the hedge. It was down in that first hollow—"

"How do you know he was murdered?" Julia asked.

"Suicides or people who die naturally don't bury themselves, Cousin Julia," Ben said. "Not that it was such a fancy job of burying. With the body laid flat in the bottom of the hollow, all whoever buried him had to do was pull down sand from the dunes on each side. He didn't even have to dig a grave."

200

"Never mind the details of disposal, Benson," Julia interrupted. "Did you find anything to indicate murder—bullet holes, knife wounds, a crushed skull?"

"We didn't examine the body," Ben said. "As soon as I saw it *was* a body, I took Lark away, and we came to phone the police."

"That man was killed before I ever came here," Marianne protested.

"That's up to the coroner to determine, Missus Seymour." Aubrey's mouth was grim. "Oscar came in Thursday night and you came Saturday. He may not have been killed until yesterday, for all we know."

"I don't think, by the looks of—"Ben began while Lark whitened.

Aubrey held up his hand. "Okay, Ben, let's leave it to the coroner. This whole thing should be turned over to the authorities, Miss Paget."

"Right now," Mr. Rollin croaked.

"That will do, Edward," Julia snapped. "And the same to you, Aubrey. I do things here as I see fit. If I choose to let no one leave or telephone, there's nothing you can do about it… that ought to comfort you timid souls so afraid of breaking the law."

Rowena came in with her glasses halfway down her nose and gray curls every which way. When she saw Ben, she gave a cry of joy and ran around the table to him.

"Sit down, Rowena," Miss Paget said. "Oscar Fry has been found—"

"How nice," the little woman beamed. "Then, with Ben back, everything's perfect."

For a moment, the only sound in the room was a crash of waves.

"Perhaps not exactly perfect," Julia drawled, "since it happens that Oscar Fry is dead."

"Oh, the poor thing!" Rowena said. "Did he go over the cliff too, Julia?"

"He's been murdered," Miss Paget said coldly, "and his body buried in the dunes."

Rowena gave a little squeak.

"Where were you, Rowena," Julia demanded severely, "a week ago Thursday night?"

"A week ago Thurs—why, Julia, wasn't that the night the man got in? This very Oscar Fry?" Rowena said.

"That's why I'm asking where you were," Julia said.

"I don't see—Good heavens above, Julia Paget, you don't think *I* killed him?" Rowena's teeth began to click together.

"I didn't say you did," Julia said. "But I want to know where you were that evening."

Ben laid a big hand over his mother's shaking small one. "We don't know that he was killed that night, Mother. Cousin Julia's starting from the beginning, I suppose. You and Lark were together all evening, weren't you?"

"Well, not quite," Rowena said. "You remember Julia and Aubrey went back to the library to work, and then you went out, Ben, and you were all gone a long time. You came back first, and then Edward came in a few minutes and took you away. After that Lark left me a while. I played several games of solitaire while she was gone—"

"You were there by yourself?" Julia interrupted.

Rowena nodded. "But after a while Lark came back, and then you came in, Julia, and sent us both to bed."

"Your memory for detail is remarkable, Rowena," Mr. Rollin declared.

"Nothing else in her head," Julia said crossly.

Ben stood up. "Cousin Julia, I resent—"

"Sit down, Ben." His mother tugged at his sleeve. Her shaking had stopped. She bowed as graciously as the Paget best toward Mr. Rollin. "Thank you for the compliment, Edward. Julia, dear"—she settled her glasses—"I remember so many things."

Again, that sea-swishing quiet filled the room.

"It's taking Leo and Adam ridiculously long," Julia scolded. "As long as you're up, Ben, set five chairs at the other end of the table. We waste so much time getting started... no, not so near the table. Back about a yard."

Of course it would never do to have servants at the same table with a Paget.

Julia, from the end where she sat alone, looked at Marianne and Mr. Rollin on one side, and at Aubrey, Lark, Ben—reseating himself—and Rowena on the other. Her eyes came back to Lark. "Where did you go, Lark, when you left Rowena playing solitaire in the Maple Parlor?"

"Up to my room," Lark said. "I felt stuffy and wanted fresh air. I did stop a minute at the door to the Egyptian Room. Ben and Leo were in there looking under dust sheets."

"How long were you gone?" Julia asked.

"I don't know," Lark said. "Maybe half an hour."

"And you, Benson," Julia said. "Where did you go before I set you and Leo to searching?"

Ben looked stubborn.

"Well, Benson?" his cousin said sharply.

"I was doing some repair work for Yep," Ben replied.

"Repairs to what?" Julia asked.

"The apple bin," Ben said.

"Why don't you tell her about it, Ben?" came a voice from the doorway.

Leo stood there holding the portières aside for Eileen and Kezzie. Adam came in smoothing the long, side locks of his hair across a shiny skull. Yep shuffled in behind him.

"Leo told me this afternoon, Kezzie," Ben said. "You and Yep want me to tell Miss Paget?"

Kezzie shrugged and Yep nodded.

"Wait a minute, Benson," Julia ordered. "I have something to attend to first. Leo, give me your garage key. Adam, your keys."

As Adam held out a clanking ring and Leo his solitary key, Edward Rollin jumped up, his bony body shaking. "In the name of the law I demand those keys!"

While the chauffeur and gatekeeper turned mystified heads, Julia took the keys from their hands. "Must I remind you again, Edward, that I am the law at Dune House?" Triumphantly she dropped the keys down the neck of her dress.

"They're hers now," Ben murmured.

Julia inclined her head, not too graciously, toward the five waiting chairs and her standing employees. "You may sit down."

As Mr. Rollin subsided, muttering, they filed past the table.

"Very well, Benson," Miss Paget said while the five chairs filled. "Now, what is this secret you seem to share with the servants?"

"I didn't find out, myself, until this afternoon when Leo brought me home. I didn't have time to tell you, Lark—"

"That can be settled later," his cousin interrupted. "What's so mysterious about repairing the apple bin?"

"You sure you want me to tell, Yep?" Ben repeated.

Yep's face creased into parallel ripples. "You tell them, Mister Ben. It's not true anyway. It won't hurt ol' Yep."

"That's a fine recommendation for my story—not true anyway." Ben turned back to Miss Paget. "Thursday afternoon a week ago Yep came up to my room immediately before dinner—no, your dinner wasn't spoiled, Cousin Julia; Yep had everything planned in advance. He asked me to build a false bottom to the apple bin—"

"You had something to hide, did you, Yep?" Miss Paget's tone was harsh.

The old man nodded several times, grinning as if what he had done would please her.

"He gave me a hard luck story about getting too old to keep up the work and how he had to think of ways to help himself out," Ben said. "He said that one thing he'd been doing was to buy jellies and preserves at the store and let you think he made them."

"Why, you old rascal—" his mistress began.

"But that's not true, Miss Julia," Yep said. "It's not true. You wait; Mister Ben will tell you."

"He said he had a standing order at the grocery to send out anything especially choice that came in, and that day a large order of watermelon preserves and brandied peaches had been delivered," Ben said. "He wanted to get them out of your sight, Cousin Julia, and was in a big hurry because you'd been prowling around looking for a radio that morning. It never occurred to me to connect the singing Lark heard the night before with the false bottom in the apple bin."

"But, Ben—" Lark began.

"Go on, Benson," Julia ordered.

"There wasn't time before dinner, so as soon as we were through and you and Aubrey'd gone to the library, I went down to the cellar and fixed the apple bin," Ben said. "I had no idea the old fraud was planning to hide something else there."

"Hide what?" Julia demanded.

"A phonograph," Ben said.

Lark gasped. "You mean—?"

"That was the voice you heard singing, Lark," Ben explained. "My friends, Leo and Yep, thought you were going to disinherit me, Cousin Julia, and make Lark your heir. They were trying to think of some way to prevent it when Kezzie produced this scheme to scare Lark. She knew you'd be so annoyed if Lark ran away that you'd see she didn't get anything, even if she could prove she was Ulysses' granddaughter. Leo smuggled in the phonograph, and Kezzie brought the records the day you took Lark shopping, of a soprano voice singing Venetia's pet arias."

"Then it wasn't—" Lark began.

"I told you there weren't any ghosts in Dune House," he said. "That voice was canned, and Kezzie took good care that you and she were the only ones who'd hear it. I didn't get there the other night in time to catch her. She heard me shut the conservatory door, and she pulled down the open window where the music was coming from and ditched the phonograph."

So Kezzie had been responsible for that ghostly singing. For an instant Lark's eyes met hers, and Lark found herself, in that group of people and in broad daylight, terrified all over again. Something in Kezzie's eyes that she couldn't read...

Rowena broke the silence. "How sweet of them, Ben, to try to help you like that." She beamed at the row of servants.

Julia's face turned almost as purple as Mr. Rollin's. She seemed for a moment incapable of speech. But her voice, when it came, was controlled. "Yes, wasn't it," she said acidly. "Was anyone with you, Benson, while you did this carpentry on the apple bin?"

"No."

"Did Yep show you those jars of preserves?"

"No."

"Did you see them in the groceries, Leo, when you brought them up from the gate?" Julia asked.

Leo shook his head. "I never notice what's in the orders, ma'am, unless I pick them out myself."

Julia sat looking at Yep. "You *are* getting old, aren't you, Yep? Pretty old for all this fancy cooking..."

"No, no, no!" Yep yelled. "It's easy for me. I've done it so long. I like to make jelly, pretty cakes, mock duck..."

Julia gave him a final scrutiny, heavy with threat, and glanced around the table again. "You weren't here that night, Marianne."

"No, and I see no reason—" She half rose.

Julia reseated her with a look. "All right, Edward, it's your turn. What was your story about seeing someone in the shrubbery that night?"

"As I told you, when the carriage left me at the house and drove away, I stopped to enjoy the air, and heard something in the bushes near the house," Edward said. "It was dark, of course, but I thought I saw someone near one of the French Salon windows. I called out and heard someone run, so I ran after him—I don't know how many times around this big, sprawling hotel of yours before I decided I'd lost him. I even went out past the hedge, clear into the sand."

"With you driving up, Oscar would have had to run all the way from the stable to get to the house as soon as you did," Ben said. "He arrived right after the carriage left with you."

"I don't see why he'd be in such a hurry." Aubrey's eyes were narrowed and thoughtful.

"Nor do I," Julia agreed. "But why would any of *us* run away from Edward?" Her glance swung to Marianne.

"I positively did not leave New York until Friday," Marianne said. "And I can prove it."

"I shouldn't be surprised if Ed and I were chasing each other part of the time," Aubrey remarked. "I wanted a word with him before we talked about

Miss Paget, but I didn't even see him when I stepped out to look for the carriage. I heard someone running and a sort of grunting yell, so I began to run too."

Lark suddenly remembered something. "Did you get into the sand, Aubrey?"

"A little, running around the same hedge Ed was," Aubrey said.

"Did either of you empty sand from your trouser cuffs and wash your hands in the coatroom?" Lark asked. Now that she knew about Oscar, that sand on the floor was important. The sand and the soiled towel… but either Aubrey or Mr. Rollin could have cleaned up innocently.

Both shook their heads.

"I brushed off my pant legs on the lawn," Aubrey said. "I didn't get in deep enough."

"Nor I," Mr. Rollin said.

"Did anyone use the coatroom that night?" Lark persisted. "The one on the left of the vestibule?"

The other heads around the table shook. So did the row of five not quite at the table.

Julia began on them next. "Where were you, Kezzie, the night Oscar Fry came in?"

"In my room, madam, most of the time, mending your duchesse lace scarf," Kezzie said. "Though I made the rounds of the lower floor windows each time you sent Eileen for me."

"Was Eileen with you in your room?" Julia asked.

"No, Madam," Kezzie said. "Only when she came to call me."

"What were you doing that night, Eileen?" Julia demanded.

"R-reading, Miss Paget, in the servants' sitting room. I was tired and—"

"Was anyone else in there?" Julia interrupted.

Eileen shook her head.

"No, madam," Julia corrected her.

"No, madam," Eileen repeated. "Leo and his dad came in once, late in the evening, but they only passed through. That's when I heard—" She stopped.

"Heard what?"

"They were talking about someone who hadn't showed up at the house," Eileen said. "But when I asked them what it was all about, they tried to pass it off. My chair had its back to the door, and I guess they hadn't seen me. Then later Aunt Kezzie told me it was only a dog they were talking about."

"I know how you felt," Lark said. "That dog..."

Julia gave her a severe look. "Things are bad enough, with a man in here out of his head, without having hysterics on my hands. I thought it best not to tell you."

"But why tell that story about losing your keys Saturday night and finding them in the gate?" Lark asked. "Oscar couldn't have used them—the way he was."

Julia frowned. "We don't know when Oscar Fry was killed. He may have gone out and come in again. Anything I told that policeman I shall hold to, of course."

"If your keys were gone Saturday night, Julia," Mr. Rollin said, "why didn't you tell us right away? We could have given up the watch Saturday instead of Monday. Sitting up in shifts every night..." He sighed.

No wonder he seemed thinner and more irritable than ever. A man his age... Miss Paget had no right... "Don't you know she makes things up for the occasion?" Lark cried indignantly. "The key story for the policeman—the dog story for us? Even bringing in that poor dog to be shot, so—"

"Lark, you're overwrought," Aubrey murmured. She felt his warning foot beneath the table. "Running into Oscar's body like that..."

"Go to it, Lark," Ben whispered on her other side.

Julia looked majestic. "I have my reasons for doing things, child."

Reasons lesser mortals shouldn't question. Lark burst out, "What about those stories Kezzie told about missing food? Were they true? Or did she have her reasons, too?"

"I was only trying to get rid of you"—Kezzie's voice was sullen—"for Mister Benson's sake."

"I never knew you were so fond of me, Kezzie," Ben said.

The look she sent him wasn't loving, and there was still that something in her eyes that sent shivers through Lark.

208

Aubrey leaned closer. Under cover of his shoulder he touched her arm. "Keep still," he mouthed. "Don't antagonize Julia."

How not to win friends and influence people, Lark thought. But how right Aubrey was. Here they barely got rid of Marianne, and now Lark was doing her best to scratch her own entry.

"You see?" Julia observed. "There was a basis for my fear of hysterics... now suppose we get on with the questions."

"Suppose we call the police," Edward Rollin muttered.

His hostess sat straighter. "What did you do, Adam, after you telephoned that Oscar Fry was at the gate?"

"When Kezzie told me you said to let him in, I let him in, Miss Julia, and let him walk," Adam said. He started to smooth what was left of his hair, then brought his hand down quickly. "I was there at the stable the rest of the evening mending harnesses."

Lark saw Julia's eyes rest on Leo and then shift to Yep. "Where did you stay, Yep, the night the man broke in?"

Yep's cheeks broke into their countless ripples. "I stayed in the kitchen. It was nice and warm. Excellent tea."

Julia's eyes came back to Leo. "So, Leo, you've been telling my guests I'm insane?"

His brown face darkened. "I never said so, ma'am."

"Yes, you did," Marianne shrilled. "Right out there on the lawn by the cliff. You said—"

"I never *said* so, miss," Leo repeated.

"Maybe not in so many words, but—" Marianne said.

"You must have misunderstood, Marianne," Lark broke in. Leo had done *her* a good turn today. "If you overheard Leo and me talking—"

"So now you're calling me an eavesdropper, Lark Williams—now that you've got the inside track here!" Marianne's cheeks were bright red. "I'll have you know this was our own conversation. People talk to me, too. And Leo distinctly told me the old girl was insane."

"She decided that for herself, Miss Paget," Leo said stubbornly. "I never told her."

"If you've finished wrangling"—Julia's eyebrows were high—"I'll go on with the questions. You brought Mister Rollin up that night, Leo, in the victoria. After you left him at the door, what did you do?"

"Drove back to the stable, ma'am," Leo said.

"Right away, Miss Julia," Adam added. "He couldn't have been more than ten minutes."

"Who asked you to speak, Adam?" Julia asked.

"Sorry, Miss Julia." The old gatekeeper, having no hat to touch, ducked his head. Then he looked up at his employer. "I thought you'd want to know how quick he was."

"What did you do on the way back, Leo?" she asked sharply.

"Why, he didn't do nothing, Miss Julia. Came back in ten minutes," Adam said again before Leo could speak.

"Hush, Adam," Julia said. "Very well, Leo, what was it?"

"Nothing, ma'am," Leo said. "Dad told you I came right back."

"If either of you says that again, Adam will lose his position," Julia said. "Now what about it, Leo?"

The young man shrugged. "Mine's gone anyhow. Dad better keep his. I wanted to see Ben on the q.t.—"

"Mister Benson," Julia corrected.

Leo went on. "I wanted to talk to him about that scheme we had for scaring Miss Lark—sorry, miss"—he gave Lark a small bow. "Of course I didn't know there was someone else to drive up from the stable; so as soon as I got a dune between me and the house, I hitched the horses to that iron weight Dad always puts in the carriage and went back. But I couldn't find—*Mister Benson*, and as I wasn't supposed to be there and someone might have heard me drive off, I thought I'd better get back. As it was, I nearly got run into by someone tearing around the house."

"Mister Rollin or Mister Hildreth, no doubt." Julia looked scornfully at her lawyers.

"That takes in all of us," Ben said. "Now, how about calling the police."

Julia's diamonds were throwing off sparks again as her hands stirred on the table, stirred in that clawing motion. "Oscar Fry followed Edward up to the house. As soon as Edward arrived, Leo started back—*along the road on which Oscar was walking.*"

Except for the muffled crash of the sea, the room was still again.

"Leo didn't go right back, on his own admission," Julia added. "But I'll be fair. No one can say a Paget's not fair. Did anyone see him in the house?"

That silence was broken by a quaver from Eileen. "I—I did—I think. Wh-while I was reading—"

"You were reading in the servants' sitting room, according to what you said first." Miss Paget's reminder was harsh. "Was Leo looking for Mister Benson in *there?*"

The room was given back to the swish of the sea.

"Well, ladies and gentlemen"—Julia looked only at those around the table—"do we need to hunt any farther for the murderer of Oscar Fry?"

Eileen began to sob.

Mister Rollin muttered irascibly, "Oh, for God's sake—*women!*" Lark didn't know whether he meant Miss Paget or Eileen.

Ben cried out sharply. "But the motive, Cousin Julia! There has to be a motive for murder. What possible reason under the sun could Leo have for killing Oscar?"

"The police will have to find that out," Julia said. "I've done most of their work for them now. There are always things like personal quarrels: money—women..." Julia's eyes turned toward the weeping girl.

Ben snorted.

"Not Eileen and Oscar!" Lark exclaimed.

"There's one thing you've overlooked, Julia," Mr. Rollin said abruptly. His back was straight and his face fiery red. "You haven't told us what *you* did that night."

Someone gasped. It might even have been Julia herself. She reared up like a charging stallion. "You ask *me* to account for *my* actions, Edward?"

There goes the Paget retainer, Lark thought, trying wildly to keep herself steady.

"The police will," Mr. Rollin returned. "You'll have to be prepared."

The ocean boomed and swished and boomed again.

His voice nudged once more. "Well, Julia?"

But she didn't have to answer. For suddenly Leo shot out of his chair and dived toward the dining room door.

"The curtains!" Eileen screamed. "They moved. I saw them!"

The other men all leaped to their feet.

But Leo was coming back, not running away. And he was pulling someone else in behind him.

A pair of dark slacks, a dark turtle-necked sweater—and a woman's face topped with gray-blond hair...

Everyone was up now but Julia, who sat like a queen in the royal box.

"And what have we here?" Her eyes moved up the slacks and sweater to the thin, frightened face.

Lark almost forgot its haggardness and marks of years as the woman straightened. Her voice had a rusty sound. "Don't you know me, Julia?"

"Hang onto her, Leo," Julia ordered. "Why should I know a house-breaker?"

For an instant, gone almost at once, the two looked alike. "I have as much right to be here as you do, Julia. Don't you know your own sister? I'm Venetia."

Chapter Nineteen

L ark gasped. She heard other gasps.

But Julia didn't change expression. She put up her lorgnette coldly. "You should have studied the Paget family history before making such an outrageous claim. As it happens, my sister was drowned more than forty years ago."

"But I didn't drown, Julia," the stranger said. "This isn't the way I planned to meet you"—she glanced down at her slacks, at Leo's tight hand on her arm, then back at Julia—"but we can't always run things to suit ourselves. Haven't you found that out—yet?"

They stared at each other.

"I have proof," the stranger said. "You don't have to take my word for it. I know I've changed a lot—since you tried to kill me."

Julia's face might have been part of the cliff below the windows.

"Kezzie." The woman who said she was Venetia lifted her chin, not taking her eyes off Julia.

Could this worn stranger, Lark asked herself, this haggard, aging woman, possibly be the golden Venetia with the voice of a bell? A moment ago there had been that convincing flash of Paget-like pride, and then it was gone. But now one glance at Kezzie made Lark sure.

As she stepped away from the group of servants, Kezzie was triumphant. Her face, her whole angular body, aggressively transformed to match the look so often in her eyes. She would never approach her employer like that without being certain of her ground.

"She's Venetia, all right," Kezzie said. "I saw her a few days after she went

213

over the cliff."

"Miss Venetia," Julia corrected her automatically.

Kezzie grinned. For the first time Lark saw all those sharp yellow teeth.

"I'm Venetia to Kezzie," the woman in slacks said. "She was my family for years—the only family I had."

"If you have something to say, Kezzie, say it," Julia snapped, "and get it over with. You won't have a chance tomorrow. You won't *be* here tomorrow."

Lark found she was shivering again. But, of course, all Miss Paget meant was that Kezzie was going to be discharged.

"Venetia—" Kezzie took obvious pleasure in leaving off *Miss*. She repeated savoringly, "Venetia sent me word a few days after the earthquake to come to a certain place in the park. And there, among the earthquake victims, I found her."

"I hadn't changed then," Venetia said. "I was still the yellow-haired girl she'd taken care of. The girl who used to wear that ring." The stranger pointed at the great opal ring on Lark's hand.

Lark's other hand covered it involuntarily, as if to hide something shameful. When she and the others looked up again, she saw that Julia's face was turning gray.

"She had a bad cold," Kezzie told them. "*That* was from her time in the water, Miss Paget, and her hours on the beach in wet clothes. *That* was your fault."

"A cold!" Julia scoffed, but it was almost a croak. "What's a cold—after an earthquake and fire?"

"It was plenty for your sister, madam," Kezzie said. "I got her right into a hospital tent. But the cold turned into pneumonia, and Venetia Paget lost her voice—her singing voice, I mean."

"Oh, Venetia!" Rowena cried. She, too, Lark could tell, believed. For Rowena, too, Kezzie's story was one of tragedy. That silver voice—gone.

For a moment they heard only the ocean again.

Then Kezzie said, "She didn't know until later. As soon as she was strong enough, I worked her in as nursery maid with a family going East. In New York, they helped her get a stewardess job on a French liner. She found out when she got to Paris."

"That she'd l-lost her voice?" Rowena asked.

"That it wasn't good anymore," Venetia said, "that I could never sing opera, or concerts... only lullabies..."

"You mean you had a baby, dear?" Rowena beamed.

Venetia's thin, work-knuckled hands closed on the back of Leo's empty chair. He no longer grasped her arm, but still stood watchfully beside her. She gave Rowena a brief, strained smile. "It was three years before I had a baby. There was lots of hard work in between... you really are Rowena, aren't you? Kezzie wrote that you'd married Uncle Benson... and that young man's your son Ben?"

Lark drew a breath that quivered with excitement. How hard it was to remember that Oscar was outside—dead—and the police not even notified. With Venetia back like this, alive...

"If I may break up this touching tete-a-tete," Miss Paget rasped, "I'd like the rest of your so-called proof."

Venetia closed her eyes a minute before she faced Julia again. "I kept in touch with Kezzie over the years. Sent my letters to her sister's. I changed my name, of course, and then changed it once again, when I married."

"I suppose," Julia said, but her sarcasm was only an echo of itself, "that next we'll be dragging out your husband from behind the portières."

"My husband is dead," Venetia said simply. "And my daughter's dead."

"Oh, Venetia," Rowena pitied.

"The proof," Julia croaked. "The rest of the proof."

"I'll show you her letters, Miss Paget," Kezzie said. "She may not look the same after forty years, but her handwriting does. And I've had dozens and dozens of letters in forty years. I've got pictures, too; snaps and photographs from the time she left. And Venetia has the opal brooch she wore that night, the one that matches the ring Miss Lark's wearing. She had to sell the diamond ear-bobs..."

Miss Paget's voice came out harshly. "What's your interest, Kezzie—in all of this? You act more excited than she does."

The maid's face was venomous. "*You're* the reason. To get ahead of *you*. To get even... you broke up my marriage. You took away the only man I ever wanted, the only *thing* I ever wanted. So when I saw how Venetia, with my help, could come back and face you—come back from the grave to accuse you—I gave her that help. Gave it gladly, like when I found you wanted that girl for your heir"—she looked at Lark—"I decided to scare her away."

"I thought your sudden affection for me was strange," Ben said. "You did all those things to Lark, not for my sake at all—but to keep Cousin Julia from having what she wanted."

"Of course I did," Kezzie said. "She kept me from having what I wanted... all those years."

"What loyal servants I have," Julia sneered. "My coachman tells my guests I'm insane. My personal maid lives merely to get even—"

"It's your own fault!" Venetia cried. "You make people hate you. You build hate around you like a house!"

In a house, Lark corrected silently... in Dune House. And her fingers meshed.

"I have more proof, Julia." Venetia's voice was quieter now. "Remember what I said to you that day we saw Georgette?"

"I remember what my *sister* said," Julia amended.

"Georgette was in the French Salon with Papa, and we were behind the portières in the Japanese Room. Papa was trying to buy her off. Remember, Julia, how you shushed me when I giggled and how I had to shush you every time Papa raised his offer and you'd give one of those furious sniffs? Remember how we parted the curtains to get a good peek?

Julia's face was stiff and gray.

The voice went on—like a radio in the next apartment that you can't turn off. "I told you then that Georgette's hair looked like the orange peel in Yep's marmalade, and the rest of her like a kitten pushed through an hourglass. We were all by ourselves then, Julia; no one else could have heard it, or know... and remember the time you made me go up on top of the cupola over Uncle Benson's room, and I fainted and nearly fell off?"

The lorgnette in Julia's hand slipped to the table in a clatter of platinum and glass.

Mr. Rollin took over. "If you're Venetia, as you allege, why didn't you come back long ago?"

Venetia's tired blue eyes turned away from her sister at last. "Eddy!" she cried. "It's Eddy Rollin. I'd know you anywhere."

His starchedess suddenly crumpled. "And I'd know you—now, when your face lights up and you smile like that. Why didn't you come to me, Venetia, back there after the earthquake when you had no place to go? If you didn't want to—see Julia..."

"Put myself in her power again..." Venetia shivered.

"I know." Mr. Rollin's voice was unbelievably gentle. "Even though your father's will gave you the right to a home at Dune House for life, there was always Julia. I wish you had come to me..."

Not until then did Lark remember that forty years ago, Mr. Rollin had been going to marry young Venetia Paget.

The older Venetia disregarded or didn't observe the wistful note in the usually irascible voice of Rollin, Rollin & Hildreth's senior partner. "A home with Julia," she said flatly. "I tried that kind of home once." Abruptly her voice rose. "I'd rather work as I did, and marry a poor man and go on working—than risk being pushed over that cliff again."

"You pushed *me*!" Julia cried. *You*, she said. She'd accepted her sister now.

"You pushed first," Venetia cried. "We were standing there—out in my garden by the sea figs on the cliff. You said you'd rather see me dead than on the stage. And you grabbed me by the shoulders—"

Julia's voice rose too. "I wasn't going to push you! You only thought so because we were so near the edge. I was only trying to be emphatic." Her voice dropped again, menacingly level. "But you tried to push me."

"What if I did?" Venetia asked. "Wouldn't you, if you felt the hands of someone you hated—who hated you—dig into your shoulders when you stood on the brink of a cliff?"

"And Edward asks why you didn't come back!" Julia said. "You didn't dare! Kezzie raves about your returning to accuse me. But you're the one to be accused, Venetia Paget! You're the one who pushed me."

Venetia turned to the others.

"See, I can't have any of my own father's money until Julia dies," she said. "Do you wonder I'd rather stay away—never let her know I was alive—than have a home in Dune House—with *her*?"

"Poor Venetia," Kezzie said softly. "She was always so scared of her sister. I kept urging her to come back and we'd fight for her rights together, but she wasn't brave enough. She said so herself the other day when I went downtown to meet her. She kept saying, 'I'm scared of Julia, Kezzie. I'm scared to see her again.' That's why she came in here the way she did. She wanted to see Miss Paget first—before Miss Paget saw her."

"How long have you been here?" Aubrey asked. "Miss-uh—Missus—?"

"Bouchard," she supplied. "Missus Bouchard. I've been here since—oh, it seems like a month. When was it, Kezzie? What night last week?"

"Wednesday," Kezzie said. "Late Wednesday night."

"How did you get in?" Lark gasped. "With the gate and the stable doors locked—and that fence…"

Venetia and Kezzie looked at each other. Kezzie nodded, and Venetia's faded eyes came back to Lark. She looked more worn than Rowena, Lark thought—harried, with an air of last-gasp desperation about her that Ben's mother didn't have. Venetia's gaze dropped to Lark's hands.

"You wouldn't be wearing that ring, my dear, if it hadn't been for luck," she said. "I wore it the night my sister and I were out by the cliff. I remember seeing the raw marks on my knuckle the next day where the ring was jerked off in our struggle."

No wonder it had always seemed like an evil eye. Lark quivered. Ben's hand came up toward her arm and dropped again as Aubrey's fingers closed on her other arm.

"How *did* you get in, Venetia?" Mr. Rollin asked. By now even he seemed to have forgotten poor Oscar out there in the sand.

Venetia dragged her gaze away from Lark's hand. "Why, Kezzie let me in with Julia's key."

She tossed the words out in a casual way, as if borrowing her sister's keys was the most natural thing in the world.

The others all sat up.

218

"Miss Paget's key!" Marianne cried.

"You said your key ring was missing Saturday night, Julia!" Edward Rollin cried.

Miss Paget's lorgnette had shot up. "And how did you get my keys, Kezzie?"

For the first time, Kezzie looked embarrassed. "I unpinned them from your nightgown, madam, Wednesday night."

"Unpinned—but I sleep so lightly! How—?" Julia stammered.

The maid looked even more embarrassed. "It was in your mulled wine, madam. Your nightcap. No more than a few harmless sleeping pills. I knew they'd never hurt you, and—"

"How dare you—how *dare* you do a thing like that! Suppose I hadn't had a strong heart—"

"But I knew you did, madam," Kezzie said smoothly. "The Paget heart."

"Suppose the house had caught fire, or—" Julia said.

"Well, it *was* because of what might happen that I didn't dare do it again to let Venetia out. But I didn't think of fire, madam. You see, I knew you hadn't lost your keys Saturday night. I pinned them on your nightdress as usual; so I knew that Fry man hadn't gotten them to let himself out, and that meant he was still here. If he was dangerous, like Mister Hildreth said, and he did anything to you while that drug was in your system, and the coroner found it..."

"So it was only because of what the coroner might find that kept you from drugging me again!" Julia said. "You didn't want to be implicated in murder! Then, too, I suppose, if I were dead, you wouldn't have the—pleasure you're having now."

"Quite right, madam." Kezzie's embarrassment was gone, only triumph remained. "Though it was hard on Venetia. She only wanted to look at you, unobserved, and the poor girl's been stuck here ever since, dodging in and out of portières, trying to keep out of sight."

"Was it you I tried to catch Thursday night?" Edward Rollin asked Venetia. "A week ago Thursday night in front of the house?"

Venetia nodded. "Only I didn't know it was you. I'd slid out of one of the French Salon windows to get a breath of air while Julia and that young man"—she glanced at Aubrey—"were in the library, and the others playing cards. You had me on the run, Edward—in more ways than one. It's hard on a woman my age to have to be so nimble—so often," she added, glancing at Lark.

"That day the portières were swaying," Lark began, "and I—"

Venetia nodded again. "That's why I had to stay on this floor with all the connecting doorways, so I could run when anyone made an unexpected appearance, though you almost caught me today in the Japanese Room under a table."

The dust sheet that ran away... no wonder Kezzie'd tried to get her alone this afternoon, Lark thought; she had to be scared away from the closed-off rooms. And the missing food... Venetia'd had to eat. Perhaps even Rowena's lost smelling salts...

"Why did you come back now, Venetia?" Edward Rollin asked. "All these years you've been afraid to let Julia know you were alive—"

"But if I'd written—even if I'd given no address—she'd have had me looked up. The Paget money can do anything. She'd have found me, sure as fate. And spoiled everything all over again. All I had was my husband and daughter. He—dear Felix—wouldn't ever have suited Julia Paget. She'd have found some way to take him away and hurt my little girl. Oh, I couldn't have Julia mixed up in my life again, Eddy! I had to wait until she died..."

"But, my dear"—Mr. Rollin's voice was incredibly patient—"that's what you didn't do. Julia's still alive—and you're back."

"I had to come, Eddy," Venetia said. She advertised in the paper for Ulysses' child. I had to let her know..."

Lark was surprised to see Kezzie lean forward with the others when Venetia paused.

"I don't know why I never told you, Kezzie, when you've been so good to me," she said. "I guess I thought it was between us Pagets. And then when I saw that piece in the paper..." Venetia sighed and straightened drooping shoulders as she faced her sister. "You see, Julia, when I found my voice was gone, I stayed with the boats. I had to live and could give a reference from the job I'd had before—in fact, that's how I met my husband. He was a steward on—oh, well, you won't want to hear that. I was on another French liner, not a high-class one—but neither will you care about that. Anyway, it was while I was there that I saw Georgette again."

"Georgette?" Rowena cried as Julia sniffed, "That creature Ulysses married?"

"She was only a year and a half older than when we saw her, Julia, and still had marmalade hair and a kitten face. I knew her right off, though her name wasn't Paget."

"Wasn't Paget!" Julia cried. "Do you mean to say—?"

"She married again. We might have known she would, Julia. I suppose that's why you couldn't trace her after she left the consulate. At least I suppose you tried to, before you put that picture in the papers?"

Julia nodded. "The trail was too old. After all, it was only a few months ago that those unsigned letters began to come, saying that Ulysses had left a descendant who was still alive."

"So that's what started you," Venetia said. "I wonder who... oh, well..." Venetia's thin shoulders shrugged. "I was in Salt Lake and sent a note to Kezzie, the code note we'd agreed on meaning I was coming to San Francisco. She met me, and we made our plans."

Julia's rings struck the table. "For heaven's sake, Venetia, you're as bad as you always were. Get to the point!"

Venetia jumped. A flush pinked her weary pallor. "And you're as bad as you always were, too! As soon as I heard your voice after Kezzie let me in—" She broke off and swallowed. Lark could see her fight for control. "I'll tell you what I came to tell you, Julia, and then—" She stopped again. When she resumed her voice was toneless. "I recognized Georgette on the boat, and told her I did, without saying who I was. I said I used to live in San Francisco. She was wearing Ulysses' amethyst ring with the Paget crest. She said it brought her luck and wasn't worth pawning, and she needed luck because she and her husband and Ulysses' baby were on their way out here to try to get money from you."

Julia made the sound a pig makes when it's prodded.

"But I didn't laugh, Julia," Venetia continued. "I wished her luck. No one else on board knew of her Paget connections. She was seasick all the way, and Monsieur Martin unsociable. She spoke as if they had no friends even back in France. Then we ran into fog, and that made her nervous and sicker than ever. Poor Georgette—maybe it was premonition. Because we struck another ship, and ours went down."

Now Lark was more conscious than ever of the ocean beating outside. The sound filled the room where they all sat staring at Venetia.

She gave another of those brief straightenings of her spine. "I suppose you were still thinking of the earthquake out here when those two ships crashed in the Atlantic. It happened a few months later. Anyway, an accident on a shabby French line wouldn't make much stir. Of course the passenger list was published, but I don't suppose you noticed it, and 'Monsieur and Madame Jean Martin and baby' wouldn't mean anything to either French or American papers. The ship that picked me up was bound for England; so it wasn't until I got back to New York that I found out what happened to the Martins."

"Wh-what did?" Rowena asked.

"Half the passengers were drowned," Venetia said. "The Martins' bodies were picked up and brought to New York with the others."

"Not the—" Lark began as Rowena cried, "But Ulysses' baby, Venetia—what happened to her?"

"She wasn't listed by name—but rather as the infant of Monsieur and Madame Jean Martin—drowned with them."

Lark tried to speak again, but her mouth was too dry. She wanted desperately to hide her face against Ben's shoulder and not look up until the others had gone. But she had to meet all those hard pairs of eyes at Lark Williams, whose mother was supposed to be Ulysses Paget's daughter.

Across the table, Marianne began to laugh.

"To think of all that rigmarole I went through to scare you," Kezzie cried, "when all I needed to do was get hold of Venetia."

Julia's eyes scorched Lark. "So you're *both* grafters!"

Ben jumped up.

"Sit down," Julia snorted. "Do you think I'm going to choke her?"

You'd like to, Lark thought, *and I'd almost like to be dead.* How could all this have happened? That picture... Aubrey, she noticed with the back of her mind, hadn't jumped with Ben. But what right had she to criticize Aubrey? It hadn't been her husband's shoulder she'd wanted a moment ago.

"I'm disappointed in you, Miss Williams," Mr. Rollin said coldly. "I shouldn't have thought..." He turned away. "No wonder you came back, Venetia, to save the money that will one day be yours."

"But I want it now!" Venetia burst out. "You're a lawyer, Eddy. Is there no way I can get my own money now?"

"Have you fallen on such hard times, my dear," Rowena asked gently, "with your husband and daughter both gone?"

"It's not for myself," Venetia cried. "It's for Charlotte. My daughter's daughter with a voice like mine—before that woman killed it!"

Julia made the pig-sound again. "You can't break Papa's will, Venetia, or get any Paget money until I die. And I'm still alive."

Venetia's answer made Lark shiver. "Is there anyone in this room, Julia, who wouldn't like to see you dead? Yes, you're alive, Julia Paget—so far."

Chapter Twenty

Julia's fingers tapped the table. Words came harshly from between her straight lips. "And to think I took on Lark, short of proof as she was, because Benson was getting restless..."

Because Ben—a plaything for Ben... she, Lark Williams Hildreth—then she raised her head. That wasn't true! She might have been kept for a plaything, all right, but for Julia, not Ben—a penniless girl to dangle the Paget fortune in front of, one more mouse in the game in which Julia Paget was cat.

"I didn't know," Ben whispered into her ear.

Julia was still reciting her bitter monologue. "And Marianne—I knew she was wrong, but Benson wasn't reacting as we should... I took her on to throw Lark into his arms. And it did. I was right. But..."

Lark leaned forward, her cheeks still hot. "Miss Paget, I didn't know I was asking for something I had no right to. I thought—because that picture was with Mother's things—because her name was Juliet, and I didn't know where she came from or who her parents were..."

Her voice died away. She might as well talk to the ocean. Julia stared straight ahead—tapping... tapping... tapping...

"Can you always remember that photograph among your mother's things, Lark?" Ben murmured.

"The only one that stands out for as long as I can remember is one of Mother when she was ten with a big ribbon tied on top of her head," Lark said. "Aunt Sophie wouldn't let me look at Mother's things often. In fact, I don't remember that baby picture, to be actually sure I remember it, until after I came to San Francisco and one night a few weeks ago Oscar Fry brought the family photographs over, and I got out mine..."

"How did that ring get to the Williams' chicken ranch?" Mr. Rollin asked suddenly. "There's no doubt of its being the real one, is there? You remember that chip, too, Venetia?"

"Oh, yes, well," she said. "Ulysses got into a fight outside the burlesque show one night—some man was fresh with Georgette—and his hand hit against an iron hitching post—"

"Venetia!" Julia had come out of her trance. "Do you have to advertise the family shame?"

"The family shame!" Venetia cried with sudden spirit. "That was never Ulysses' marriage. You drove him into it yourself—drove him to his death! If he hadn't had to leave home he wouldn't have been killed in that runaway on the Riviera. You brought about your brother's death. And you tried to kill me!"

"The woman's raving," Julia said coldly.

Edward Rollin cleared his throat. "You say Ulysses' widow had that ring with her on the ship?"

Venetia nodded. The blond-gray hair like her sister's straggled where Julia's was neat. "I noticed the chip while Georgette had the ring on. In fact, her having it was the reason I checked with the coroner's office after I came back to New York. Their records showed that it and her wedding ring—the only jewelry she was wearing when the ship was struck, had been appraised and bought by a Missus Geraldine Smith. She identified the body, and said Georgette had no relatives and claimed to be her closest friend."

"They had her address?" Mr. Rollin asked.

"Yes, but I had no money to spend for rings, and I'd have had to tell who I was to persuade her to sell it to me," Venetia said. "No ring was worth that. Besides, I was sour on the Pagets. The family crest didn't mean what it would have to Julia."

"Perhaps that Missus Geraldine Smith can still be found," Mr. Rollin said. "At least we'll have her looked up."

"I'll send a wire to our men in New York," Aubrey said, "as soon as I get to a phone." His voice sounded husky. He hadn't spoken to her, Lark found herself thinking, or touched her, or so much as turned her way since Venetia had told her about the Martins. He was looking at his hostess now. "What about the police, Miss Paget? You'll have to let them know about that body sometime."

"I'm still alive, Aubrey," Julia returned, "as I had to remind my sister a moment ago. And while I'm alive, I'm mistress of my own house."

"Tell us about your granddaughter, Venetia," Rowena said chattily. "Charlotte, you say? Such a lovely name."

"She's lovelier than her name." Venetia's eyes brightened. "Tall and slim and blond. And that voice—oh, Charlotte *must* have training! Her voice mustn't be wasted like mine. You should hear—"

Julia cut in scornfully. "Those two magpies! You'd think after more than forty years they'd be adult."

The chattering stopped. Outside, the ocean waves crashed against the shore.

Aubrey said abruptly, "You know, Miss Paget, if I had a chance like yours, I'd take it pronto."

"A chance for what?" Lorgnette and yellowish brows rose together.

"To right a wrong," Aubrey said. "To make up for an injury done." His tone tossed off the grave words lightly.

"You know, I think you mean that, Aubrey," Julia said. "You're as bad as Rowena—*you*"—the pronoun came out in a snort—"the last person on earth I'd expect to turn preachy!"

Across the table Marianne laughed. "I agree with you, Tante Zhulee," she said unpleasantly.

Lark winced.

"Okay," Aubrey shrugged. "If higher motives are out, I'd still give Venetia money so fast it'd leave her hanging on the ropes—for practical reasons."

"Oh, Julia, why don't you?" Rowena cried. Her glasses had slipped down her nose again, and her faded eyes were shining. "You ruined her voice and her life. Why don't you make it up to her through Charlotte? Give Venetia's daughter's daughter—"

"Venetia's daughter's daughter," Julia mimicked. "Don't be sloppy,

Rowena!"

"You ought to help your sister, Julia," Mr. Rollin said. "Quite apart from whether she has a case or not, it would look a lot better—"

"*You* may care for looks; the Pagets are above it. Or is your interest more personal, Edward?" Julia's tone was spiteful. "You might renew that old offer of marriage—if I gave Venetia enough."

Edward Rollin started to his feet, his face dark and his thin body shaking.

"Look, Cousin Julia—" Ben began.

Aubrey said at the same time, "If I were you, Miss Paget—"

Kezzie broke in. Her voice might have been Julia's own. "Did any of you think she'd help Venetia? Not the mistress of Dune House—who pushed her own sister off a cliff!"

Lark shivered. Kezzie was getting rid of forty years of venom. Kezzie and Venetia...

Mister Rollin sat down again, muttering. Lark caught something about guarding tongues and trouble with the police and then the word *murder*, before Rowena leaned forward on the other side of Ben.

"Oh, Julia, won't you—?" she began.

Both of Julia's hands slapped the table, fingers wide, rings hitting wood. "You're a lot of sentimental fools! If you think I'm going to give up half my fortune—or even one dollar—to that sniveling widow of a cabin boy, you're crazy!"

Outside, the ocean crashed.

Aubrey said quietly, "There's one thing I wonder if you've thought of, Miss Paget. A while ago I said I'd give her money if I were you, for practical reasons. No matter what her legal status, your sister could make it uncomfortable for you in the newspapers. You may not care about looks—about making an ethical appearance—but you do care about publicity, and there's no reason any more, you know, for Missus Bouchard to keep still."

"Now there," Julia said, "is the first sound argument I've heard."

"You have the money in your safe from the Santa Barbara sale," Aubrey continued. "Of you did yesterday. You could give her enough right now to last her and young Charlotte for years. And you'd be safe from attack in the papers."

Her fingers drummed on the table. They seemed to Lark louder than the ocean.

Rowena gulped and opened her mouth. But before she could speak Aubrey said competently, "You need time to think this over, Miss Paget. Why not go up to the pilothouse where none of us will disturb you? You can reach your own decision without argument. And I'm sure it will be worthy a Paget."

Julia's eyes were suspicious. "Trying to get rid of me, are you? You think if I'm gone you can sneak out to the fence and stop a car to call the police. You think you'll outwit me if you get me up there. But you won't. I'll prove how wrong you are—and be rid of the yapping and whining or mongrels that disturb clear thinking, too. You've forgotten something." She stood up, and the feeling of reptilian power packed the room fuller than the sound of the sea. "I can look in all directions from Papa's pilothouse. If one of you goes out on the dunes toward the fence I'll shoot him—the same way I shot that dog!"

She's crazy, Lark thought, shuddering. *Crazy, and what can we do?*

Julia left the room, her back contemptuously turned on all the mongrels.

"That woman!" Edward Rollin muttered as the portières dropped. "She's so determined to keep control that she won't even stop at murder. She'd kill us to get her own way."

"She's—crazy," Lark whispered.

"Hardly psychotic, Miss Williams." Mr. Rollin was very much Lark's senior employer now. "Neurotic, I grant you, and quite beside herself at the moment. There never was anyone so willful… when she comes down she'll be calm; she'll have reached a decision. But we can't cross her now."

He stood up and began to pace the carpet.

Gradually the others rose, restlessly moving about. Aubrey got up without even looking at Lark. Several times she felt Ben's gaze but sat on without stirring, staring at the grain of the walnut table. At last he got up and went away. Finally she, too, pushed back her chair and, with eyes straight ahead, walked to a window.

The lawn—as plushy green as the Paget livery, with a rickrack of hedge sewed to the cliff top—after Venetia went over... the sea, green-blue today, clouds spotting it with ink blots...

Lark turned the latch and leaned out. The sea roared. Wind blew her hair...

She must tell Aubrey. It wouldn't be fair not to—now that she knew what to say. Actually she had known, though she wouldn't admit it, ever since she'd run for Ben this afternoon. It hadn't been Aubrey she'd wanted when she had that fright, any more than she'd wanted the shelter of Aubrey's shoulder at the shock of Venetia's disclosure. Her marriage had been a mistake, one of those things built on a young girl's romantic notions and an older man's reach for youth, she supposed, not on love.

But she owed him loyalty, if he still thought he loved her. Lately she'd felt he was more interested in the Paget trust fund than in her. Perhaps seeing him with Marianne had made her realize it, or maybe her own feelings for Ben had opened her eyes. Now that the money wasn't coming to her, couldn't come to her—if it was the money Aubrey cared about... anyway, she must let him know how she felt as soon as Julia and Venetia stopped lashing at each other and everyone in Dune House pacing up and down like caged beasts—like lions and tigers, as someone had said.

Unless Aubrey still wanted her, couldn't she go to another state and get a divorce as quiet as her marriage had been? Or wait until Mr. Rollin retired and then get it? Divorce or merely living apart—just so it was far enough away from Ben, what did it matter now? If only he hadn't—done what he'd done in the war.

When she closed the window and turned around, the room was empty, the restless pacers gone. Had Venetia only been a ghost? Had Lark imagined those bitter words with Julia?

Then she heard a crash. Not the crash of waves—a splintering sound, like glass—and a terrible, sickening thump.

For a second she couldn't move. She hadn't imagined the bitter words. She hadn't imagined—enough.

At last her feet began to go—running toward the hall—though the portières—almost to the pillars...

Something wrong with the light... the gilt core of the hall—it wasn't all gilt. A down-shaft of clear light that wasn't yellow...

Her feet dragged—stopped... everything within her squeezed together.

When she comes down she'll be calm, Mr. Rollin had said. Julia was down now... calm... *so many falls*... one more fall in the Paget family.

She lay prostrate with her head toward the stairs—toward the lamp statue.

But she wasn't adoring the golden figure. Julia Paget was past that... past even hate.

Chapter Twenty-One

L ark's eyes climbed three stories. In the Chinese hat was a gaping hole, And the sky was blue above it.

Her head bent. Red... the carpet at the bottom of the arched colosseum galleries was so red that the stain around Julia looked only wet. Blood in the arena...

Lark reached for the nearest pillar—and her hand fell back. The marble was red...

She saw the others now. How long they had been there or where they had come from, she didn't know. Ben was kneeling by Miss Paget, touching her wrist; Aubrey standing above him. Rowena was behind them wringing her hands in the unnatural silent way of the old silent films. Mr. Rollin and Venetia stood part way out in the disk of light at the edge of the jagged patterns that had lost its gilt. Marianne and the servants were half in the bright circle and half in the dusk beneath the galleries.

Ben stood up. "She's dead."

"Did you have to take her pulse to know that?" cried a woman's voice, so strained that Lark didn't recognize it.

The servants drew closer, as if, now that they were sure Julia was dead, it was safe—only now that they were sure.

Lark crept forward too. They formed a rough ring about Julia.

"She couldn't take it," Marianne said. "She must have known the police would find out she killed that man herself."

Kezzie's head jerked up and down in affirmation, jerked like a marionette's. "She'd rather be dead than on the front page of the papers for murder."

"But do you think—" That was Lark's own voice. She didn't know how the words came. "Do you think Miss Paget would—I can't believe she'd ever be willing—herself…"

"You mean she's not the suicidal type," Mr. Rollin said, "and I agree, but faced with two evils—"

"Miss Paget would *never* kill herself," Lark insisted. Even if Julia had killed Oscar Fry, she'd expect to wriggle free. She'd never believe that a Paget would be punished. A sacred Paget…

Suddenly Lark found that her head was turning toward the other Paget—Venetia.

Slowly other faces turned toward Venetia.

The tarnished gold head jerked up, wild eyes made the rounds of the faces. "But I didn't! I might have wished she was dead, but I didn't—I wouldn't—do that!"

Inside the gilt circles splashed jaggedly with light that seemed platinum by contrast, the ring of faces was still.

"I didn't!" Venetia cried. "I didn't! I tell you—"

Mr. Rollin laid his hand on her arm.

She whirled. "You don't think I—did that, do you, Eddy? I'm not the only one who's injured. There're those two girls she was playing against each other. There's the coachman she accused of murder. There's Rowena who's felt her whiplash all her married life. There's Rowena's son… there's Kezzie… there's—"

"You were the one most damaged, Venetia." Edward Rollin kept his hand on her arm. "That's why you must be careful."

"You hated her too, Eddy," Venetia said. "You know you did. Everyone here—"

"Missus Bouchard," Aubrey broke in, "if it's suicide there's no use saying things you'll be sorry for later. I'll get the police and—"

"How could anyone who knew her think Julia would commit suicide?" Rowena quavered. "She'd no more give up all the years she had left to make people squirm in than—"

Her son interrupted. "I can't believe it's suicide either, Aubrey. But that's not for us to decide. The police—"

"Julia's not the only one dead!" Venetia's eyes had a queer, glazed look as if she were seeing private pictures. "There's that man buried in the sand."

"But if Miss Paget killed him and then killed herself to avoid arrest—" Aubrey began.

Venetia's voice cut into Aubrey's. The glaze that walled her off from the others still covered her eyes. "But I saw—I heard you tell in the library how he was killed by a bust from the house—that bust of Napoleon in the hall. And I saw it taken! I'd just slipped back in the house while Eddy was running after me outside. I was in the French Salon where I'd left the window open and I ran over to the door to peek into the hall, and saw an arm snatch that bust off the table by the vestibule—and it wasn't Julia's arm."

"How do you know it wasn't?" Aubrey demanded. Lark had never seen him look more alert, more ready to pounce.

"The sleeve..."

Aubrey pounced. "The arm wore a sleeve? Then you couldn't know—what kind of sleeve?"

"It was like a man's dark jacket," Venetia said. "Only there was something funny..."

"It could have been a woman's coat," Aubrey said. "You didn't see any more than the arm?"

Venetia shook her head. "He—she—was in the vestibule and reached back for the bust. But it wasn't Julia's hand. I'd have known that hand, even if I do need glasses."

"So you need glasses, didn't recognize the hand, and the arm was covered by a coat sleeve?" Aubrey asked.

"I didn't get a good look at the hand," Venetia said. "I barely noticed it. I didn't want to be discovered, and there seemed to be something funny about the sleeve—something, I thought afterward, that didn't fit in with Dune House."

Ben spoke before Aubrey this time. "What do you mean, *didn't fit in with Dune House?*"

"I—I don't quite know?" Venetia said. "I tried to figure it out later to keep from thinking too much about Julia and the past while I was alone, hiding. It seemed somehow as if the sleeve was dirty..."

"But if the owner of the sleeve was picking up the bust to do in Oscar, his clothes wouldn't be dirty—yet," Aubrey objected. "Not until after—"

"But, Aubrey—" Lark began.

"Keep out of this, Lark," Aubrey said. "It's something for a lawyer to handle. Missus Bouchard has been under a great strain, terrified of her sister and hiding about the house for over a week, and now—this." Aubrey gestured toward the figure sprawled on the red carpet with the darker red growing. "If it isn't suicide..."

"Damned if it's suicide," Ben said bluntly. "Someone shoved Cousin Julia, up there in the pilothouse. You know how it overlooks the skylight. The police'll find out who went upstairs and—"

Aubrey's voice lowered. "You're a fool if you don't keep plugging suicide yourself, Ben."

Ben's already tense body went tenser.

"Wh-what do you mean, Aubrey?" Lark gasped.

He didn't even look at her. "I'm going for the police."

"But the keys," Rowena wailed as Aubrey turned toward the front of the house. "They're on her! All the keys are on Julia. How can you—?"

He glanced back. "Don't worry, Missus Drew. I wouldn't want to—hunt for them there any more than you would. I'll stop a car at the fence."

Ben strode after him. "Wait, Aubrey. I'll stop that car."

The man in front turned. "Do you think I'm nuts? Let you out of the house—after all you've engineered? If this isn't suicide..."

"What do you mean, Hildreth?" Ben asked.

The cluster by the stairway began to struggle toward the men at the door. Lark tried to catch up with Rowena.

"You wanted to be the fair-haired boy with Miss Paget, didn't you?" Aubrey's face was dark red, as dark as the frame around Julia. "So you planted that picture on Lark and sent those anonymous notes to your cousin. I don't know whether you knew about the picture Marianne had or not, but that wouldn't matter—the more, the merrier. You must have known

Ulysses' baby had drowned; so Miss Paget's ad would have no legitimate takers. What you wanted to do was show up someone else, or any number of others, as grafters out for Julia's money, to get yourself solid with her and make her execute that will in your favor she'd been coy about signing. After all, we're her lawyers, and that will's in the office right now—still unsigned."

"How can you say such things, Aubrey?" Lark choked. "It must take an evil mind to think such evil! Anyone who'd believe—"

"And that dinner pail talk, that big play you made for independence—part of camouflage—" Aubrey said.

Lark stopped listening. Her thoughts were frantically racing—recognizing this… recognizing that… her own words had been her answer. She knew how Aubrey could say such things. She knew now why she hadn't been able to remember the Paget baby picture among her mother's things; why Oscar had fallen from a seventh-story window; even why the sleeve on the arm that picked up the bust had looked funny to Venetia.

She turned her head and met Aubrey's eyes. Bright eyes. Hard eyes.

He took another step toward the vestibule. "Well, I've got to flag a car. You folks keep an eye on Ben—and each other."

The bronze doors clanged behind him.

"Eye on Ben, hell," Leo muttered as he started forward.

Ben's eyes met Lark's, and he shook his head at Leo. "Skip it, fella."

Old Adam grumbled. "Don't know why Mister Hildreth was so all-fired bent on calling the cops himself."

But Lark knew, knew with a sickening sureness. The sleeve that Venetia had seen didn't fit into the evening formality of Dune House and looked dirty to her faulty vision because it hadn't been the black sleeve of a dinner coat. That sleeve had been dark blue tweed.

Lark knew, and let him go.

Chapter Twenty-Two

Boarding the Powell Street cable car on her way to work, Lark found a seat on the front platform. It was good, after all the notoriety in the papers the last few months, to go back to being an inconspicuous stenographer among other stenographers and bank clerks and telephone operators. She sat down beside a fat man who looked like a chef and smelled of fish and garlic.

The cable car lurched along between Russian and Telegraph Hills, and Lark, looking away from Coit Tower on the skyline, watched the crowded small houses, children on their way to school, green patches of park, and church spires topped with gold crosses. How good it was to be back among people.

Her eyes caught a newspaper headline farther down the long seat: "Murder suspect held." Her lids closed. She sat grasping an upright and trying not to shiver.

She was back there again, back in Dune House, while she and the others waited—they, for the sound of the police siren at the gate; she, for the sound of a shot. It must have been nearly an hour, with neither siren nor shot to be heard, before someone thought of looking in the pilothouse to see if Julia had left the keys there. It wasn't until later that anyone knew she'd used them to open the safe.

That part Lark hadn't known either. She'd been sure that Aubrey'd pushed Julia, but she hadn't known why. Several things she hadn't known reasons for, then. All she'd felt blindly was that if the man she married had killed two people, he should be allowed the chance to kill himself.

But the shot hadn't come, and finally, after the police arrived, she had learned that Aubrey was trying to escape. They caught him, hours later, in the pass between Bakersfield and Los Angeles, and they had to shoot. The car had gone over the grade, and Aubrey lived only a few hours.

Long enough, though, for him to explain. No use leaving things in a mess, he'd said, when the doctor told him he couldn't live. Lark knew now that when his mother was ill and he went East to be with her after his discharge, she had given him the sea horse ring and told him the story of Georgette and her baby. His mother was the Mrs. Geraldine Smith that Venetia had mentioned. He knew it would only be a matter of time before the detectives found out. When his mother died he had come across the picture among her things, and, remembering Lark's history—already known at the office—he'd seen how everything would fit. The divorce was started as soon as he got home; with the prospect of the Paget trust fund, he could offer Ninon tempting alimony. Then he'd married Lark—secretly, to avoid suspicion; but securely, to make sure of the money.

He'd done the same things he accused Ben of doing, except Aubrey had had Oscar to help him. Oscar planted the Paget photograph among the pictures Lark's mother had left, and then made sure Lark would see it by his ruse with the photographs—that evening they'd gone sentimental over old albums and family things, just a few days before Oscar's fall.

Poor Oscar, doing Aubrey's dirty work had cost his life. Aubrey hadn't expected to have that photograph printed. He'd sent Miss Paget the anonymous notes to rouse her interest—a Paget heir for an aging woman steeped in Paget worship—and then expected to "find" the child they were looking for, astonishingly, in his own office. But Julia had taken things into her own hands, for the Paget cause overcoming her hatred of publicity, and the picture was about to come out. So Oscar had to die.

The window cleaner's ladder at the foot of the light well had been an unexpected block. Aubrey must have been terrified that Oscar had seen him and would be able to say, if he came to, who had pushed him. The note to arrange the meeting in the empty office had been typed, of course—over Mr. Rollin's name. Fortunately for Aubrey, Oscar hadn't seen him, but the note, supposedly from Edward Rollin, plus Aubrey's finagling, must have been what sent Oscar to Dune House—to tell Miss Paget she was dealing with crooks. Or he might have gone to warn Lark after seeing Dune House, or in one of the papers when his nurses thought he wasn't conscious, the mate to the photograph he'd planted on her. What took him to Miss Paget's would never be known, because Aubrey had met him on the road.

As soon as the hospital telephoned the office, Aubrey had hurried out to Dune House, and after Adam called that Oscar was at the gate, Aubrey had said he must see his senior partner—but he'd have used any other excuse—picked up the bust of Napoleon in the hall, and walked down the road. All he needed to do was crouch behind one of those big lupin bushes where Leo wouldn't see him and Aubrey would see Oscar—first.

As for Julia insisting that she give Venetia money had been only Aubrey's way of getting Julia alone. He had followed through the bedroom door that was never locked when Julia was inside, velvet-footed on the carpets, stocking-footed on the iron stairs—up to her father's pilothouse. There, above the central skylight, out of hearing if she screamed, he'd held her up with his own automatic before she could get Papa's revolver and made her open the safe and give him the money and keys. Then that hard push through the window over the skylight, and the run down the back stairs to join the others. If they'd waited long enough, or the authorities had been slower, he might have crossed the border with his loot and the stolen car. He had taken it and left his own among the Saturday crowds on the beach.

Lark sighed, as she had so often in the last few months. If Julia Paget hadn't lived in an antiquated house with a skylight, she couldn't have been pushed through it; if she hadn't kept her money in an 1880's safe, there would have been no reason to push her; if she hadn't been the kind of woman she was, none of this would have happened.

And Aubrey... Lark sighed again. She'd always told him he should have been a salesman. Now, from this distance, she could see how he had sold her on their secret marriage. Dazzled by his being her boss and the way he left both socialites and working girls breathless, she had been high-pressured into it. It hadn't been at all the way she felt about Ben.

Ben's face shot suddenly into her view, then the rest of him—running. No kite above him today with its chili-pepper tail floating. Something must have happened to make him run like that...

She shook herself back to reality. She wasn't at Dune House any more. That period was over. It was really Ben she saw, running for the cable car while it jerked along Nob Hill a block above Chinatown. Below, down the steep side streets, on Stockton and Grant Avenue, she could see red pagodas and gold lacquer and black Chinese heads.

It was the first time she'd seen Ben in a month.

He leaped on the step and slid into the seat the fat man had vacated. "What a break to catch the car you're on! I was hoping, of course"—his grin was strained—"but you don't always get what you hope for."

Her answering smile was forced too. "What are you doing in this neighborhood this time of day?"

"Moved here yesterday," Ben said. "I was lucky enough to find an apartment. I'm on my way to work, like you."

"You're moving up so fast at your job, Ben," Lark said. "Past the dinner pail stage a month ago."

"The forge in the basement paid off, all right. Though I don't think I'll ever be as good at my job as Leo is at his. Too bad you couldn't come to his wedding last night, Lark. Eileen was a mighty cute bride. The doctors say his scar'll be almost gone in a year if he keeps up his treatments. He and Eileen have one of those stucco houses out on the dunes—"

"Oh, Ben, how can they bear it, after all those years behind the Paget fence?" Lark said.

"But they're not behind a fence now, and they like the ocean air... have you heard what's happening to Dune House?" Ben said.

"I don't even want to hear that *name* again!" Lark said.

"But it's being torn down," Ben said. Venetia said there'd be too much evil in that house to leave it standing anywhere on earth, let alone stuck up there on the cliff where everyone has to see it. Every tower and chimney and board of imitation stone is coming down. The first thing she did was uproot the fence. I knew you'd be glad to hear that. The land's going to be sold for building lots and she gave all the furniture to the museum."

Lark drew a long breath, and they rode by the next street in silence. Far out in the water, but looking as if it pierced the houses in the next block, the Bay Bridge thrust its long probe. Once Lark had thought of it as a child's needle threading wooden beads; but that had been long ago, all those months ago when she'd dreamed of having children herself.

She shook her head and straightened. "You see a lot of Venetia, don't you?" she asked quickly.

"Naturally—since Mother's living with her," Ben said. "It's fun to see those women blossom out. Venetia went back for Charlotte, you know, and now the three of them have the biggest suite at the Fairmont."

"I'm glad Venetia has the Paget money, Ben," Lark said. Glad, too, she added silently, that she herself wasn't a Paget after all, that her mother's people must have been ordinary people like the Williamses. Lark wouldn't want any Paget blood or any of "that Georgette creature's."

"Venetia's put me down for a million in her will," Ben remarked, "which is more than Cousin Julia ever got around to doing. But I'm not counting my chickens until they're hatched, any more. Basically, I'm glad Venetia's got it, too. God knows she deserves it, and it probably would have finished making a no-account of me."

"You're not a no-account!" Lark insisted. "The thing she could least forgive Aubrey for was his backing Miss Paget in that lie about Ben and the thyroid. It wasn't Ben who had stolen the druggist's big bottle; it was Kezzie, under orders from Miss Paget. Julia had put trial amounts in Ben's coffee to see how much it would affect him, and doped him accordingly when the right time came. Kezzie had seen, and finally told.

Aubrey's lie about the night watchman catching Ben and being bribed had been made out of whole cloth to influence Lark. Aubrey didn't know then that anyone else alive knew that the Martin baby who'd been drowned was Ulysses Paget's. He knew that the ring he had hidden at Aunt Sophie's would be found any day, and that it was only a matter of time before Marianne would be shown up. Lark was still useful to him then, and he'd been determined to keep her.

After Kezzie straightened out that drug-taking business Lark had stopped having one kind of nightmare, but Ben was still strained and formal and avoided being with her alone. It must have been a shock to meet her on the cable car—for all the light touch he'd been using, a heavy light touch. Well, he'd have to stand it—as she did.

She shoved her hands into her coat pockets so he couldn't see they were clenched, and kept her eyes on the bridge. "What's Charlotte like, Ben?"

"What makes your voice so funny?" Ben said. "Don't tell me you're jealous!"

"Don't be silly," Lark said.

"I knew you'd say that," Ben said. "Charlotte's a beautiful girl though, Lark—with her grandmother's golden hair and voice, and a pair of Irish eyes she picked up somewhere, and a figure that's out of this world. And she's seventeen—almost grown up."

"And only your first cousin twice removed, I believe," Lark said.

"What you were supposed to be—if you'd been Ulysses' granddaughter. That's a good sign, you know, Lark—to remember the things I've told you."

"What's become of Kezzie?" Lark asked quickly. "Is she with Venetia?"

"Venetia offered her a home," Ben said. "Said she and Mother and Kezzie were the three Cousin Julia'd done the most harm to. But Kezzie sent regrets. She went to her sister's when they started to dismantle Dune House. You know, I believe that, with Cousin Julia and Dune House both gone, Kezzie's kick out of life's gone too."

"You think she only stuck by Venetia all those years to get even with Miss Paget?" Lark asked.

"Looks like it," Ben said.

The cable car reached the summit and tilted downhill. All the passengers slid toward Market. Lark found herself wedged against the front window, with Ben and the others sliding closer.

"Why waste time on Kezzie," Ben murmured, "when we could talk about us—how nice it is to sit so close—"

Exercising that heavy light touch again—darn his buttons! Why couldn't he go on being formal when they had to see each other?

"I'm sorry, Lark," Ben said. He must have felt her stiffen. For she felt the stiffness in him, the same tenseness of shoulder and thigh jammed against hers that she heard in his voice. "I guess it's—too soon."

"Too soon for what?" Lark asked. "To go to work or to catch the car? Of course if you'd caught a later one you wouldn't have to ride with me." It was all spilling out of her now, and she couldn't stop the flood. "It's too bad we have to tip downhill like this or you could at least keep your distance. Well, it's only two more blocks."

"Lark!" He gripped her arm. As he bent toward her the other passengers slid that much closer. "Do you know what you're saying or are you opening your mouth? Are you actually trying to pretend you don't know what I mean?"

For a moment Lark was still in her tight little corner. Then she asked, "What *do* you mean, Ben?"

"I thought—in your grief for Aubrey, you'd consider it too soon for me to... you loved him so much," Ben said.

"What makes you—think I did?" Lark asked.

"You married him, didn't you?" Ben's mouth was grim. "You couldn't wait to marry him openly. You were so crazy about him you had to go through a secret ceremony..."

Then more spilled out. Fast, half-whispered words, so the man on the other side of Ben wouldn't hear. Words about high-pressure salesmanship and Aubrey's plan.

"I know that plan of his, Lark—now," Ben said. "But your face—I'll never forget your face there at the door when he was leaving. You looked so lost I couldn't stop him, or let Leo."

"You can't send a man to his death lightly, Ben—not any man, whether you've been fond of him or not," Lark said. "I'd realized that Aubrey had killed Miss Paget and Oscar before that, and I thought—how much better it would be for him to administer his own justice. I thought he wanted to kill himself."

Ben's hand on her arm moved gently. "At least he cleared everyone else before he died. You have the satisfaction of knowing he did that much to the good."

"Isn't that rationalizing?" Lark said. "Of course I'm glad he saved the rest of us that much unhappiness, but it can't make up... I—maybe all I've been telling you is why he married me, not why I married him. He was my boss, you know, and all the girls were crazy about him..."

More half-whispered words, these broken, hesitant.

"You mean"—Ben's hand on her arm was so tight that it hurt—"you mean you didn't really love him—at all?"

Lark nodded. "Of course I thought I did until I found out—" She stopped, scarlet.

"Found out what?" Ben asked.

"You've been avoiding me, Ben," Lark said.

"I thought you wanted me to," he said. "I thought you hated me. Tell me what it was you found out."

"*Hated* you?" Lark whispered. "Hated *you*? That's what I found out—that I didn't, right before Julia—fell, when I was leaning out the library window. That's how I knew what love really was."

"Lark—darling," Ben said.

"Aw, why don't you kiss her?" muttered the man in the next seat uphill.

But Ben had Lark's hand under her coat, holding it there between them on the seat of the cable car—while they rode five blocks past their stop.

A Note from the Author

Eunice Mays Boyd was my, Elizabeth Reed Aden's, godmother and Marilyn Reed Roberts was my mother.

Dune House is set in the Sunset District of San Francisco and written between 1948-1950. While I don't remember the dunes of the Sunset District, I did a lot of horseback riding down Ocean Beach to Golden Gate Park and the Cliff House. I knew people living next to the Great Highway, the road separating the beach from the houses, who had converted their garages into stables.

Eunice's mother was born in 1879 and I think that many references in the book are based on pieces of furniture that were in their Oregon and Berkeley homes. It may also have been a way of making the story and its descriptions relevant to her quasi-bed bound mother, Mabel Ainsworth Mays.

When Eunice, or "Nana", died on February 4, 1971, she left me many things. Some jewelry, a framed *Pennsylvania Gazette* from 1758, and unpublished manuscripts. When the estate was settled and the articles in the will were distributed, I was in graduate school on the East Coast. My mother relieved me of the burdens of dealing with Nana's bequests and stored my inheritance safely at her house for decades.

At the time of Nana's death, she was working on a novel set primarily in Carcassonne, in the south of France. I read a draft of that novel in 1970, and she left me her working draft in a clipboard. I kept those hundreds of yellowed pages with me in a safe place for the next 40 years. In 2014, my husband Mel and I traveled to Europe, and I insisted we visit Carcassonne. After Mel returned to the States, I reread a scanned copy of her book set in the restored medieval walled city. I stayed at one of the hotels Nana mentioned and visited some of the places Nana described. I communed with her that day in April over croissants and café au lait.

When my mother died in 2016, I discovered three more of Eunice's unpublished novels in a cardboard box while cleaning out my mother's house. Nana was very important to me, and a cornerstone figure in my life. I wanted to honor her by publishing her novels. I have made some necessary edits to modernize aspects of the work.

Eunice was born and raised in Oregon. She graduated from the University of California in 1924 after her family moved to Berkeley. She also spent twelve years living in Alaska. Her published books are: *Murder Breaks Trail* (1943), *Doom in the Midnight Sun* (1944), and *Murder Wears Mukluks* (1945). Among the unpublished novels *One Paw Was Red* is the fourth mystery also set in Alaska featuring her amateur detective, F. Millard Smyth. She was the "E" in Theo Durant, a group of authors, who each wrote a chapter in *The Marble Forest*, which was made into the movie *Macabre* starring Jim Backus in 1958.

Acknowledgements

I want to thank the following people who have helped me bring *Dune House* to life. My editor, Jim Gratiot, for his patience and persistence. Laura Duffy took on the challenge of designing a series of covers for these Vintage Mysteries by Eunice Mays Boyd. Elina Cohen who designed the layout. I also want to acknowledge the very helpful guiding hand of Alan Rinzler who suggested republishing Eunice's earlier works. Special thanks also go to Eunice's nephew, Harry Watson Mays and her grandnephews John and Kirk Rademaker and their sister Erica for their support and permission to publish these novels.

About the Authors

Eunice Mays Boyd (1902-1971)

Eunice was an award-winning mystery writer during the Golden Age of Agatha Christie. Her books are intelligent, cozy whodunnit murder mysteries with many twists and turns. She loved to read mysteries and prided herself in identifying the murderer well before the end. After graduating from UC Berkeley in 1924, she moved to Alaska where she lived for 12 years. Circa 1940, she returned to Berkeley where she wrote the Alaska-based F. Millard Smyth mystery series: **MURDER BREAKS TRAIL** (1943), **DOOM IN THE MIDNIGHT SUN** (1943), and **MURDER WEARS MUKLUKS** (1945). These will be republished in 2022. A fourth book in the series, **ONE PAW WAS RED** will be forthcoming (2022/2023). She co-authored **THE MARBLE FOREST** that was made into the movie "Macabre" (1958). Her new cozy murder mysteries are: **DUNE HOUSE** (11/23/2021), **SLAY BELLS** (12/7/21) and **A VACATION TO KILL** FOR

(2022). These books are published with her goddaughter, Elizabeth Reed Aden. **DUNE HOUSE** and **SLAY BELLS** are set in San Francisco, California, and **A VACATION TO KILL FOR** is set primarily in Carcassonne, France.

Elizabeth Reed Aden

Eunice inspired Elizabeth "Betsy", her goddaughter, to write her own medical thriller *The Goldilocks Genome* (2023), highlighting the importance and impact of personalized medicine. Betsy has a doctorate degree in anthropology. Her forthcoming book *HEPATITIS Beach* (2023/24) describes how a young woman's experiences living on a remote island in Melanesia where she studied the transmission of hepatitis B virus, changed the course of her life and career. She treasured and guarded the draft of *A VACATION TO DIE FOR* which she was given when Eunice died. In 2017 she discovered three boxes containing *DUNE HOUSE, SLAY BELLS,* and *ONE PAW WAS RED.* Eunice was an important person in her life and she is proud that she is able to share Eunice's intelligent, cleverly constructed murder mysteries from the Golden Age.

SOCIAL MEDIA HANDLES:

Facebook: Elizabeth Reed Aden Author

Twitter: @eliz_reed_aden
Instagram: elizabeth_r_aden

AUTHOR WEBSITE:
www.elizabethreedaden.com
www.eunicemaysboyd.com

Also by the Authors

Other books by Eunice Mays Boyd
Murder Breaks Trail (1943)
Honorable Mention, 3rd Mary Roberts Rinehart Mystery Contest
Doom in the Midnight Sun (1944)
Murder Wears Mukluks (1950)

Co-author of:
The Marble Forest by Theo Durant (1950)

Other books by Eunice Mays Boyd and Elizabeth Reed Aden
One Paw Was Red
Slay Bells
A Vacation to Die For

Other books by Elizabeth Reed Aden
The Goldilocks Genome
HEPATITIS Beach

CPSIA information can be obtained
at www.ICGtesting.com
Printed in the USA
LVHW102158050622
720561LV00003B/217

9 781685 120610